LAST FLIGHT OUT

LAST FLIGHT OUT
JENNIFER VAUGHN

EDITED BY NIKKI ANDREWS

Published by SciArt Media
www.SciArtMedia.com

This book is dedicated to my family.
Beginning with a Mom and Dad who have blessed me
with more love and support than one girl could ever ask for.
I love you from the bottom of my heart.

To my husband, Brad, who picks up any slack I leave behind.
I could do none of this without you.

And most of all, to my children, Brody and Darby.
Your mom loves you more than all the words inside this book.
Thank you for making me complete.

Foreword

I was a fan of Jennifer Vaughn before I came to Channel Nine. I first saw her on the air a dozen years ago. At that time I was hosting a show on New Hampshire Public Television.

Over the years I had seen dozens of television reporters come and go. Jen was someone special. She wrote clear news stories that had punch. She had a good voice. She understood the camera. In short, she was a natural.

And she was good looking.

When Jen told me that she had written a novel, it came as no surprise. With her competence I knew her book would be readable and fun.

Which, I am delighted to say, it is.

And her novel is not just a read, it's a romp; a fascinating, funny, scary, romantic, touching romp with all the characters larger than life.

Jen's story slams us back and forth all over the world; from England to Iraq to the White House to New York, Los Angeles, and Florida.

It all comes together on an airplane ride as good as a rollercoaster.

What fun!

Fasten your seat belt, you are in for a hell of a ride.

Fritz Wetherbee
Acworth, NH
January 2011

Acknowledgements

This is new for me. Writing for television news is one thing; writing a book is quite another. I have asked so many questions along the way I very likely annoyed a good many of you, but in any case, your overall gracious acceptance of my persistence has meant the world to me. I offer my sincere and heartfelt thanks to Jeff Bartlett and Alisha McDevitt at WMUR-TV. You both, along with my entire television family, have had nothing but support for my new venture. To Josh Judge, for helping me land with someone who would get my very first book out into the world. To Maryann Mroczka, your enthusiasm has touched me so deeply. To Kirk Enstrom and Doug Perry, who entertained all my technology questions that always began with, "But would it be plausible if…"

To every journalist who has traveled to the places I have yet to get to myself, and chronicled what you saw and whom you met. I could not have created the characters in this book without your stories, your pictures, and your insight. Anna Badhken, and Molly Hennessy-Fiske, your exceptional work made me feel like I was right there with you. A very special thanks to all my early readers, who let me know if I had any right doing something like this. I am humbled by your support, and so grateful for your honesty, especially Andrea Craig Alley. You are a grammatical goddess. To James Maynard, and Nikki Andrews, my thanks for holding my hand down a path that I've never walked before. To Shawn Dixon, your talent is grand. Your cover was everything I wanted it to be, and more. To Erica Auciello Murphy, and Scott Spradling, your guidance and suggestions are so greatly appreciated.

Finally, to every pink warrior who has permanent space inside my heart. You have displayed more courage, grace, and bravery than anyone should be asked to. Beginning with my aunt, Melodie Figueiredo, I have seen this disease take too many of you away. I write this in your honor, and in your memories, because you fought the good fight. May we, one day soon, carry your precious spirits across the finish line with a cure.

A portion of sales from each copy of Last Flight Out will be donated to the Elliot Breast Health Center in Manchester, New Hampshire, and to BreastCancerStories.org.

Jennifer Vaughn
February 2011

Prologue

They say the best stories are the ones you live to tell. As I sit here with every muscle in my body tensed tighter than a circus high wire, I am not sure which way that will go. We are at 37,000 feet and heading *somewhere*. There is silence in the cabin, save for moments when you can actually hear passengers trying to gulp down the fear that sits lodged in their throats like a boulder. Everybody has been allowed to keep his or her cell phone except me. The pilot said they would not work anyway. Sure enough, try as they might no one has been able to get a signal.

How is that happening?

He took both of my phones, which is not a good sign. How did he know about *that* phone? No one is supposed to know about that phone. The most powerful people in the world are going to be exceedingly pissed off at me. If I survive this, *my mother* will kill me.

He has told us almost nothing. For the first time in my life, I have seen someone die right before my eyes. I have seen the exact moment when death seeps in like a flood of dark water under a locked door. I had to look away from the frozen eyes staring at me as I choked back the coffee that was turning sour in my stomach.

At this moment, I sit at a crossroad. What I had envisioned as the biggest catastrophe in my life now seems almost delicate as I wait for the click of the intercom system that will signal the pilot is ready to speak again.

Please, tell us something, *anything*.

The big, warm hand grips mine again. He tells me for the hundredth time that everything will be fine and we will make it out of this. How is it that I have met this perfect creature on what could be the final day of my life? Is fate that cruel that it would give me mere hours with the one person who just might be able to scale my impossibly high walls?

His face is the only thing I can focus on as I nod back with a shaky smile that feels more like a grimace. He puts his head back on the seat and looks me square in the eye.

"Ella," he says. "Trust me. We will live."

God, I hope so. This could be really good.

Just then, I hear the intercom *click*.

The pilot is about to speak.

Chapter One: Ella

Don't ever let anyone tell you Irony isn't an evil bitch. The day my life hit the skids should have been murky and overcast with a pelting rain and icy chill. Instead, it was postcard perfect. Everything went down the crapper on a brilliant early fall afternoon with gently blowing air that felt as soft as a cotton ball. The sun had reached that spot high enough in the sky to make you sweat in the long sleeves you threw on that morning when old man winter felt like he was tucked into the bed right beside you. In the moments just before my cell phone rang, I focused on drawing the air deep into my lungs in a lame attempt to flush out the fear that felt like quick sand.

I closed my eyes against the sparkling blue sky. The warm breeze felt like the tiny hairs of a paintbrush, feather light strokes that tickled my cheeks, my forehead, and my chin. I wished I could stay in that moment forever. With my eyes closed, hair blowing in the wind, no one wanting anything from me. Right that second, I felt healthy and strong. I wanted to hold onto that for as long as I could.

And…time's up.

My cell pulsed in my right hand. The foreboding almost so powerful it felt paralyzing. I braced my body for the words that would crush my spirit like a hammer on a walnut. The pieces smashed into such tiny particles there would be virtually no hope of putting them back together again.

No one knew what was happening. Not a single person was aware of my personal crisis unfolding right there on a ridiculously tiny patch of grass in mid-town Manhattan. Sounds strange, I realize, and my explanation for not sharing is relatively simple. I'm just not very good at being the center of attention. I get all flustered and uncomfortable, and start to scan the room for a wall to hide myself behind. Sure, I have an interesting worldview, and I can easily weigh in on lots of topics, just as long as none of them is about me. I understand basic human nature, I get that most people need constant validation. I'm here to give it to them.

I can deliver the belly laugh at the end of what is supposed to be a rip-roaring hysterical story with flawless timing. I'm a master of the wide-eyed "*wow*" as I properly celebrate someone's latest accomplishment or bemoan their ultimate betrayal. I add the exclamation point at the end of someone else's paragraph, and I am just fine with that.

So having the starring role in my own drama was particularly unappealing. None of it made any sense. At twenty-eight, I assumed I was in a grace period of sorts for something like this. My lifestyle was clean, my habits boring, and I could think of nothing I had done to support the potential revolt happening inside me right now.

The incessant buzz of my cell reinforced the tingle in my fingers and the teeth-rattling shudder of my heart. It did not matter that I was sitting there all alone, with no awaiting hand to close around mine, or a shoulder turning toward my falling chin. I needed to answer the phone; the news would not wait.

For once, it had to be all about me because my life depended on it.

My finger pressed the button.

"Hello," I said, trying to pretend my voice wasn't quivering.

"Hi, Ella, it's Doctor Sturgis. Are you free to talk?" Oh sure. Free and clear, and ready for you to swoop right in and attack my life as I knew it.

I had attempted to steady my voice again before I replied, even though it felt like I had just taken a karate chop to the larynx. I had already made my doctor promise that no matter what the tests revealed, I would get the news over the phone. I explained that it would be easier for me that way. I simply could not take his sympathetic eyes planted on me in anticipation of my emotional breakdown. If there were to be any kind of breakdown, it would happen about as far away from the consult room of a doctor's office as I could get.

"Yes, Dr. Sturgis. Free and clear, so just lay it on me."

Please, be gentle.

"Okay, Ella." Long pause. Just that alone told me all I needed to know.

"Unfortunately, the tests revealed a malignancy. You do indeed have breast cancer."

I guess the very first thing I realized is that you don't actually drop dead right then and there. You're still among the living, even though everything about you is suddenly different. Somehow, I managed to get through that phone call, pick myself up off the grass that had begun to feel like thumbtacks in my rear, and go back to work. It may be a blur of events, but no one referred me to the psychiatric unit that day so I must have managed to keep up some sort of charade that everything was fine and dandy.

I am a few days into my cancer diagnosis and this new life still feels surreal. Even when you have a sense of yourself, and how you react to certain situations, this is different. No matter how prepared you think you are it still feels like a backhand across the jaw, a leveling blow that catches you off guard and takes you down before you even know what hit you.

Now I know exactly what has hit me. It is a formidable opponent with potentially deadly intentions. My doctor and I have begun to map out my treatment plan but it is so daunting I think half my brain checks out during these conversations. I guess that's a typical reaction because Dr. Sturgis keeps asking if I need any anti-anxiety medications, or sleeping pills. I have denied all of it; I need to stay lucid and clear-headed. There is a lot at stake here after all, not just my health but also the pristine image of my family. For any other woman there would be that whole force field of patient confidentiality and medical privacy rights keeping word of her deteriorating health on the down low.

I, on the other hand, do not have that kind of luxury.

My diagnosis may very well be front-page news in the near future, the lead story at six. Every person I confide in brings me one step closer to the big reveal. Ready or not, I will soon become the topic of discussion at dinner tables across America.

Across the world, even.

Everyone is about to find out the vice president's daughter is sick. It's just not right. My mother would rip a man's balls clean off if she caught him leering at her own breasts. Now she'll have no choice but to discuss mine.

Thanks again, Irony, you little witch.

I suppose some portion of the population will feel sympathy for us. Then there will be those who whisper in small circles at the bingo hall or in the produce aisle of the grocery store, who click their tongues over our hardship, but secretly give praise to the deity of misfortune for finally leveling the playing field.

Politics is like that. So is celebrity. So is my family.

Of course, we knew the nation's first female vice president would be polarizing. We prepared ourselves for the onslaught, braced for the impact. My mother knew she would be both beloved and reviled. She spent her entire adult life cultivating the image that would take her straight to the top. She put in her time as a state legislator in upstate New York, and then started to think about the United States Senate, though Washington had no idea what it was getting. Off she went, this hot, young mother of three with America's favorite former quarterback staying home to raise the kiddies. All over the country, women began to look at their beer swigging, lazy-ass husbands snoring on the couch with a brand new perspective.

"Why can't you be more like him?" they would ask.

With my mother taking D.C. by storm, Brett Sheridan became the poster child for domestic daddy-hood. A tasty piece of eye candy for all the housewives sick and tired of cooking dinner, hauling laundry, and playing taxi driver while their husbands went for cocktails after work.

Soon enough, heavyweight names began to sniff around, looking to get involved with this rising star from the ground up. They worked on polishing her message, getting her ready for the big time. She was everything they had been looking for. Better yet, she was willing to go all the way no matter who went down in flames around her.

That would be us, to a certain extent. To fit the brass ring firmly on her finger, my mother had to sacrifice. Serious contenders need a singular focus. So systematically, we were lead along a gilded path straight to the guillotine. My mother knew what this life entailed, and she entered willingly, fully expecting that we were all in on the big secret. That this journey can be a whirlwind of good fortune but we had better be prepared to accept the short straws that come along, too.

Not that I ever had a choice in the matter.

Do I sound bitter? Am I? Probably, a little.

I had to come to terms early in life with the idea that I may have fine clothes, and smart people around me teaching me important things, but I did not have a mother who met me at the door with chocolate chip cookies fresh out of the oven.

Not even once.

I'm the oldest child in this family of five. I love my sister and brother but because my mother was on this meteoric rise from the time we were little, there was some dysfunction planted long ago. Just like the sunflower that sprouts in late summer, you can bet it has grown tall and strong ever since. You wouldn't know it just by looking at us. From the outside, you might just think we had it all.

While my mother's career was exploding, my father's was unwinding. They have been together a long time, the golden couple. Her opponents made a good case that she was nothing more than a sports wife who had benefited by national exposure and strong name recognition. In some circles, that stuck, but spend two minutes with her and you'll see she is no slouch in the brains department, and by all means she is her own woman. She had a bunch of degrees hanging on the wall and had already logged long hours in a law firm when she first met my father. He was a few years older, had that whole *professional athlete* thing going on, and came at her with the kind of swagger only a few men can legitimately pull off. The rest, as they say, is history.

Theirs is a good kind of love, I suppose. They have each other's backs all the time. When you get one, you get the other and God help you if you try to come between them. All these years later, they are still each other's biggest fans.

Two of a kind, success stories crafted out of pure human will.

I remember being thrilled when my sister came along, then my brother after that. Kelby and Kass are just a year apart, so we are all pretty close in age. I love them both, but we are very different. On the other hand, maybe I'm the one who is different. In many ways, they're actually a lot alike.

My dad had just about ripped his shoulder apart by the time he was forty, and *thank God*, he had the wisdom and humility to step aside while he was still whole. Somehow, he avoided giving in to that nauseating ego that keeps aging athletes in the game far past their expiration dates. He admitted toward the end it got harder to get up from beneath the bulk that had just pummeled him into the turf. He began to worry about the blitzes. He knew he was losing his touch. At just the right time, he hung it up. Once he retired, my parents built a sprawling but comfortable ranch on fifteen acres in a small town. After all the adulation, glitz and glamour they were ready to slow down and raise their kids.

Or so they said. In reality it didn't slow down, not for long anyway. Political ambition has a funny way of turning into the elephant in the room. Once that world came calling on bended knee we were off and running again.

It's not like we were ignored, or raised by a gaggle of nannies, or even homeschooled. Sure, they were busy but my parents were involved during those early years. They were authentic in their hope that we would see parts of the real world their wealth and fame might otherwise have buried from sight. They told us early and often that we all had a responsibility to live with dignity, respect others, appreciate what we had, and work for what we wanted.

It is because of my parents' almost altruistic shove into Mrs. Dupont's second grade class that I found my dearest friend. I consider it an act of fate because there would have been absolutely no conceivable way I would have met Lauren had I gone to any of those private elementary schools that kept girls in pigtails, plaid skirts, and bad attitudes for their entire adolescence.

Lauren was bold and brash, almost cocky if you can say that about a seven-year-old. She was as irresistible to me as a cold Popsicle on a hot summer day. In no time, we were inseparable.

Our small town was unable to keep her around for very long. Blessed with the voice of an angel, Lauren is one of the most naturally talented women I have ever known. She packed her bags, hopped on a plane, and headed to the West Coast the day after we graduated from high school. She had contacts rather than friends, and about enough cash on hand to rent some shitty East Hollywood apartment. She would call me every Tuesday, reverse the charges, and spill her guts in ninety seconds or less. She found a part time job in some trendy Melrose second-hand clothing store, so her afternoons were open for auditions. Soon enough, she was singing jingles for TV commercials and doing background vocals for up and coming bands. Her wings were spreading, but it was a grind, and Lauren had about as much patience as a junkie in a church pew. She struggled for a while, trying to stand out in a sea of equally talented, physically flawless competitors. Who actually got the part was a crapshoot because for the most part she was as interchangeable as the rest of them.

It was a vicious, twisted world that snuffed out too many dreams, but every now and again, the magical mix of opportunity and timing paid off. It happened right before her self-imposed Hollywood age limit was set to expire. Lauren made a promise to herself she would pack her bags and her ego if nothing significant had happened by the time she was twenty-five. About six months before that fated birthday arrived, Lauren's agent got an interesting offer. The executive director of the longest running soap opera, *A Life in Progress,* caught a glimpse of Lauren's demo reel and fell in love with her dark, stormy face and her deep, perfectly pitched voice. The part was meaty, much more challenging than Lauren had ever imagined, and she became a true soap star in no time, earning two Daytime Emmy nominations, a significant extension on her original contract, and a steady paycheck that kept her on the good side of the Hollywood sign.

Best of all, Lauren has not changed one little bit. She sends a good chunk of her paycheck home to her two sisters and mother, volunteers for community music programs, and keeps her feet firmly on the ground. Never once have I found her floating too close to that stratosphere of self-importance that hovers over L.A. like smog. Lauren is real, she is true, and she is always the first person I confide in.

Although this time, the news really sucks.

This brings me back to my previously discussed dysfunctional family.

They handle good news really well. Bad news, not so much.

There are a slew of reasons to avoid having heavy discussions with them. First, they are all tremendously busy people. Already pulled in a hundred different directions, they live under the earnest assumption that we can all take care of ourselves. There are no cracks in their system, so trying to squeeze my cancer into a hairline fracture is like trying to stop a nosebleed with a single sheet of discount toilet paper.

I am not the only one who thinks the family chain link is ridiculously strong. Enterprising reporters and paparazzi armed with telephoto lenses and unscrupulous sources have searched for the weak spots for years. There just aren't any.

Sorry folks, it sucks for me, too.

Our closets simply don't house any skeletons, hideous or otherwise. As hard as the media has tried, it has never been able to dig up anything that would jeopardize or shame my family during my mother's campaigns. Countless reporters have taken a whack at it, and one of them got pretty darn close. It was during my senior year in high school, a flying soccer ball caught me right upside the head. Our team was playing "away" at the time, so how some photographer managed to find the obscure field and snap this one nasty shot is beyond me. But he did. He clicked away at the exact moment I whipped my body around, grabbed hold of the offending midfielder's long ponytail and dropped her flat on her ass. Sure, it was a knee jerk reaction and I should have cooled down on the sidelines, but I popped her. In a way, she popped me right back.

The next day, I appeared on the front page of every rag across town. Teeth bared, muscles tensed, hand clearly seen wrapped around the long strands of brown hair. We almost laughed it off, but then the national media picked it up and played me off as Senator Mel Sheridan's brutal beast of a daughter who obviously needed anger management intervention before someone else got hurt. My mother never addressed the picture directly, but her office did release a statement saying something to the effect of... "*Our family respects the rules of all organized sports, and would expect the coaches to dole out the proper punishments for anyone caught breaking them.*"

My mother was fiercely protective of her children, but she did make me well aware that the ponytail smack down was not acceptable behavior and she hoped I had learned a valuable life lesson that this type of crisis resolution did not work on the soccer field or in the real world.

Being Mel and Brett Sheridan's daughter meant lots of little life lessons and discussions about better ways to handle those unexpected moments.

Inasmuch as I say we are a dysfunctional family, follow me here.

Imagine what it feels like to live up to someone else's expectations every stinking day of your life. Let me tell you, it can be daunting, frustrating, and just about impossible. It makes me weak, but I crawl back every time. Where else am I supposed to go?

Certainly, dysfunction is not always so subtle. It can come in the abusive taunts you hear hollered from the sidelines of a football game full of ten-year-olds. It can be the absentee mother, the only parent not to show up for the third grade Halloween party. It can be all of those obvious things, or it can be more refined and keen, cutting swaths of pain through your psyche deeper than a serrated edge can slither through skin.

I should know. It's been happening to me my entire life.

I grew up denying my emotions, cutting off their air until they were insignificant enough to ignore. I may not be the same person I am today if I had been allowed to cry, or scream, or feel sorry for myself... *just once*. When you develop your personality based on other people's expectations, you can't help but wonder where you might have wound up.

Or with whom.

I have chased many a good man away with my inability to share, or indulge the give and take of a normal relationship. I have been told I'm far too independent, way too self-reliant, and much too eager to take on the role of the provider.

That's pretty much more than enough to scare off almost anyone, and who could blame them anyway?

I'm a total drag. Now I have cancer.

Can I have a table for one? For the rest of my life.

Time has come for me to tell someone. Cancer is a tough thing to sit on for too long, and there is so much information to wade through I need a second set of eyes to understand it all. I've ruled out telling any of my family members first. I think that needs to wait until I can get them all in one room so I don't have to keep repeating the shitty details of what's to come.

Of course, getting the vice president to lock in on a place and time is a bit like walking through a corn maze with a blindfold wrapped around your head.

Whenever I need to speak to my mother, I usually start with my dad. At least he is easier to keep track of these days, and I don't have to start with the chain of command to get him live on the phone. He keeps himself busy with several business ventures and a ton of charity work. My favorite is the non-profit he runs for inner city athletes who show real promise but are saddled with crack whores for mothers and fathers who beat them up.

He is always available to us, just a phone call away, albeit on a highly safeguarded phone. As the *second-husband* and all, he is constantly under the protection of Secret Service, but he insisted on maintaining a personal Blackberry for business purposes and for family necessity. It's not your typical Blackberry, of course. This one has encoded GPS, and an emergency line that connects him immediately to the Situation Room at the White House. All incoming calls are cleared from a list of known or suspected terrorist extensions, and the line is untraceable.

That's about as private as it's going to get when your wife is the vice president.

All of us live with certain measures in place to ensure our safety. We also have secure cells, and our addresses are kept off the public information rolls. I get a monthly update from the national security investigators on any attempted breaches, as do my sister, brother and grandparents. This was a point of contention early on in the president's administration. Apparently, it was a novel idea to share security information with civilians, but my mother insisted her family receive notification if they were in imminent danger. She also demanded each of her children receive a version of my father's tricked out Blackberry, and even made a few attempts to extend Secret Service protection to us, even though technically we didn't qualify for it because we were all adults. What Mama wants, Mama gets because eventually the White House relented on the phone, but not on the A-Team. Personally, I prefer the whole ignorance is bliss theory, but my mother is the *antithesis* of ignorance and bliss, so the phone goes everywhere I go. Same drill for my brother and sister. At least we don't have the men in black trailing us around.

Kelby, most of all, will hate that I am about to become a talking point, she is quite used to claiming that all for herself thank you very much. She loves that she is the spitting image of my mother with striking yet classic features, a wide genuine smile, and a cascade of honey blonde hair. She is tall enough to cast a noticeable shadow when she enters a room, yet beguiling enough to make her your best friend. Instead of envying Kelby, you just want to bask in her light. Until she burns your skin off, that is. Kelby is by no means evil, but she is opportunistic, self-serving, and completely obsessed with one thing.

Herself.

All those life lessons our parents forced down our throats have been kicked back up in Kelby's case. I deal with her a couple of ways. I never expect too much, and I keep a safe distance. She's wrapping up her last few semesters of grad school, then lord help the poor soul who gets her next.

Then there is Kass, my little brother and my hero. He is also a mirror image of our mother, but that works for him. Tall and strong, Kass is like the guys on the Abercrombie & Fitch murals at the mall. Ripped muscles, broad shoulders, long legs, Kass is the total package. Throw in a couple of perfectly placed dimples that look like God gave his cheeks a quick pinch before sending him down here to earth, and Kass is just about perfect. He also happens to be the best man I know.

When we were little Kass was always the one who wanted to linger at the soup kitchen, who stood up for the nerdy kid who couldn't catch a baseball with an eight-foot net, and really took to heart the pious message our parents preached from the time we were old enough to hold our own sippy cups.

If there were one family member I would consider dropping this news on first, it would be Kass. He would rush to my side, hold my hand, and spew forth well-intentioned happy lines that I know he would honestly believe. That I would be fine, that this would make me stronger, that my chemo-ravaged hair would grow back better than ever. I know he would be there for me, but I don't want him to have to be. I want him to continue on his journey of good will, to stay shiny, happy, and untouched by the shower of shit that is about to pour down on me.

Kass may look like my mother, but everything else was transferred directly from my father's DNA. Good genes have delivered to him a bomb of a right arm, so it took no time at all for Kass to blow right by kids his own age in every sport he ever tried. By high school, the buzz on him exploded. Recruiters would line the metal fences of the baseball field, or the upper bleachers at the Friday night football games, scratching down notes or whispering into their cell phones. Not that there is not hard work involved, although I think that if there is any percentage of a successful outcome that depends on the hand of fate scooping up your ass at just the right time, the fingers are permanently cupped for Kass. Not too long after being drafted into the NFL, he shut down the critics who said he was nothing more than an entitled kid with overinflated expectations. This boy can *play!*

Sometimes Kass will bring his government issued cell into the postgame press conferences, dial up the White House and put the phone on speaker so the Sunday afternoon VIP crowd gathered at the other end can hear the whole thing.

He's a regular chip off the old block. My father could not be more proud, and honestly neither could I. On game days, I am always the last phone call Kass makes before he drifts off or gets on the plane for the trip home. For a while, he would try to put in a call to Kelby but always got voicemail and no return call, so he figured he'd catch her later. I told him the later, the better.

Even though he and the rest of my family will have to know eventually, I decide that Lauren will be first.

I figure the best way to do it is face-to-face. With that, I start looking at my schedule.

How soon can I book a flight to Los Angeles?

Chapter Two: Dezi

"You're an asshole, and don't *think* I won't tell everyone I know how much you suck," the lovely woman with the angelic face bellows at me from the opposite side of the kitchen. That's pretty much what she's become, a fine object to look at but way too prickly to touch. I focus on the path of least resistance to get her the hell out of my house.

"Listen, Bridget. Sometimes things just don't work out and I should have told you sooner I wasn't ready to live together." I make a quick decision that now is not a good time to mention that I think she needs a therapist more than a husband.

My goal is simple. Get her out, don't get smacked in the face, make sure all her shit is gone so she doesn't need to come back.

It takes another fifteen minutes for her balloon of rage to lose its air. Then, as the tears begin to trickle down her chiseled cheeks, her bottom lip quivers and she thrusts herself at me hoping to meld her curves into me and bring this dispute to a close right there on the kitchen floor. I should be all over the invitation for a self-serving quickie but all I can see is a twisted, sad girl who needs to be someone else's problem.

I gently pull back, hold her shoulders and tell her it's time to go. Five more minutes after that, with several broken dishes scattered about and a stream of insults trailing behind her, Bridget exits my life. *Jesus Christ!* By the skin of my teeth, I survive another round of girls gone wild. I look down at the shattered glass and my eyes trail up to the screen door pulled from its hinges. If this is all the damage done, I got lucky again. I know it won't always go my way; one of these days my luck will run out.

I vaguely remember hearing my cell buzzing on the coffee table as breakup chaos was unfolding in my kitchen. I walk carefully over the glass to check my messages. Melissa, my secretary, was letting me know she had booked a shoot in Los Angeles this coming Friday. Not just any shoot, this was *the* shoot. My hand grips the phone, my stomach doing a quick spin as I listen to her voicemail detailing the job. This is a deal I have been working for months now, an exclusive spread for *Time* magazine featuring the senator from California who had been caught shagging his staffer. There had been such a strong early buzz on this guy, pundits were talking presidential potential. He blew it, *quite literally*, and now the schmuck actually agreed to sit down with a reporter and have his mug splashed across the cover.

Of course, he'll been doing it simply for the right to tell his side of the story, which we all know by now means blabbing about how his marriage had been cold and distant for years, but he couldn't imagine putting his young children through a heartless divorce. Sure, it's *so* much better for the tykes that you sniff around your assistant rather than be straight up with their mother.

Whatever.

I don't care what sorry excuse this dog has for fucking up, it isn't my problem. All I need to worry about is taking a photo of him that has the perfect mix of apologetic, shadowy angles that will entice the average grocery shopper to stop at the checkout and throw the magazine into the cart.

I feel my eyes narrow as I begin to set the shot in my head, already noting how the light needs to hit from the side, his chin down, eyes looking straight ahead. I will make this asshole look like a million bucks. It's why I got the call; my stuff is rock solid and I know it.

It's not like a life calling or anything like that. It's not brain surgery or rocket science and I'm not saving puppies from the high-kill shelter. It's more of a comfortable fit. I have an eye, I suppose.

Once I blew out my right knee during a college football game I had to find a Plan B for the rest of my life. Sure, I had dreams of the big time, worked my ass off from the time I hit puberty and realized I could grow muscle. While the other guys were out smoking pot, funneling Bud, or getting laid in the back seat of their parents' car, I was at the gym. My body was strong and lean, but my mind thought it knew it all. I was a naive, stubborn bastard. I totally dismissed the trainers and coaches when they would tell me to pack on more body fat, add some weight to support my overworked muscles. I'd laughed at them when they told me to focus on what they all believed to be my true God-given talent, if you can call it that. I resented them for thinking I couldn't make it, or for suggesting a sport that I had long dismissed because it wasn't nearly sexy enough to handle everything I had to offer.

Baseball, they had all told me. Your future is with baseball. Make it work, Dezi, listen to your body.

Instead, I had listened to my ego, and it was way too loud for its own good.

Even though they were the very same people who trained kids like me for a living, I ignored them like they were the village idiots. To me, baseball was the girl next door. Sweet and loyal, always there for a good night kiss on the cheek. But football was the hot chick that wanted it rough and dirty, who bit and scratched me raw. I kept slithering back for more until she just about ripped my heart out.

One injury turned into another, then another, until finally, the ligaments snapped and my leg began to resemble something like Jell-O. I found the best surgeon I could, and gave him the green light to get in there and fix me up. The surgery was a success, but the results were not. The rebuilt knee was perfectly fine for a regular guy's life. It did not work for the running back that needed that extra burst of speed and agility to make the play.

I tried to take it like a man, make an honorable exit from the game and move on even though it was like a knife through my gut. Just like that, everything I had worked for and dreamed of, taken off the table faster than a Thanksgiving turkey.

After graduating from college with a degree in business, I did some soul searching. I knew I had blown my one chance of living my passion, so I needed to find something that wouldn't bore the crap out of me, while keeping me fairly well-funded. Through the years, I had started looking more closely at the action shots that filled my *Sports Illustrated* magazines. How the photographers were able to make the colors explode from the page. How they could capture the bead of sweat rolling down the pitcher's face, but blur the faces in the background into nothing more than smudged dirt. It began to stir me, how a moment in time could be captured but the perspective was fluid.

I decided I wanted to learn more about it. Then I set out to become the best.

My technique varies. I change it up depending on what the subject is. Sometimes it's a straight forward, no bells and whistles, what-you-see-is-what-you-get kind of shot. Typical for portrait work, still subjects like landscapes, that kind of thing. As I developed my skills, I realized I could actually elicit an emotional response simply by adjusting my light, angling the forehead, the chin, or an ear. Catching a flash of honesty in the eyes of someone you are photographing has become my touchdown. A moment of personal glory so deep and powerful, it's like a bolt of lightning running up my back and piercing my heart on its way out. Gives me chills just thinking about it.

For a few years, I took every job that came my way. Catalogue stuff, stills for commercials and films, even a few high school senior portraits and modeling portfolios. I needed as much practice as I could get given I had started this from scratch. I made my family and friends promise to be straight up with their critiques, and I took it all in with no ego, which was new for me. I gave myself room to learn, but none whatsoever to fail. There would be no way in hell I would let myself drop another ball and slide back to square one. This time it had to stick.

By now, it has. At this point, my work has gotten enough attention that jobs typically come to me. That's why I had to hire Melissa a couple years back. I just couldn't keep track of where I was, where I needed to be, and how to get my stuff shipped to all the right places at all the right times. She's great. I fully cop to being completely dependent on Melissa to keep my professional life humming. She keeps my calendar in order, books my shoots, and even makes my deposits for me. She gives me the freedom I need to keep this fun. All the other shit that comes with finding a bit of success is a drag.

Just dealing with the women in my life gives me all the drama I can possibly stand. Work stress is unacceptable.

This L.A. job, however, took some time and patience to put together. I was on a short list of photographers *Time* and the senator were willing to contract with for the photo; now the pressure is on for me to deliver the goods.

Shoot is scheduled for Friday, today is Tuesday. I need to book a flight and get my ass out to L.A. I also remind myself to get *Time*'s West Coast editor on the line and work out the details. We need to find a mutually agreeable location for the shoot, although I am already planning to be flexible on this. Let this bonehead choose the location. I inject my terms of the deal when I steady my gaze through the lens and summon forth his soul. It won't be my fault that it's dark and sinewy, like the snake he is.

Hey, it's not like I haven't done my fair share of sowing oats, because I have. The foul-mouthed hottie who just hoofed it out of my house isn't the first casual fling I've enjoyed. Women are appealing to me, but I make no promises. I am who I am, and at this point in my life, I can't imagine having the intestinal fortitude to wake up to the same face day after day, year after year. I enjoy knowing I can watch them come and go with few complications and limited expectations. Bridget is an exception, I let her get a little too close and I got burned. Usually, I can keep them at enough of an emotional distance to make sure they don't start in on the demanding girlfriend routine. I am all about the fun, not the strings attached. Even though I have nothing against those tied down, so-called happily married couples who manage to smirk out a smile during Christmas dinner as long as they're deep into their wine by then, I don't want to have what they're having.

I want more.

I want to travel the globe, documenting the bizarre and wonderful things I find in faraway places. I want to capture the Amazon at sunrise, shoot along the Serengeti as wild gazelles dart by, and lift the door tarps of huts deep inside an African village to expose the world of starving families who can't fill their rice bowls more than three times a week.

I want my camera to be a searchlight, to seek out the guilty and the innocent, the powerful and the meek. I want to honor nature and humankind with each click of my shutter. Then maybe I will think about finding just the right girl who is enough like me to make it work.

For now, I'll focus on a philandering fuck-up who might have been president.

Chapter Three: Ahmed

It will be hard to leave the boy. He is as gentle and sweet as a newborn lamb. His intentions are pure; his need is great. There are moments I find myself lost in his half moon eyes. Their color is liquid velvet. A brown so deep and translucent it can resemble ebony, then catch the morning sun and appear almost like spun gold. My heart aches with pride, and sadness that I will never see him become a man, or a father.

I know I must sacrifice in the name of my mission. This path has been awaiting my sure foot for many years, brought to me long before my child's mother became my mate, and many years before I would hear his rapid-fire heartbeat in those first few weeks of life in-utero. At times, I must remind myself to remain resolute in purpose, because there is a portion of this that has left me unsettled. The boy will not know my reasons. He will know my name, he will know my actions, but he will never know the thoughts that have kept my mind focused and my vision clear for all this time.

I have thought about writing to him. Putting this all down in words that he will read one day when he is old enough to wonder who I was. I often whisper to him, using verse he cannot yet understand to explain how I became who I am. I describe to him the life I used to have. I try to speak deeply into his tiny ear, to send my words directly into his developing brain as if I can leave my own personal imprint on his earliest memories. These will become the days that will undoubtedly haunt him. When his father was close, and he was good, and he loved him with gentle hands and a full heart.

There will be those who will tell him I was evil. His mother may curse my very existence and work to erase me from his life entirely. I shall not blame her for that will be a natural reaction to what is about to unfold. She does not share my desire to punish the one who started all of this; she does not even know of it. The woman has no power over me, but I will regret hurting her and abandoning our shared responsibility with the child. But she was chosen for such a purpose. She had shown she had the adequate skills to recover from tragedy and move on to raise our boy. At least I will leave with a sense of peace knowing they will make a strong life. That he will have all he needs to learn and grow. The child in no way resembles me. He is the image of his mother, and that will make it even easier for me to fade entirely from his life.

My memories are like tidal waves. They rise, fall, and leave me breathless with renewed energy, or soundly defeated with sadness. They mostly come at night and take me right back to the blackened city as it exploded into chaos. The day it all changed plays out behind my closed eyes. In my mind, I can see the red sky so vividly I feel like I am still there. I can smell the fire in the air; I can hear explosions so loud they rattle my brain. I let the present go. I allow myself to go back in time, to feel her again. Her hand was shockingly strong as it grabbed me with an urgency I had never felt before. It had always been so soft, gentle as it stroked my cheek or brushed back my hair. She had hands that were trained to save lives, just not her own.

She was beautiful and kind, and taken from me in the blink of an eye. My mother had become a doctor when few women had the courage to try. She left her home at eighteen, disappearing into the night sky never to return to her family. Her father was a traditional Iraqi man, with a heavy hand. Her mother and sisters were much like the other females in the village, largely illiterate and expected to serve their men and keep the home. After the invasion, many of these women were left to raise their families all by themselves. The men simply vanished into the dust of the desert. From what I have heard, I doubt many of them were missed.

I knew of my mother's family only from stories. She was aware that by leaving her home, she would never be welcomed back. At the heart of the role of an Iraqi woman is a belief that her family's honor is tied to her modesty and faithfulness. She had violated both.

My mother told me the public shame my grandfather felt by her sudden departure must have burned inside him for years. She knew even her mother would struggle to accept her daughter's choices. It was not as she was raised, and not as they had planned. There was much repair work to do following my mother's exit. Her second cousin had already selected her for marriage, and the family had been building her dowry and the alimony they would provide against the chance her future husband abandoned the union. He would go on to receive the money, of course, as a means of payment for his suffering by her abandonment.

It had been an excruciatingly difficult decision for her to leave, and extremely dangerous. She had explained to me the risks involved with being a woman alone on the streets of Iraq. Often times, they vanished, only to suffer horrible, inhumane fates. She told me of one friend she had known from the early days at her neighborhood village school. She had defied her father, going to the town square by herself without the protection of her brothers. In the days following her disappearance, news began to trickle back to her family that she was dead. One night, my mother told me she had awoken to hear her father speaking to her friend's father outside the front door. He told him his daughter had been found, her body stuffed under the bleachers at a nearby sporting field, bloodied, battered, and riddled with bullets. They began to talk of vengeance and retribution but the conversation was tempered by the realization that she had violated her family's code of honor. There would be no need to seek the perpetrators of such horrific violence. The girl had brought it upon herself by leaving without permission and not allowing a male family member to accompany her into town.

The next day my mother and her sisters were brought before their red-faced father. Invigorated by his neighbor's disgrace, he came at them with a fury they had never seen. Their mother cowered in the corner of the room, not even welcome to sit at the table with the rest of her family. He addressed them as fiercely as he would a battalion of soldiers.

"From this day forward," he started. "If any of you dishonor me I will bring forth my own justice. I will remove the tongues that you speak with, I will take the hands you wish to work with, and I will cut out your disloyal hearts." That was the day my mother began to plan her escape.

Very late one night when the skies were particularly dark, she quietly pulled out the small bag she had stashed beneath her mattress, kissed her sisters lightly on the foreheads, and crept downstairs. The house was silent, and she told me her footsteps had felt leaden. Every muscle was tensed, every sound felt like an explosion inside her own head. Opening the door was like Russian roulette, at any moment the chamber would fire and she would be hauled back inside. The door only mustered a lame creak before swinging wide enough for her to slip right out.

As the darkness closed in around her, my mother ran. Her heart pounded in her ears, her breath came in short, sharp spurts that burned her lungs. She ran until her house faded into the black of night. She ran down the deserted city streets, counting off buildings and alleys, until she thought she had reached the right one. She turned into the small space that fell between a store with iron bars on the windows, and another that had once housed a butcher shop her father took her to on weekends. She flew down a flight of steep stairs, rolling her ankles, tripping on the impossibly narrow steps, and losing stray fibers of her hastily packed bag to the shards of concrete sticking out from the water-stained walls.

Finally, she stopped at the bottom of the stairs. Turning toward a gray door with rust eating away at the knob, she told me she had knocked upon it three times. She closed her eyes tightly and whispered a prayer that what she had been told was true. She prayed she had chosen the right alley, and salvation was waiting as a reward for her bravery. She opened her eyes as she heard heavy footsteps approaching on the other side. As she exhaled the air she hadn't realized she had been holding, the door opened and dim light spilled out into the alley. My mother was whisked inside. As she looked around, she saw faces just like hers. Females of all ages swathed in black, standing together and looking back at her from inside a small, windowless apartment.

One by one they opened their arms and moved in together to welcome her into their solemn sisterhood. My mother noticed many of them were visibly scarred. One young girl had a vicious red slash under her right eye. My mother later learned she had been gang raped and beaten by her brother's schoolmates then left to die by the side of the road. Another woman was missing her left hand. She explained how her father had forced her into prostitution at sixteen. One day, a client had paid extra for the pleasure of tying her to the bedpost. As she lay there, he burned her with his cigarette, backhanded her when she cried out in pain, and left her there helpless to free her arms and legs. Her arm later became so infected from the loss of blood flow, doctors had no choice but to remove it from the elbow down.

The stories were horrific, and vivid, and full of disgusting abuses that permeated their culture like putrid air. In some way or another, they had all been given a second chance. By trusting in rumor and a secret network of survivors known only through word of mouth, each woman had put enough faith and hope into the possibility of freedom that they risked certain death in search of the dark door at the bottom of the concrete steps. This modern-day Underground Railroad had existed for generations to lead women brave enough to trust in it down a new road.

In this coven, there was no rape, no fists of rage or dishonor in denouncing evil tradition. Each woman buried her past and re-emerged as a strong, purposeful, and proud human being. From the moment my mother stepped into that room lit by nothing more than candles and the spirit of love and generosity, she never looked back.

Right up until the day she died, she held a permanent place in the circle of women who opened the door as often as a knock came upon it, seeking to rescue new souls that otherwise would have been left to wither away and die.

She was saved that night, but another wicked presence would find her soon enough.

My mother's time on earth would still be brief.

Chapter 4: Ella

I began to hate my computer. Against my doctor's advice I Googled my diagnosis, read blogs, and soon discovered that as far as my laptop was concerned I would be dead soon. The lump that I had found buried under my sports bra several months ago had now begun to throb. Dr. Sturgis warned me it might, because it was sitting directly under my muscle near my chest wall. He was optimistic we could remove the affected tissue and get enough of a clear margin that a full mastectomy might be avoided. Here's the kick in the ass, however. He also warned me to be prepared that once they got in they might find more affected or suspect tissue and the breast would have to come off.

As in, *say goodbye to your boob, Ella.*

How vulgar!

I started verbally attacking my cancer. I told it how much I hated it. I yelled at it, and tried to summon all those antibodies that are supposed to seek out and destroy foreign cells in our bodies. The ones we hear so much about on the cartons of green tea, and vitamins, and fortified sports drinks. Why did they let me down when I needed them most?

I have explored the cancer blogosphere full of stories from millions of patients all over the world. Some of them are funny, and they make me laugh. Others give me a knot in my throat I can't swallow down for days. Now that cancer has invaded my own space, I find myself pissed off and totally amazed that we are still treated much like lab rats when it comes to conventional medicine. Sure, I get the end game, but why do they have to brutalize our hair follicles, make our teeth gray, and send us to the bathroom with wracking chills and violently heaving intestines? Why do they make us too weak to talk, shatter our hopes for children by crippling our ovaries, and drip poison directly into our veins? Just when they think we can't possibly take another moment of the torture, *oops, I mean treatment,* they lay us down and zap us with skin-searing radiation that we can only hope doesn't get too close to our lungs. If that happens, we could have an even bigger problem on our hands.

"But we're trying to save your life," they will tell me. "Be thankful you are young and strong and more importantly, are able to pay for what we are about to charge you because as we all know, cancer is a cash cow and if you want to live to see Christmas you better be prepared to feed the whole farm."

I hate them already, the doctors, nurses, and receptionists who will look at me with downcast eyes and sickeningly sweet smiles as they watch me deteriorate into a bald, shriveled, radiated, and potentially boob-less corpse.

Am I feeling sorry for myself?

Maybe at this very moment I am.

It does not last long. I switch out the *why me*, and consider *why not* me? It's true I guess, to a certain practical extent. At least I can afford cancer. At least I will get the best torture/treatment available. At least I have some hope that I'll survive this. At least I have a good plastic surgeon on standby just in case I need him. Don't think I won't have the last laugh. I will design the perfect breasts, and they won't budge an inch for the rest of my life.

How many women can say that?

Once I've had enough of the online cancer world, I switch sites to look for flights out to Los Angeles. My mother freaks out when I book my own flights, so I never use my real name when I buy tickets. She's convinced potential terrorists regularly hack into airline manifests to scan for high profile passengers. I have learned the best way to avoid a national security event is to be as inconspicuous as possible. I don't travel all that much; most of my trips are out to the West Coast to hang with Lauren. I never get away with it and always promise not to do it again. I do it again, only because I have to. I mean really, do I honestly need White House clearance to board a plane? I appreciate her concern but I think my mother is giving me more credit that I deserve. No one in the real world gives a shit about my travel plans.

I have cleared my schedule at work for the next couple of weeks so I can head out anytime. My job at a publishing house is a bit of a joke. Sure, I'm diligent and qualified and give it my full attention, but

I could come in drunk off my ass, throw up on my boss's desk and still be employee of the month. I had my pick of jobs out of college and floated around Manhattan for a couple of years before settling into Hyde House. The company's president is my dad's former frat brother and runs a tight ship. When it comes to everybody else, that is.

I was hired around the same time my mother was inaugurated so name recognition was at a crescendo. Alan Shiro was already a giant in the industry so I was caught off guard when he offered to give me the key to a back door entrance so I didn't have to slink by the paparazzi staked out at the front door every day after hearing of my hire. He even offered to send his personal driver to my apartment each morning so I could skip the subway. I remember thinking at the time that he didn't have a clue what he was suggesting. Did he really think shuttling the ass of the twenty-four –year-old newbie in the company limo would go over well?

I kindly, but firmly rejected all his offers and even had my dad call him personally to ask him to back off. Alan is a good man, but I know he was angling to watch his stock rise by employing the daughter of the vice president. In the end, he had the most successful business in town, with the most exciting up and coming writers to preview, and it just worked. I'm always granted first glance at the new manuscripts that come in and usually have the final say before Alan or one of his partners signs off on a contract. It's a small but satisfying sense of purpose that I have grown to really appreciate. It makes me so proud when a nondescript author surfaces on my watch and becomes a star. It's almost like I had a hand in molding the future of a perfect stranger.

I really do love my job. It's just me and my manuscript, and when it's a story worth telling I can kick back and read it all day long. And, of course, get paid for my bliss.

Does it get better than that?

When I left a voicemail for Alan, I explained I'd be away from the office for awhile, but I'd finish proofing and editing and email in any changes directly to the authors. He quickly texted me back saying no problem, take as long as I need, and call him if I need anything from him.

See? Job stress is definitely something I don't pretend to deal with.

It's almost like God said, "Let's give her the office with the view and the famous family, but make her path cross directly into a giant pile of dog shit."

Best of all, let's name that dog Cancer.

I have a small window to book my flight before my mother becomes aware of my airline transaction. We are supposed to alert Secret Service whenever we travel on commercial planes, trains, etc. My brother gets a pass on this because he generally flies charter to and from his games. Kelby follows the rules, but does so grudgingly because it's just another step in the process and any extra work pisses her off. When I book my ticket, I'll use a fake name but I'll have to charge it to my real credit card and it will only be a matter of time before the numbers ping the watchers in Washington. I've learned that it can take up to twenty-four hours for the transaction to process so I will wait until the absolute last minute to pull the trigger. That way, I'll already be in the air when my mother gets the alert that one of her chicks has flown the coop. As soon as we land and we're allowed to turn on our electronic devices, mine will be screaming at me all the way from the White House.

The whole notification of movement thing can be such a bitch.

I've left a message for Lauren letting her know I'm on my way. She puts in super long days on the set so I know she won't get back to me for several hours, factoring in the time difference. I will be on my own getting to her house; she can't just skip out of work to meet me at the airport.

I arrange to rent a car at LAX, again using my fake name but my real credit card, another security alert that will take my mother from zero to ten in a heartbeat. I do believe, however, that once I drop the C-word, my travel transgressions will be forgiven.

Part of me feels a twinge of guilt that I'm about to disrupt Lauren's world with my big announcement. I can almost see her happy grin slowly slip downward until her chin trembles and she struggles to keep it together because she will want to be strong for me. I absolutely despise having to do this to the people who love me. Watching their faces go from concern to dread to fear and then struggle to climb back up to the surface. What I would really like to do is keep this little secret all tied up inside and put the next year on fast forward just like my TiVo. Skip right through the battle scene and pick it back up at the victory party.

I punch in my credit card information, hit confirm, then print out my itinerary and shut down my laptop. Flight is booked for Friday morning leaving JFK at 9:45. I will only fly direct flights, especially anything over two hours. I also splurged and booked myself into first class, where the seats are bigger and I can help myself to some sweet bubbly to pass the time and quell my nerves.

Honestly, I *can't stand* flying. I feel every little bump, every drop in altitude, every punch of power when the engines accelerate. I can never fall asleep, can't focus on a book, and anxiously await the pilot's voice booming through the cabin when we reach our cruising altitude. I *need* to hear his voice telling me he's doing just fine, we're not going down, and he's got it all under control.

Even on those rare occasions when I've been onboard Air Force One with my mother, I still need to have confirmation from the pilot that all is well at the front of the plane. If I don't hear from the pilot, I swivel frantically in my seat looking for the flight attendants to pop up and begin hoisting their drink carts down the aisle. That's another signal to me that everything's okay.

Of course, these days I also find myself scanning the faces of my fellow passengers. I'm looking for potential terrorists and for the thick-muscled men who will jump up and take back our plane if they dare pull out a box cutter or begin muttering under their breath about impending *jihad*.

It takes a lot of energy for me to get through a flight, and I always end up with a raging migraine once I finally get off the plane. I remind myself to pack some aspirin. As I head to my closet to pull out my suitcase, my cell buzzes from my kitchen counter. It's my "government issued" phone, so I hustle over without hesitation to see who is calling. Just like Pavlov's dog, this is how well we've been trained. I feel a moment of relief when I notice it's not my mother's line or my father's, but then tense right back up when I recognize the number as Kelby's. Because she's calling on this line I feel like I have to pick up, even though she's burned me before with phony private line calls that are supposed to be strictly reserved for family emergencies. Kelby's "emergencies" have included a broken zipper on her favorite jeans, and a less than flattering write-up on Perez Hilton's website.

Why do I trust this time will be any different? I pick up the phone and give her a quick hello.

"*El-La*, where in the frickin' world have you been?" she shrieks at me. "You've left me with no choice but to call you on this stupid line because I knew you'd pick up."

I think I hear panic in her voice, but I can't quite tell yet if it's *real* panic, or just *Kelby* panic.

"Hey, Kel, been busy, what's up?" I keep my tone light but firm to discourage any dramatic prelude leading up to the purpose of her call.

"Seriously?" she begins. "Seriously, *El-La*?" Kelby tends to separate my name into two syllables when she's got a bone to pick. "You are *sooooo* inconsiderate to not even think for a moment that I might *neeeeed* you," she whines, stretching out every other word like an immature brat who thinks the world has just let her down again. My fault for indulging her for far too long, yet I step right back into the role of her personal enabler. I curse myself for having a weak moment and actually answering her call. I try to maintain my patience as I ask her what's wrong.

"Well, Jesus Christ, *El-La*, what do you *think* is wrong?" I shuffle through a mental list of the possible disasters that have just unfolded and I zero in on something I suspect might be spinning her out of control.

"Uh," I start, "is it your dress for the state dinner?"

I hope I got it in one guess because I think I can disentangle from this conversation fairly easily. The dinner is still over two months away but Kelby's wardrobe selection process is already well underway.

I lose focus for a moment, figuring by then I'll be totally bald. What color dress goes best with bald?

My mind snaps back when Kelby's voice wails on.

"*El-La*, don't you *get* it?" she brays. "They will never let me bring Harris to the White House, and he'll be pissed at me if he can't come. Like, what the fuck am I supposed to tell him that won't feel like I'm pulling off his dick with my tweezers?"

Hmm, the image of that certainly gives me a chuckle. Harris is Kelby's professor-slash-lover, and it's not going over very well with my parents. They consider it highly undesirable for Kelby to be dating someone related to the university, and they refuse to acknowledge the relationship. In fact, the university has already censured Harris for taking up with a student. They both insist that because Kelby is of legal age of consent, there is no conflict of university policy but that's not completely true. Harris is crossing the line and no one is fooled that the attraction is strictly due to Kelby's charming personality and intellectual prowess.

Hardly!

He thinks she's hot, and she's the daughter of the vice president and he's ready for his fifteen minutes to start ticking.

Unfortunately for all of us, Kelby doesn't quite get this yet and she's doing all she can to insert him into our family landscape like a thorny rose bush.

Sweet Jesus. Like I need this now.

The call turns out to be much more complicated than I had hoped, leaving me no easy way to get out of this without tackling it head on. I remind Kelby that we are advised *not* to bring guests to White House events and she can easily blame it on protocol.

Kelby is usually able to weed through the wannabes who sniff around her like horny giggling hyenas, but for some reason Harris has her fooled. Even Kass hasn't been able to unlock the strange hold he has over her, not that she's more apt to listen to him over me. We both know Kass likes just about everyone. You have to be a serial killer, child molester, or a left tackle that can't block for him *not* to give you the benefit of the doubt. My parents are no help either. By *not* approving, they've pretty much given her a green light to enter the rabbit hole that is paved with velvet. She just can't help but slide right down into the abyss.

Kelby is giving me good practice for the day, if it ever comes, when I have to deal with a petulant child who is always one "no" away from a meltdown. Chances are my uterus will be nuked dry by my impending radiation. My kids could come out with one eye and three arms. Truth is, they probably won't come out at all.

I move on to try a new tactic with my persistent sister. I remind her that Harris is under administrative watch and he really shouldn't be flaunting their relationship. I spin it to make the point that it is for Harris' own professional good to stay away. Not that Kelby gives too much thought to what's best for someone else, but at least she may take a bit of responsibility for helping him keep his job. If Harris went from simply being unsavory in the eyes of my family, to downright unemployable, well then she'd have no choice but to cut him loose.

"Yeah, I guess you're right. It just sucks that this has to be so hard for me. I mean *seriously*, *El-La*. Kass can show up with whatever skank he's banging at the time. Tell me how that's fair? Not that you can relate, when was the last time you even had a *date?*"

Kelby flows into personal insult territory as swiftly as she glides into her white Mercedes. There is virtually no change in the tone of her voice, so you almost have no way to prepare for the hit. I deflect the question to which there is no easy answer and bring the conversation back around to her, which is how we both prefer it, really.

"Kel, if Harris is really the great guy you think he is, he'll understand. Otherwise, I just don't see how you could pull it off. Maybe if you guys stay together for awhile, Mom and Dad will come around. Look, I gotta go. I'm flying out..."

Oh shit, I think, as I pull back the words that almost tumble right out of my mouth. Maybe it's a stray cancer cell infiltrating itself into the part of my brain that controls verbal stupidity.

Sure as a cold sore on your wedding day, Kelby pounces.

"*What* did you just say?" she barks. "*Flying* out of *what? Where* do you think you're going, *El-La*, and why don't *I* know about it?" Then she goes in for the TKO. "Does *Mother* know you're going somewhere? Are you taking a *commercial airline?*" She says it like she has rotten mustard on her tongue. I quickly scan my options, realizing there are few that can level out this mountain of crap I've just stacked up for myself. I just don't have access to a bulldozer at the moment. I'm on my own.

"Look, Kelby," I begin, "it's no big deal. I'm heading to L.A. for a couple of days to visit Lauren." I pray silently in my head she'll accept this and shut up. The less she knows about this trip the better. She goes fishing for more.

"*El-La*, really…*AGAIN?* Haven't you pushed her far enough, and shouldn't you tell someone *when* you'll be leaving? You know Mom will have to inform the flight crew if you're going commercial. *El-La*, you can't *not* tell her."

Technically, Kelby's right and I've violated the rule the most. We've all been reminded time and time again to clear our commercial itineraries with our mother's office. The fact that Kelby is now sitting on this golden nugget of a secret could be a disaster. All it will take is a phone call to our mother for the whole trip to sink, and I'll be given yet another lecture about presidential protocol, and my personal responsibility to myself and my nation. My mother is forever worried about us being used to inflict greater damage on the country. That's why our flights must be cleared individually from the gate, and then monitored on White House radar from takeoff to landing. That's also why we are forced to use these ridiculous encrypted cell phones to call each other. She has *no* patience with us when we attempt to skirt our way around the rules.

As much as they have told us our whole lives that we are just like everybody else, no special treatment, in reality we are *not* like anybody else and special treatment now dictates our every move.

Without even trying, I add yet another dilemma to my quickly crumbling life.

How in the world can I get to L.A. without my mother alerting the National Guard?

Chapter 5: Dezi

From my office, I make arrangements to overnight my lighting equipment the day before I fly out to L.A. I connect with *Time*'s West Coast editor several times, exchanging emails and ideas on how to make sure the shoot goes flawlessly. The senator also emails me to discuss the day, and we work out the location details and wardrobe. Even though I spend hours planning each shoot in my head, I never share my exact vision with my clients, preferring them to be pleasantly surprised with what we end up with.

Damn, I'm good. With the touch of a button, I can enhance a shade of pink to either side of the color wheel. I can pump it up to a color that borders freshly drawn blood, or blush it down so gently it's soft enough to wrap around a newborn baby. I love that alone time, when I'm inside my dark studio playing on my computer with the edge of an eyebrow, or the shadow that falls along the side of the mountain. The tricky part is keeping the subject real, while enhancing its deepest elements. I see it behind my closed eyes before I lay it out in final print. I memorize the tone and texture and wait for the moment of impact when I know it's just...about...perfect.

Some of my absolute coolest shots have come when the NFL commissions me for a game. This is typically when the Giants or Jets are home and I'm listed as a good local contact. Given my vast knowledge of the game, and my fantasy football expectations, I have to remind myself to stay focused on the players and not the game itself. Not easy. These days football is larger and more violent than even I can remember. Guys seem to be bigger, and I mean that both in size and personality. Gone are the gentle end zone dances, or harmless spikes into the turf. Now, they prance in from the five-yard line, teeth bared, ink blazing on each exposed arm, even in sub-freezing temperatures. I especially dig the huge tangle of dreadlocks some of them are sporting now, long rows of black syrup that fly in the wind and give me the most insane shots. On a good day I can grab the exact moment the dreads rise and spread out like the tentacles of an octopus. They look animalistic, wild, and so fucking intense it makes my head spin. *Goddamn it,* this sport kicked my ass then handed it back to me in a sling. I don't want to, but I still love it with all my heart.

No matter the shoot, no matter the day, I rely solely on instinct and seamless preparation so there are *never* technical glitches that pop up. I plan the entire shoot in my head, how I'll have to make sure the shot is as sharp as possible, limit the light if I'm working for a clean black and white. The art of photography can be daunting to learn, so I've really tried to pave my own way. I take risks with my subjects, placing them in uncomfortable positions that may seem awkward but are guaranteed to churn out the most stunning results. I remind them that my lens works much like our retinas, registering an image as particles of light, which complete each other upside down. The camera's inner wiring operates like our eye muscles do to flip the image right side up, fusing all those tiny particles of light to complete a picture. It is virtually the same way our brain processes what our eyes see to form a memory.

By then they are staring at me, open-mouthed and dazed. Once I have thoroughly captivated them with the very entrancing process they usually stop the grumbling and contort to any level I ask.

I prefer to fly solo when I take a job, no assistants on site. I also think it helps develop a certain level of trust between my subject and myself that might be lost when too many eyes are watching. As my reputation for exceptional work began to develop and I took on more high-profile clients I made a promise to myself to keep work entirely separate from my personal life. No dating clients, no heavy flirting on a shoot, or inappropriate nuances. My work is intense on its own merit. We work hard together, and while I might dig at my clients a little, I want them to leave feeling as if they gave me a glimpse of their souls and I treated them with respect.

Melissa's role is to stay put in New York with the busy work and we both like it that way. She's a young single mother who needs the freedom to dart off midday and check on her son at daycare. She knows I'm meticulous about the details of my schedule, but not a total dick if he needs her, too. He's a cute little guy, comes in sometimes to mess around with some of my pocket cameras. No father to speak of, asshole took off when he found out Melissa was planning to keep the kid. She never speaks of him, and I always make sure to spend a little bit of man time with the boy to show him all guys don't suck.

I box my equipment and walk it over to Melissa's desk. She's on the phone so I leave her a quick note with the shipping address in L.A. She already knows the drill, she's done this a hundred times, so I give her a wave and head out of the office. My flight leaves early tomorrow morning out of JFK. I'll hook up with the editor once I land, scope out our shoot location, and make sure my equipment is locked and loaded. Then I'll head off to my hotel to chill, try to relax, maybe even hit the gym for a run if my legs haven't been entirely cramped during the six-hour flight.

Working out is still an important part of my life; you need a strong body to keep up in the world. I keep myself fairly well toned, but I'm not lugging around the bulk I needed on the field. Nevertheless, the old body isn't getting any younger, and it's endured more than it should have. It aches to high heaven whether I'm on a treadmill, or sipping a beer on my back porch.

Experience has taught me that the hours leading up to an important shoot can be tense. I have developed a routine of sorts to settle the nerves; beginning with one glass of red wine which I will sip slowly to savor the warm feeling that spreads into my head. After that, I'll pull out the one thing I refuse to travel without, my heating pad, and lie flat on the floor with the thing wrapped around my knee on high. One 800-milligram ibuprofen later, I will crawl up to the bed where my bones will let go and I'll collapse into the soft mattress. No matter where my camera now takes me, I'm always just one step off the football field. Forever damaged by my own conceit, my body will never let me forget just how close I came. Sometimes, the memories hurt like a motherfucker with a rotten sense of humor.

I head home to pack up a few things--some jeans, a decent-looking shirt and my favorite pair of Nikes. I bought them for my very first shoot, and wear them only when I'm working. My good luck charms that keep me grounded no matter who is sitting in front of my lens.

Early to bed, and I surprise myself by sliding into sleep easily. Before the sun rises, I am up and in the shower, giving my knee a couple extra minutes under scalding hot water to loosen it up for the flight. I lock up my apartment, check my bag one last time and grab my cell phone and wallet. I glance down at the phone to make sure there are no new messages, then put it on vibrate and tuck it into the pocket of my coat. I switch off the lights and pull the door shut behind me.

Here goes, I think to myself as I turn and walk down the steps to the street. I raise my right arm to hail a cab. As I climb in the driver catches my eye in his rear view mirror, offering no words but silently telling me he needs to know where I'm heading.

"To JFK," I tell him, but in my head, I'm thinking...*to the biggest shoot of my entire career.*

We slide through mid-town traffic, starting then slowing again but overall making pretty good time.

L.A. is waiting.

Just a few more hours to go.

Chapter 6: Ahmed

The old stories came to me only because I asked. I wanted to know why I was the only child who didn't have cousins, or two sets of grandparents. Why didn't my mother's family want to meet me? How was I half-Iraqi, but looked anything but? Why did my mother leave her home?

Enough of her culture had seeped into my young brain by then to tell me I was living a very different sort of life. In spite of how my parents were raising me, with love and opportunity and generosity and kindness, I felt like a part of me was missing.

After escaping her childhood home my mother spent only a brief time with the women who welcomed her into their underground world. After a couple days of rest and preparation, they handed her a small cardboard box that held travel documents and enough money to buy food and clothing. The rest, they told her, was up to her.

During yet another dark night, the journey to her new life resumed. The women had arranged for her safe passage out of the country, but she needed to figure out how to get to her final destination. Hitching rides from kind strangers, and sleeping under the stars, she finally made her way to England, where she quickly enrolled in school. At night, she worked at a ground level pub along a quiet one-way street. The family who owned the place allowed her to sleep in the back room that was equipped with a bathroom and a small sink. They were kind and never asked questions my mother was not prepared to answer. They had a good idea that she was on the run from someone or something, but never pressured her to divulge her secrets.

They had a son, who was a few years older than my mother and studying medicine at university. They often spoke of how proud they were of Easton and his brilliant mind. My mother listened politely at first to the glowing stories, but over time began to genuinely look forward to the tales they told of the fine stranger who seemed destined to spend his life saving others.

By the time Christmas rolled around that year, my mother was fully engrossed in Easton and spent many hours dreaming of the moment he would arrive home for holiday break. The family had invited her to spend the holiday with them at their country home a few miles outside of the city. My mother had no car, so the husband decided he would help her close the pub early the evening before, then take her home with him. His friendly ways were unfamiliar to my mother, but she accepted this gracious invitation out of respect and curiosity.

What was this Christmas all about? She wanted nothing more than to learn.

Plans changed, however, when a last minute snowstorm blew in, canceling Easton's trip home. Through their disappointment, the couple carried on with their plans, giving my mother her first glimpse at a tradition that celebrated light and promise and the sanctity of family. She spent several minutes carefully unwrapping what would be the very first gift ever given to her.

It was a necklace on a gold chain with a tiny bird in flight. Its wings spread out, with sparkling diamonds at their tips. My mother told me she wore it every single day, for years after. In times of great stress, I would see her stroking the bird, as if it gave her enough strength of purpose to press forward.

Although she had still not met their only son, my mother saw the love that had raised him. At times, she would catch herself staring at the handsome couple as they entwined their fingers or laughed together at a private joke. There were never harsh words, no fists ever reached out in anger, and happiness seemed to seep in from every direction. Hands worked together at this business, no one ever shouldered all the labor, and my mother quickly became a valued member of the team. The couple always padded her paycheck with a few extra pounds, saying they had no idea what the future might hold and my mother needed to think about moving on to something more important than the family pub.

They took notice of my mother's impeccable attention to detail, and the steady hand she used to complete her daily work. They had no knowledge of the nightmare that had chased her from her native home, but they were determined to give this young woman a fighting chance in her new life. They noticed that although she was intelligent and caught on quickly, she seemed to have very little in the way of a formal education.

As the weeks turned into months and my mother breezed through her lessons, the wife decided she needed more of a challenge. For two hours after school each day, my mother would continue her studies at the pub. Having gone to university before settling down with her husband, the wife dug out her old textbooks and designed a lesson plan full of world history, mathematics, and English.

As a young woman, my mother spoke clean English but tended to miss nuance, innuendo and social cues. The wife also knew that she was innocent in the ways of the opposite sex. My mother admitted to even me that she was completely oblivious to the gawking eyes that watched her move along the cobble stone floors inside the pub every night. The couple had an inkling that their sudden spike in business was not due to the foamy beer from the tap, but instead because word had spread throughout the city of their comely new employee.

The wife had found a burka buried deep inside my mother's tiny room, underneath a load of dirty towels. Because of her long black hair and olive complexion, the wife assumed she was of Middle Eastern descent but she had the most sparkling green eyes the wife had ever seen. Lined by thick black lashes, and as wide as a meadow in the springtime, they forced your own eyes to blink in an effort to clear away what seemed like a mirage along the desert sand. She was a vision, and yet she was *entirely* unaware of it. As my mother explained to me how the couple debated the best way to have this delicate conversation with her, she would laugh as she recalled how they described the unintended but very real effect she was having on their patrons. The couple had noticed that my mother shied away from men, refusing to engage in their playful banter, scurrying away from their touch. She would unintentionally cower at the sound of a raised voice, or shudder at the clank of a beer goblet on the wooden bar. She had not yet learned that not all men were so brazen in their attempts to appeal to her. But she was about to.

In those early months with the sweet little family, my mother took only if she had already given. She walked the streets with a quick step and lowered head, unwilling to meet the gaze of the passers-by who inevitably stared at her lovely face. She came fully prepared to each lesson with the wife, completing each assignment ahead of schedule and above expectation. Her teachers routinely advanced her to the next level, the next grade until the day came when they told her it was time to begin her secondary education.

This was my favorite story of all. I would beg my mother to tell it over and over. It never got old.

It was the day she received what is equivalent to a high school diploma. Wearing a fine dress given to her by the couple, my mother joined them for dinner at an elegant restaurant she had heard about only in stories. Someone else folded her napkin, someone else gently placed her exquisite meal before her, and someone else paid the bill that came delicately wrapped in a leather binder at the end of dessert. She told me that she had made a decision that night. As she looked at the faces of the two people who had become like real parents to her, she took a deep cleansing breath, and spoke from the most private place buried inside her heart.

She started softly and slowly, the story of her life. She owed them that.

She told them of the family she fled from, the sisters she left behind. She told them of the murdered girl who had been her friend, the vengeful rage of her father, her own fear of becoming what her mother already was.

She explained how she became desperate to run away, single-minded in her driving need to escape the torture of being passed from one heavy-handed man to another.

She watched their eyes, locked on her as she described how she hatched her final plan in a matter of days, her destination guided only by rumor and word of mouth among the women. She said she had prayed that night that if she did not find the door at the bottom of the stairs, God would take her home.

If salvation was nothing more than false hope, she preferred death.

She tried to find the appropriate words to describe to the couple the moment she stood on the edge of the doorway, getting her first look at the outstretched arms of the angels on earth standing just inside. She wanted them to understand the risk these women were taking. One wrong step and there would be no time wasted bringing any one of them to swift justice. How they all knew there would be no acceptable form of punishment other than a violent and bloody death. In spite of that, they risked it all.

The couple held her eyes the entire time, only looking down occasionally when the horror of my mother's truth seemed to strike so deeply they could barely stand to listen. She will never know what they were thinking that night, because they never asked a single question during the entire time my mother spoke. They were silent as she told of the bold courage of the group. How they hid their soul-saving work from the human corruption that festered just outside their front door.

God's hands move in many directions, the women had told my mother. Sometimes they push you down to make you fight harder, and sometimes they lift you up when your own mortal resolve has failed.

As the night wore on, and their fellow patrons pushed their chairs in and left the restaurant with the glow of wine and good spirits, my mother's words began to slow. She looked into the misty eyes across the table and uttered the words she had never had cause to speak before. Three little words she should have known her entire life, but until then had felt as foreign on her tongue as a new language.

"I love you both," she began, "for giving me hope and kindness and a place I shall call home for the rest of my life."

The couple did not realize they had been holding tight onto the other's fingers. For the next few seconds, the fingers froze then tightened, exchanging more than words ever could. The couple who had been blessed with only one child, but had enough love for a dozen, had already given this woman-child a permanent place in their family and in their hearts. The daughter they did not create, but one who came to them as if on a path from above. They told her they had waited for this moment, knowing that she kept her heart guarded, never asking for it to be included or assuming it was even welcomed. Without intending to, she had brought them a peaceful kind of joy; an unexpected gift they could never have prepared for, but couldn't imagine not getting.

In the months spent with the couple up until that point, the most important piece of this puzzle had been missing. My mother described to me the final moments of her celebration dinner and the surprise that followed, as if they were guiding her to the next fork along the road of her life. She would recite for me what the couple had said to her, word for word.

"Dear, we have loved you from the moment you knocked on our door," the husband and wife began, each finishing the other's words. "We don't know the people you came from, but from this point forward you will always be our daughter." The husband looked down at their locked fingers, as a single tear slid slowly down his cheek.

"We love Easton in a way we could never imagine feeling again. Yet, we do…for you. We have arranged for you to join him at university. We have saved enough money, and the school is granting you a scholarship to make up the difference. We have kept it a surprise, because we knew you would never ask for our help. Everything is paid for, your place is being held, and you will begin in one month."

"Easton will meet you at the train, settle you into your new apartment, and help get you ready for classes to begin." The wife picked up her napkin and dabbed her eyes before continuing. "We will respect your wishes to do as you see fit once you get to school but if I could make one suggestion…" she began tentatively, hoping her words would be welcomed advice. "I see in you some of the qualities we saw in Easton. You are calm and steady, you have a disciplined mind, and you wish to help other people," she stated firmly, forcing my mother to accept this as fact rather than compliment, which she refused to acknowledge most times. "These are qualities best put to good use among physicians. Doctors must be calm, they must be confident, and above all else seek to ease the pain and suffering of complete strangers." The wife then focused her eyes directly at my mother. "You are going to be very important in the lives of others, I can just feel it. Where you go from here is completely up to you to decide. It doesn't matter who told you otherwise, but in this life there is always free will. We will always be here for you, but the world is also waiting for you to take your place in it."

My mother held the wife's gaze firmly, feeling the sting of tears behind her eyes. She had never known the physical phenomenon of joyful tears. She spent so many years fully in control of her emotions that not even her sisters had ever witnessed the fall of a tear from her face.

Like a door swinging wide open, my mother's iron resolve shattered and she was overcome by gratitude. She had a flash of the fear she had felt the night she left her father's house. The blind rush of adrenaline that had propelled her down the dark empty streets to the safe house. She briefly recalled sharing bread with mothers and children huddled under heavy blankets in the back of rusty old trucks traveling away from the abuse their families had nurtured for generations. She wondered what had become of them, and offered thanks yet again for the blessings she had been given.

As the family prepared to leave the restaurant that night, emotionally spent and ready for the warm comfort of home, they each heard the moan of the heavy wooden door as it was pulled open. They chuckled to each other as they expected to hear the loud happy conversation of a couple heading inside for a final toast of the night.

Instead, all was quiet as the tall man entered. He was wind-blown, his cheeks dusted with color from the early spring chill. His eyes darted around as he adjusted his collar and raked his fingers through thick blond hair tousled by the breeze.

My mother described this to me many times. I always closed my eyes as if to drop myself into this memory as a quiet bystander watching from nearby.

She told me how she felt a tug deep inside her stomach that hitched her breath and forced her mouth wide open in search of air. No words formed inside her head as she felt a swarm of butterflies spread their wings along the sides of her chest. This was good, she had explained to me, because she could not have spoken anyway.

As the tall man looked in their direction, she could not help but stare. Then she could hardly understand why he suddenly broke into a trot, heading straight for her table. As he swept the wife into a bone-crushing bear hug, a lightning bolt of realization shook my mother to her very core.

This glorious man with the wide white grin and strong shoulders was none other than *Easton!* The doctor-to-be and beloved son of the two most treasured people in her young life was then turning toward my mother.

She extended a shaky hand in his direction only to have him bypass her outstretched fingers in favor of a chest-to-chest embrace. Her skin pulsing with what felt like electricity, she returned the hug feeling hard muscle and soft gentle hands on her back.

Finally, she stepped back and looked up into the face of the man who would become her husband.

Soon enough after that, he would become my father.

Chapter 7: Ella

There are days when I flat out adore New York City. I often get up early in the morning, taking a stroll during the time when the fog is still sticking to the sidewalks. I can be a gypsy here, free to float around the city at will, nameless and faceless and unrecognizable under my broad shades and torn jeans.

There's nothing I can't do here. Broadway glows twenty-four hours a day, and there is always a spotlight if you're interested in standing under it. People follow their dreams to get here, and many times, they lose all hope during their stay. A dichotomy of life greets you at every corner. The stretch limo double-parked along the Avenue, idling in park and blowing through gas like water. Just down the way is the drunken bum who has not a penny to his name and no desire at all to do anything more than just watch people walk by. Every now and again, the elegant businessman hustling out to his awaiting car catches the eye of the poor downtrodden sucker laid out in his own vomit. They look at each other, but *right through* each other. Their lives intersecting for a moment in time, before one goes back to abject poverty and the other to his penthouse on the Upper East Side.

That's New York for you, the best and brightest a heartbeat away from personal disaster.

I have a little time to kill before I have to head to the airport. I'm traveling pretty light, just a few pairs of jeans and t-shirts, couple of bathing suits if Lauren has enough time for a trip to the beach. There are no cute little dresses or stilettos included on this trip, I doubt either one of us will have the heart to leave her house once I suck out all the joy like a wind turbine in reverse.

I didn't sleep all that much last night, my thoughts slamming around my head like marbles on a driveway. I tried to focus on the noises of the city, the coughs, the laughs, the blaring horns all rising through the air.

Lauren is under the impression I just needed a break from New York, some space to spread out and just chill. I wasn't very generous about the details of my quick trip, basically just telling her I wanted to see her and catch up. This is the part that still tears me up inside. Aside from the chance that my boobs are about to be whacked off, and that horrifying feeling I'm trying to prepare for, when I run my fingers through my hair and it's not there anymore, it's the full disclosure I'm dreading most. Lauren will get an instant impression that something is wrong. She is so intuitive it's spooky, especially about me. One look at my drawn face, and she'll know all is not well. History will have her assuming it has something to do with my family. She knows they are a load and dealing with them is exhausting.

I walk with my head slightly angled down, lost in my own thoughts. It's still early so the sidewalks are quiet as I stroll down to the twenty-four-hour CVS to grab a few things I need for my trip. As always, I am tucked away from my fellow streetwalkers by sunglasses that cover half of my face from my eyebrows down to mid-cheek. I'll admit my sister has taught me one valuable thing as my family's fame grew. For some odd reason, and one Kelby has a fiery anguish about, I was blessed with some rather unique eyes. "Blessed" is not the word I use, it's hers, and it's always preceded by "fucking, fricking, or goddamned" depending on how foul her mood is at the time. Kelby is herself one hot piece of ass, but apparently my single blessing really stings. I guess in her reluctant attempt to love me in spite of it, she has insisted I wear big dark sunglasses whenever I'm out alone to keep the ever-present and always annoying paparazzi off my heels. When my face is partially covered, my hair tucked under a hat, I can pretty much carry on unnoticed. Besides, New Yorkers are hardly the type to look at one moving object too long. My coworkers at Hyde still get a kick out of walking out the front door with me and getting a flashbulb in the face. Sometimes they even find themselves featured alongside me on *Page Six*, but being the most boring member of the Sheridan clan, that doesn't happen all that often.

I'm careful to keep my eyes low as I pay for my travel size toothpaste, Excedrin to ward off my all for certain migraine when I land in L.A., and a new paperback to keep my mind off being suspended too far up in the air for six hours. I hope that the flight won't be fully booked and I'll have the entire row of first class to myself. In reality, there is a fat chance of that ever happening. Almost every single flight headed from New York to Los Angeles is packed tighter than Kelby's ass in her True Religion jeans. That's one of the reasons I splurged on my first class ticket, to lessen my chances of having to make small talk or even worse, get recognized and gawked at.

My travel attire would make my mother's jaw drop in disgust but it is a great way to stay unrecognizable. I always follow the same routine. I stuff my hair deep under a baseball hat with a dark brim; wear my famous face-shielding sunglasses, and my oldest pair of worn jeans with a long nondescript sweater. With half my body covered, I can usually pull off a clean break from airport to airport, with only a small flicker of recognition from an alert flight attendant.

On this JFK-to-LAX route heavily traveled by celebrity types, the flight attendants can be your best friend or worst enemy. Get a young giddy one, star struck and skittish, and you're swarmed by the time you hit cruising altitude. The more seasoned attendants barely even blink in your direction, and my secret is always safe with them.

To make sure Kelby was not going to tattle to my mother, I had to do some hard negotiating. I agreed that if she kept my trip under wraps I would talk to my parents about their boycott on Harris. Not that I ever really will, but at this point I'd agree to just about anything to keep Kelby's trap shut.

Sometimes I feel like I'm still ten years old, getting caught with a cigarette lighter or muttering a forbidden word under my breath. The wrath of my parents is still fearsome for all three of us, often used as a bargaining tool for one of us to get what he or she wants from the other. Probably not at all healthy and somewhat immature, but it always does the trick. For Kass, it's always a plea for us to help keep his penchant for sleazy women a secret, even though I'm certain my father at least is well aware of this. After all, he's been there. Did not partake quite as much as others, but at least watched the strange and seductive dance of the beautiful people from afar for many years.

One day, I'm sure Kass will meet the perfect girl who is just the right mix of sexy and smart. It's not like I think it's fabulous he's acting like a major player, and I tell him all the time to steer clear of the really dirty girls who just might be hiding a Flip-cam in the corner of the hotel room. Kass has enough of that Sheridan guilt plugged in to worry about showing up naked on YouTube, someone's Facebook page or on TMZ. He's also smart enough to make sure any girl he's photographed with would come up clean on the government database. No arrest warrants, no outstanding charges, not even a parking ticket. Disappointing my parents is not an option; even as adults we do what we can to keep them happy.

Is that love? Or flat out fear of being cast out of a position of good-standing. Either way it's not a place you'd like to be. It is always cold and icy, and your feet can't get traction to climb back up.

I adjust my sunglasses, thinking that if our eyes are the windows to our souls maybe that's why I'm so good at hiding mine from the world. Under my sunglasses, or below the brim of my hat, no one sees that I'm just average and make a lot of mistakes. No one can see my cancer, or my fear, or the fact that I've come up short, yet again.

Maybe Kelby knew something I didn't all those years ago when she bought me my first pair of obnoxiously oversized Dolce & Gabbana sunglasses. Maybe she knew that one day I would be carrying a burden so large it would look like a billboard.

I grab my plastic CVS bag and leave the store. The sun is just starting to break along the horizon, brilliant enough to warm my face before my shades dim it down to a soft gray. I check my watch and realize I have to pick up my step if I'm going to catch my taxi to the airport on time. My bags are packed and ready to go at my apartment. I have two manuscripts packed into my carry-on, just in case the paperback doesn't hold my attention. I don't feel much like editing, but I chose two that are demanding a lot of my time right now and I feel guilty setting them aside.

One is from a woman in Las Vegas who has already signed on with Hyde, more because of her potential than her actual progress. She's under contract to send me her work in progress chapter by chapter. Instead, I am getting bits and pieces that lately seem to have no rhyme or reason. When I called her gently out on the carpet she explained that her three-year-old son was recently diagnosed with autism and her heart just isn't in it at the moment. I have chosen to keep that potentially deal-breaking morsel from Alan and give her some space to deal with life. I know I can't keep her protected for much longer, because in this high pressure world if you don't produce you get kicked to the curb. As much as they pour out their hearts in their written words, authors are still a commodity and when their stocks take a dive, the market cleans house.

Amanda Southerby, personal disaster aside, is skirting dangerously close to being sold off.

The other manuscript is one I am helping the author tweak almost page by page which is unheard of, but I have a soft spot for him, too. He has an enormous gift but is kind of like Jim Carrey, a rubbery artist with a raging case of ADD. His tale of a Boston detective caught up in a murder for hire investigation manages to hook the reader almost immediately with violence and such disturbing human behavior I've had to ask him if he was tortured as a child. He has assured me the horrific twists and gory turns are purely the result of an overactive imagination. He rounds it all out with an ending that readers will dissect word by word because they just don't want it to end. Sam Burton may be skilled with his words, but he's reckless with everything else. I feel like I'm correcting the work of a brilliant second grader. Sure, he's clever, but his crayon just can't seem to stay inside the lines.

Sam's grammatical minefield and Amanda's family crisis notwithstanding, my work is like the angel on my shoulder right now. At times, with my glasses perched at the end of my nose and my pencil wound around my ponytail I completely forget I will soon become a fixture in the chemo room of New York General Hospital. When I'm reading about Sam's mobsters making back room deals in some greasy old North End Italian restaurant with plush red leather seats and checkered tablecloths, cancer doesn't even register. There just isn't room in my cerebral vortex, and *that* is like happiness on a stick.

I can totally ignore the ache along my chest wall when Amanda tells me how the doctors began to suspect her son was on the spectrum when he couldn't muster more than one word by the time he turned three. I feel her pain, rather than my own when she tells me he can't look her directly in the eye and tell his mommy that he loves her.

Maybe this is why I tuck these two particular manuscripts inside my bag.

My gift in return for theirs.

But really, how can you ever properly thank someone for giving your brain a moment of peace, when it is otherwise fully engaged in the fight of its life?

Chapter 8: Dezi

Eyes closed, my breathing smooth and relaxed, I give myself a personal moment in the back of NYC Yellow Cab #524. Part of my work strategy is to look ahead to a successful outcome. I used to do this before each football game with my helmet pressed firmly into my locker. I forced myself to take deep steady breaths. After a few seconds, the noise around me would fade out until all I heard was the sound of my own breathing and the rush of blood in my ears following each heart beat. I would envision the final play of the game as a sprint that would take me down field on a direct path for the end zone. My fingers would clench with the weight of my imaginary football and my legs would tighten as they anticipated the motion of full speed ahead. Slowly, I would come back around to the present but I would bring that feeling with me.

Only then would I be ready to go for real.

I am a firm believer of mental preparedness in life. Too many people just don't listen to that gut feeling that we are all born with. The small voice that keeps you from getting behind the wheel when you've had one too many, or that pinch of pain when you ask your heart to open back up to the flame that burned it once before. Call it intuition, instinct, or just plain common sense. Whatever it is I respect the hell out of it, and listen ever so carefully when it speaks to me.

That's why I just can't shake this uneasy feeling kicking around my head. I have triple checked my equipment, making sure it has safely arrived at the airport and is being held for me until I get there to pick it up. I even had the baggage handler check the tracking number twice to make sure it matches my receipt. I left a final message with my contact, making sure he will be there to pick me up, and asking him to confirm our shoot location for the full six hours I requested.

I have no reason to believe I'm missing something, but *the voice* is whispering. I just wish I could hear what it was trying to tell me.

I reach into my coat pocket for the itinerary printout Melissa left for me. I give it a quick glance then chuckle as I realize she booked me into first class, a luxury I rarely allow myself to enjoy during business travel. She knows how hard I worked to land this job, and this is her unobtrusive way of joining in on my celebration. Hey, I can afford it occasionally so why not take advantage of some extra space, fine food, and creature comforts we sacrifice in coach. Nothing I hate more than a screaming kid or someone hacking just over my shoulder, sending all their germs straight into my personal space. Do I really even have to bring up the bathrooms? I always feel an especially poignant sense of sympathy for the sorry suckers who are stacked into the seats next to the lavatories. Their necks craned toward the windows, as if every extra inch they can put between their nostrils and the swinging bathroom door is a step up from the level of purgatory they're stuck in.

We continue our crawl to the airport. Even this early in the morning, the highway is packed and the line snaking its way toward departures is just limping along. Damn, there are too many people in this world. I have always hated crowds. They make my body temperature jump and my muscles twitch. Actually, I cannot stand the entire airport experience. The mad rush to get there, followed by the herculean effort to hand off your bag without being tagged for going over the weight limit. Then, it's a waiting game. God only knows when bad weather will keep you grounded and you're stuck curled up on one of those flimsy chairs connected by metal bars to the next guy doing the same thing.

My grandfather used to be a pilot and when he'd fly in each Christmas my mother would bring us to pick him up at the airport. My younger sister and I would walk down to where his plane was unloading and watch the passengers getting off. Back then you didn't have to clear security to get down to the gates, you just went. No questions asked. No U.S. Marshalls standing by with guns holstered to their hips, no need to dump your liquids in the trashcans, no need to take off your shoes or be patted up, down and all around. It was a kinder, gentler world in those days.

We would scan the group of weary-looking travelers, anxious to see the tall gentleman with his three piece suit and smart leather briefcase by his side. When he earned his pilot's license there was a certain class to the business of transportation. Folks dressed for it.

Men wore suits, women wore skirts, and no one would be caught dead in ripped jeans, flip-flops, or wrinkled tees.

I look down at my own jeans, freshly ironed though they may be, and offer up a quick apology to the sky. *Sorry, Gramps.* I am not the gentleman he was, not on my best day.

My driver barks back at me in broken English something that I figure is either the amount I owe him, or a warning that we are approaching my drop off location. I dig back into my coat for my wallet and come up with the right amount of cash, giving him a few extra for his trouble. With my gear already waiting for me in L.A., I'm traveling with only one carry-on bag. My cell buzzes in my coat pocket and for a moment, I feel a sense of panic sweep through my chest. *Oh shit*, could this be why I have had this sickening sense of dread all morning? If this job falls apart, someone will have to bring a dolly to roll me out of the nearest bar.

I don't recognize the number but I try to calmly grab the call, praying to high heaven everything is on track.

"Hey, baby," I hear in a whisper soft voice. *What the fuck?* How did Bridget not get the message that…*I'm out?* I suck back the vile words that I almost let fly as I struggle to hold the phone, my bag, and my temper. I thought she was long gone.

Now what do I do?

With few options that don't involve me threatening a restraining order I figure the best way to set her straight is not over the phone on my way to a job that requires my full undivided attention. I tell her hello, but firmly explain I can't talk right now and I'm heading out of town. Bridget tries to dig the details out of me. Where am I going, is it for work, or *pleasure?* She rolls the last word off her tongue with what she hopes is a seductive little trill. Instead, I feel like I'm trying to outrun a coiled rattlesnake that could strike at any moment.

Back away gently, don't engage and live to fight another day.

I have followed very firm rules when it comes to women. I may not be the best boyfriend when it comes to promises of a future full of picket fences and kids playing in the backyard, but I am as kind as I can be when it's time to call it quits. I like to think of the women who come and go from my life as someone's little sister. Having one of my own, I know what I would do to the asshole that broke her heart. It gives me a sense of restraint even for psychos like Bridget who are as thick as bricks.

I press my tongue into the roof of my mouth to make the sudden pounding between my ears stop. The kitten voice on the other end keeps purring. Why is she still talking?

I check my watch and realize time is running out to get to my gate on time. I sigh loudly as I figure out her new strategy, which sounds like it came straight from the break up section of Men's Health magazine. She's full of quirky little anecdotes and all pumped up on what she perceives as insight into my typical male reaction and my emotionally shattered state. She tells me I am not properly dealing with my hurt over losing her.

Losing her? I thought I willfully gave her away.

I'm also supposed to appropriately mourn the loss of our relationship and even cry out my feelings if I need to.

"There's no shame in crying, Dez," she says in her little girl voice.

Yeah, I agree. If she keeps talking, I just might.

She goes on to tell me how women are more likely to use straight talk when they break up, and men just can't follow their logic. She tells me that's what happened in my kitchen the other day. I simply missed the boat.

If that's the boat she's on, I'd rather drown. I give her a few more seconds to explain to me that if I continue to repress my feelings they'll linger longer than the mold on the Chinese food in my fridge. Finally, when I've had about as much as I can take, I tell her my flight is boarding and I have to go. She tells me to think about what she's said and that she'll be ready for a nice quiet dinner and a long talk when I get back.

Great, I'll look forward to that like heart surgery.

I click off and put my cell back into my coat pocket. As I find a seat at the gate and put my bag down next to me, I slide into the hard plastic with such force the entire section of seats shifts. I get a couple of annoyed glances before people look away and shimmy their asses over to fit back into the uncomfortable curve.

Jesus Christ, do I really need this right now?

I begin to anticipate the first full swig of the Bloody Mary I'll order when we hit our cruising altitude. I can almost feel the vodka work its magic on my central nervous system. Usually, I stay far away from the booze cart when I fly, but these are extraordinary circumstances. Isn't it just like life to give you the golden egg with a huge crack right down the middle? Everything you have worked for spilling out around you like hot tar. One wrong step, with the wrong person, at the wrong time and you are stuck in place forever.

I push my forehead into the palm of my hands, visualizing the end zone one more time. Mental preparedness takes you three quarters of the way; I am almost in the home stretch. Why is the voice still here? What is it trying to tell me? Is it Bridget? Is it this job? I can't shake this sinking feeling that I'm missing something, and it's the biggest something of my entire life. Tension builds in my neck, along my shoulders, and even down to my hands as I work to keep them quietly in my lap as boarding begins. First class is called so I grab the leather strap of my bag, swing it around my shoulder and pull out my boarding pass.

The flight attendant waiting at the top of the boarding tunnel says a warm hello to the woman in front of me, revealing a perfect row of straight white teeth. There were times when I would have taken full advantage of that as she slides her eyes in my direction like smooth glass. I dig eyes. Eyes get me off more than anything else does. It doesn't matter if they're black as charcoal, brown as tree bark, or as blue as the ocean at midnight. I just really appreciate a good set of eyes on a beautiful woman.

For some reason, on this day her smile gives me a sense of calm as I approach her with an outstretched hand. She takes my ticket, rips it in half and hands me back the stub. I smile, getting a good vibe from her end. Even so, I decide not to engage. There is way too much on my plate as it is. On another flight, on another day, maybe we would have had a good time.

Just one more reason to get the hell away from Bridget. I never start a new relationship until I have completely ended another. It would seem I still have some ending to do with her.

I board the plane, find my seat, and settle in for the long trip. I turn the volume down on the voice in my head to stifle the part of me that just won't shut the hell up.

Chapter 9: Ahmed

My earliest memories are happy ones. My parents logged long hours at the hospital as they finished their residencies around the time I was a toddler. I would stay with my grandparents at their pub, playing in the back room or singing along to the piano man on Thursday and Friday nights. Those were the best nights when I stayed up until ten o'clock laughing and enjoying the company of my family.

My father seemed like a giant to me. He would grab me with his huge hands and swing me atop his high shoulders. They seemed strong as boards as I reached down to wrap my small fingers around his whiskered chin. He had the widest grin I had ever seen and the boom of his laugh would fill an entire room.

My grandparents gave me the nickname Little E, because I looked just like my father. Although my mother refused to acknowledge much about her Iraqi heritage, my father insisted she give me a name that was significant to her culture. He never asked her to divulge more than she wanted him to know, but he was aware of the pain the men in her life had inflicted. He told her their son was a way to change that. He would grow to learn of the people he came from, but he would live a kinder, gentler existence. Perhaps one day he would even spread his message to other young men who had yet to see a world of love and peace.

With that, I became Ahmed. My mother told me she thought for many days about what I should be called. It was difficult for her to accommodate my father's wishes that I receive a traditional Iraqi name, because she wanted to protect me from what she had known. Finally, when I was about to begin my fifth day of life my mother made her decision. She explained to my father and grandparents that many male names are based on physical prowess or individual power. In Iraq, women have little value and virtually no opportunity. That, she explained, could never have been God's intent. She wanted her son to listen to the words of his maker over those of his fellow man, as he followed a path of righteousness into his own life. My mother was very literal at times. "Ahmed" in its true meaning is "one who constantly praises God." My mother could think of no more perfect thing for me to remember each day of my life.

My father and grandparents sat mesmerized by her words, as they often did. They looked upon me and spoke my name together for the first time.

"Then Ahmed he is," they said happily as they beamed down at their much adored child with the downy blond hair, pink cheeks, and bright blue eyes. I looked no more like an Ahmed than my father did, and that has served me well as I prepared to carry out my life's true mission. I do not think of what my mother might say if she knew of my intentions, I only hope she would understand them as I do.

My father became a surgeon. One of the best among his graduating class, he quickly found permanent work at a London hospital. Although the hours were long and the job rigorous, he never stayed away from me for too long. From time to time, he would take an entire day off to bring me to the tiny fishing village on the outskirts of his hometown. Together, we would sit along the dock, casting our lines out into the shallow water and occasionally hooking a tiny sunfish or two. He would tell me of his own boyhood spent fishing in the very same waters with my grandfather.

I had many questions for him. I would ask if he always wanted to be a doctor or if there was a time when he unsure of what his life would bring. I wanted to know how he knew he would marry my mother. I asked what it felt like to be a father, to fall in love. He would patiently answer all of my questions then ask what else I wanted to know. He would hold my hand when we walked back to the car, gently rubbing small circles around the knuckle of my thumb. He would wink at my mother as he told her I had caught "the big one" but threw him back to find his family. I never did catch "the big one" but I would have loved the chance to keep trying.

It was not to be. Although I did not know it at the time, fate would intervene and take my father from me long before I was ready to let him go.

My mother's childhood had shaped her in many ways, but what she could not erase was a sense of duty to the women of her homeland.

She became an obstetrician, determined to start each new life with the care and comfort she never had. It was not long before she and my father began to speak of moving to Baghdad where medical technology was several steps behind the modern world.

For generations, women labored at home with only the assistance of the village *qabilas*, or midwives. They were untrained at best, and had learned their limited skills from their own mothers or village elders. She told me the story of her youngest sister, who barely survived her own home birth. Her father had been anticipating a son and frantically paced the front yard of their small home waiting to hear his child's first cry. It did not come for a very long time. Day passed into night with my grandmother growing weaker by the hour. Finally, the child was born. It was not breathing. Sabeen, my grandmother's *qabilas*, tried something she had seen only once before, and had never done on her own. As my mother watched in utter fascination from the doorway, the midwife shook the infant, blew into her mouth, and lightly trailed a fingernail down her cheek before tickling the newborn's ashen ear. Only then did the first cry come. My grandfather had rushed into the room after hearing the wail of his child. My mother scurried out of his line of sight as he roughly brushed back Sabeen to hoist his newborn son high into the air. She quickly stepped aside too, unwilling to be the one to tell him a daughter had been born. The air in the room was still as his eyes glanced down, and disgust twisted his mouth into a tight line. He laid the infant back down at the foot of the bed, without even looking at his tormented wife covered in blood, dripping with sweat and regret at her inability to bring forth an heir. Overcome with disappointment that he had fathered yet another daughter, he stormed out of the home and did not return for days. There was no concern for his exhausted wife, fragile newborn or two other youngsters trying to survive on their own. He never apologized nor was he expected to, and he never forgave my grandmother for failing to give him a son.

My mother's sister was named Sabeen, after the woman who had saved her life.

Although many Iraqi women still relied on the village *qabilas* there were maternity wards springing up in the largest cities. My mother watched all this from England, with a growing tug of responsibility to help them any way she could. It would take a few more years of perfecting her skills before my mother felt she was ready to return to

Iraq. She had done countless hours of research on the state of Baghdad, where it was safest for children. Although she knew it was risky to bring me, she could not bear leaving me behind and my father wouldn't dream of letting us go alone. So together, they reached out to the largest hospital in the heart of Baghdad. The hospital director was a wealthy man originally from Kuwait. His family owned half of the Arabian Peninsula, and was quite willing to fund his effort to get the facility to a level that could keep pace with medical advances elsewhere. It was no easy task.

At the time, Baghdad was war-ravaged and poverty-stricken. Only very limited funds were available from the government, so the hospital had no choice but to become self-sustaining. The Kuwaiti man and his family invested much of their vast personal wealth and tried to attract some of the best doctors in the region. My parents were part of that vision.

The man promised them a safe place to live, and an opportunity for me to go to a hospital-sponsored school with the other employees' children. He told them of the important work they would be doing, that they would be helping in the rebirth of the country. So with the blessing of Easton's family, who had always believed my mother had a purposeful place in this world, we moved to Iraq.

Even though my grandparents held onto the firm belief that their family would one day return home to them, I would never see their kind and loving faces again.

Chapter 10: Ella

I hail a cab easily this morning, a good sign. Usually, I have to wait around at least a few minutes before an empty one sidles up next to me on the sidewalk. I toss in my small suitcase and climb shoulders first into the back seat. I tell the driver I am heading to departures at JFK and we move out. The sun is even higher in the sky now making me thankful to be under the full protection of my sunglasses.

I can almost smell fall in the air today. Soon the leaves will signal the official change of season and our entire skyline will look like the inside of a Fruity Pebbles cereal box. I love fall. Even though it means I am that much closer to sloshing through brown snow on the city sidewalks, hiding from the biting wind whipping my face, and trying to avoid the ten pounds that will settle on my couch-bound ass.

This fall, of course, will be different. Dr. Sturgis has insisted we begin treatment the minute I get home from seeing Lauren. He has already lined up my first appointment with my medical oncologist, telling me to block out two hours for this one meeting. I have also learned that I will have *several* oncologists, and many appointments with all of them.

First up will be the *surgical* oncologist who will have the pleasure of digging into my chest wall in search of all things that resemble cancer. This doctor may also earn the unique opportunity to actually rid me of my breast altogether. *Lucky guy.* I wonder if he has nightmares of all the breasts he has ever chopped off coming back to haunt him. A gang of them carrying fiery torches and storming his giant cancer-funded castle looking for vengeance.

Next, my team will whip me up a nice cocktail of chemicals that just might churn my guts into shredded cheese. Then, my radiation oncologist joins the party, ready to trip the light fantastic and beam it straight into my chest like a light saber. Of course, I hope it's not the same one that sliced off Luke Skywalker's arm, but beggars can't be choosers after all.

So ideally, I should consider us one big happy family that should all be on the same page. I have been advised to bring a family member or close friend to my appointments. Dr. Sturgis is especially adamant about this, and is quite disturbed that I have not told my family yet. As if I really want to throw out this can't-miss opportunity. Who wants to hang out with my cancer and me? We're really fun. We sleep all day, might throw up in your lap, and enjoy long talks about the afterlife. Anyone? Anyone? Bueller?

I kick around my options, yet again. Kelby? *Yeah, right.* Maybe if one of the oncologists looked like Brad Pitt and told her what nice boobs *she* had. "Too bad your sister is such a mess," he would tell her. She would agree, thankful that *someone* understood how hard it was for her to deal with her sister's "situation."

No, Kelby is definitely out. Kass is also a firm no. No matter how much I love him, I don't think you'd be able to find a woman alive who would want her brother to know *that* much about her breasts. Several wonderful friends have come along in my life. Many of my college girlfriends are still some of my favorite people, but most of them have husbands and small children and lives of their own. As if I would really ask them to drop everything and rush to my side.

Sure. *That* works.

My colleagues at work are also some of my closest friends but they are more the type you bitch about your job to, or discuss their husbands over a cocktail on a Friday night. Plus, there is still the whole bombshell announcement thing. I just don't completely trust that my work comrades, well intentioned as they may be, won't rush out to spill the cancer beans to the world.

Sorry guys, love you…but it's true…don't take it personally.

If Lauren weren't a superstar who worked a hundred hours a week, she'd be a no-brainer. But she is, and my bedside is just too far from L.A.

With that, the demoralizing process of elimination brings me back to my parents. I feel that all too familiar tightening in my stomach as I consider how in the world you ask the vice president of the United

States to play nurse. I can just hear myself asking my mother to take a personal day and come with me to the doctor. I'll remind her to bring a notebook so she can jot down things I'll need to remember, and then we'll order takeout and do each other's nails.

Could I ask my father? Probably. Will I ask my father? Absolutely not.

That pretty much leaves me with no one. Thanks again, cancer, nicely played.

God, I need some coffee.

I check my watch and hope the driver can get me to the airport in time for me to run to the Starbucks inside and order up a dose of spirit-strengthening caffeine. I check my wallet to make sure I have some cash handy. Although it won't be long before my mother gets wind of my credit card activity, I can at least limit how much I choose to shove in her face. No debit card at the airport. Luckily, I see a couple of twenties, which is also another good sign. Usually, my wallet is entirely empty. I have a bad habit of never carrying cash. To this day my father still slips me a small wad of dough each time I see him. His way, I suppose, of trying to take care of me. How I wish he really could.

The driver checks in with his boss, telling him he's almost pulling into JFK. *Good,* I have plenty of time to check in and make a quick beeline to the coffee counter. I can almost taste the first sip of the steaming brew and hope the line is relatively tame this morning.

I exit the cab, walking straight to the counter to check my small bag. I avoid the woman's eyes as I adjust the cap of my baseball hat, pulling it lower as she hoists my suitcase behind her and plops it onto the conveyor belt. She quickly looks to the person waiting behind me. I double check that I remembered *both* of my cell phones and that they are on vibrate. I put my personal cell into the pocket of my sweater and tuck my Bat-phone into my carry-on. That one I will leave well alone until I arrive in L.A. It hasn't chirped at me since Kelby's call, so I am cautiously optimistic she is keeping her word and hasn't yet run to my mother to play *I've Got A Secret.*

JFK is bustling today, the flying public having perfected the art of balancing their bulging leather bags on their shoulders, with their tiny cell phones hanging off the tips of their fingers. No wonder half the population has back problems. We are all twisted up into these impossible positions because we refuse to get off the damn grid. *Hang up*, I want to tell them. Hang up your goddamn phones and watch where you're going. *And lower your voices.* I don't want to hear about your kid's seventh grade science project, your dinner plans, or your boss's affair with his secretary.

I close in on the Starbucks counter and feel a small sense of satisfaction as I notice the line is downright small. Just a few people *on their cell phones* in front of me so I drop my bag down, dig out my cash, and wait my turn. The young woman quickly churns up my order and I head off to find my gate. At least I am on time today, less stress when there's time to kill. Passengers are waiting to board and it looks to me like it will be a full flight. Oh well, there goes my hope of grabbing the entire row to myself. I find a seat and the one next to it for my bag to sit on. I rifle through it, looking for one of the two manuscripts I threw in for the long flight. Sam's Mafia mobsters, or Amanda's tale of unrequited love, which story will it be today? I decide to go with Amanda's because I know once we get airborne I'll be too distracted by my freakish awareness of my surroundings to really focus on Sam's jumble of clutter.

I know that keeping the welders' glasses on when I'm inside buildings only draws more attention to myself. And it looks stupid. Why don't celebrities *get* that? That they look like total attention-sucking sycophants with their bloated lips and feigned annoyance at the world. I tuck my shades inside my bag, but I do keep my hair entirely stacked up under my baseball hat. Wouldn't do to have someone's cell phone camera snap a shot of me and then tweet about where I am at the moment. That would surely put my mother on my tail long before I am ready to deal with her.

Advancements in our technology make it increasingly challenging to stay anonymous. Everyone is now a potential threat to my effort to live inconspicuously. The whole Twitter thing especially, feels like yet another way for already self-consumed people to feel more important than they are. Wait, that sounds cruel. More important than they *wish* they were. Even my mother's keepers maintain a Twitter account for her, as does the president, and almost three quarters of the United States Congress. Kelby tweets incessantly, mostly about herself. Kass does so occasionally, but he has to follow NFL social media rules that limit the content. He is forbidden to post during actual games, as if he has the time, and he can't post about teammates, coaches, or strategy. Duh, why would he? It would be like offering up the perfect interception to the other team. My brother is ultra-competitive and the consummate professional. He easily follows all the rules. On the field, that is. Off, not so much.

Oh Kass, I hope you find a girl soon. A nice girl. It's time.

The plastic chair is about as comfortable as sitting on a block of ice. I shift around, trying to encourage my butt cheeks to find the most comfortable angle. There isn't one. There was such an early fall chill in the air this morning I pulled out my clunky old Ugg boots for the flight. I can just see my mother's mouth fall into the tight disapproving line I get whenever she doesn't like a particular piece of my wardrobe, or my entire wardrobe which is more often the case. Today, there is not a single thing I have on that she *would* approve of. Uggs included. My mother hates Uggs. She thinks they're lazy and sloppy and quite unattractive.

Sorry, Mom, I will give props to the few things in my life right now that fit. My old Uggs fit *perfectly*.

I sip my coffee and look around the gate at the people waiting for boarding to begin. None of them is aware of me, which is good. Off to my left, at the end of the row of chairs, is a man who appears to be in pain, or completely hung over. I can't tell which. He has a battered leather jacket on with jeans, his strong hands wrapped around his face on either side. He appears to take a deep breath then run his fingers roughly over each cheek before throwing his entire weight backward, straining the plastic chair and making the whole row of seats groan. He takes out his cell phone and smirks at it. I can see him clicking around the keypad, muttering at the same time. After a few minutes, he puts the phone back inside his jacket and leans forward with his elbows on his knees.

He looks oddly familiar to me, though I can't for the life of me figure out where I might have seen him before. *Celebrity?* Possibly, there are so many so-called celebrities these days. Reality TV star? I quickly think not because he doesn't seem to be waiting for someone to notice him. His agitation is almost palpable. I can *feel* the energy rolling off him in waves. Something is troubling him, and it's starting to make *me* nervous. Like, who needs the unstable guy hopping up to board the same plane you're on?

He doesn't *look* like a terrorist, but then again who does these days? *Anyone* could be a terrorist. Some disgruntled dude pissed off at everything and ready to blow up the world. I drag my eyes off this man, who is actually quite nice looking in a rugged athletic way. His coloring is a little darker, but in many ways, he reminds me of Kass, strong bulky arms, thick legs. His hair is stylishly long but he doesn't have that metro vibe at all. As I assess him from afar, I start to wonder what his story is.

Not a celebrity, not an obnoxious reality TV star, not a terrorist. So who are you? More importantly, what's got you so upset?

Why the heck do I care?

I notice the flight crew approaching the gate, all of them laughing and joking together as they pull along their rolling suitcases behind them. They greet the attendant and then turn to walk down the loading bridge. I always try to pick out the pilot, the guy with the most stripes on his jacket who will be responsible for my well-being for the next several hours. I hope he looks old enough to have enough experience, but not too old that he'll drop dead of a heart attack. I hope he has a wife and kids who keep him focused on the control panel like his life depended on it.

Like my life depended on it.

It's easy for me to pick out the pilot in this group. He's the young looking guy who is standing at least five inches higher than the rest. He seems completely at ease as he allows his crew to walk just ahead of him, pulling up the rear as he gives the attendant at the gate a subtle signal that soon she can start calling passengers.

Jennifer Vaughn

He looks good to me, I think. I take another sip of my coffee and wait for the call to begin boarding.

Chapter 11: Dezi

I shuffle past a few people as I make my way to my seat, avoiding any unnecessary small talk. It's early so the plane seems to be filled mostly with guys in khakis and ties who are likely heading to the West Coast for a business meeting.

I find my row, slide off my jacket and stuff it into the overhead compartment. It feels good to sit down in the plush first class seat and I say another silent thank you to Melissa for padding my ass with soft cushions for the long flight out. I have packed my iPod but I'm thinking I might try to grab a few winks given the time change and the level my nerves have hovered on for the past few days. I am trying not to over-think this job, and just let it happen. I have prepared flawlessly, my equipment is safe and waiting for me to pick up in L.A., and soon enough Bridget will be thousands of miles away. Temporarily, of course, but the distance will feel like a cold beer on a hot day. Smooth and sour, with just the right kick in just the right place.

I'm surprised at how agitated she's gotten me. Usually, I can climb out of the female spider web with ease, before the lovely long legs spin their death yarn around my neck. This time, however, I feel like I am all hung up in the gummy network of tangled strings. *What the hell? Why am I so fucking distracted? A nut job like Bridget is really* what's got me all tensed up? Part of me refuses to give her that much credit. Sure, she was fun while the sanity lasted but I've known where this was going for a while now.

The bad feeling is settling back in my gut like a lava rock. I reach into my bag and pull out my iPod. My eyes are hot and I think sleep will be about as elusive right now as a million dollar scratch ticket. Maybe some sweet Alicia Keyes will ease the strain in the back of my neck and put a splash of cool water on my fiery stomach. I would love to photograph this girl. Not only is her skin as smooth as the surface of milky mocha, she has a grin as bright as a constellation in the night sky. She is at the top of my list of dream jobs. I could forgo every trick I have ever learned, use a disposable camera from a convenience store and she would still light up the shot like the sunrise on a summer day.

I notice my cell buzzing again. I grab it then let it go to voicemail when I see it's only a buddy of mine probably looking to make plans for the weekend. I have been so caught up in this job I haven't even told anyone about it yet. I'm kind of superstitious like that. I only tell people in my life about the important things *after* I've already knocked it out of the park. That way there's no risk of disappointing anyone with unexpected failure.

I'll never forget the look on my parents' faces the day I collapsed on the field with a busted knee. The play had been simple enough. A quick hand-off from the quarterback, not even a sneak, and I was supposed to find the hole and shimmy up for a first down. What I couldn't have seen was the middle linebacker move at just the right moment to take me out at the waist. Of course, middle linebackers can be quick to read the attack, and move in on you in a surprisingly nimble way, every cocky running back in the world has found that out the hard way. Being cockier than most, I never even gave him a second glance as I saw myself shoot right up the gap. His enormous arms came out of nowhere, snapping my head back as he wrapped himself around me, pulling my torso in one direction while my legs stayed planted on the turf. I heard a sickening pop and knew in that moment I was down for good. The ligament tore clean through, taking with it every ounce of hope I had for my future.

It felt like an eternity buried under the heap of bodies pressing down on me, twisting my knee to impossible degrees as each monster hauled his massive bulk off me one at a time. There is no worse feeling than being at the bottom of a tackle. Fingers reach through the protective grate of your helmet, poking your eyes, forcing their way up each nostril. Your bones rattle under the weight of the pile. Your hips press deeper into the turf, hands crushed, lungs burning as they try to find air.

Most days I could shake it off. On that day, it was as if my brain and my knee weren't connected to the same body. My brain told me to move. My knee said no way. I could do nothing more than roll onto my back and shut my eyes as I waited for my trainer to deliver the crushing news that deep down I already knew. And he did. He took one look, and then lifted my leg with one hand under my calf, the other gripping my thigh. The final test that told him there was nothing holding it together in the middle. He bent his head as close to my ear as he could to make sure no one heard it but me.

"It's over, Dez. I'm going to walk you off this field with as much dignity as I can give you. Keep your helmet on. Do not look up. Do *not* give the fuckers the satisfaction of looking them in the eye."

My memory may blur at times, and there are certain events in my life I can't remember for shit. But the words he spoke to me that day are seared in for good. I can still hear his voice booming in my eardrum, and I can still see the fury in his face as he got under my shoulder and lifted me off the field for the last time.

After all, on that day he lost a lot, too.

The locker room was like a morgue. No one spoke; the mood was dire. I remember the lights blazed in my eyes, as I lay flat on the table, biting a towel to keep from screaming out in pain. The team doctor met us inside and quickly cut away my pants to get a better look at my knee. He put one hand on my thigh and pulled the shin forward, looking for shifting. I have had doctors do this a hundred times before to test the flexibility and give, but this time I could barely stand him touching me. His fingers felt like hot pokers as he bent my knee up about ninety degrees, looking at the stability of my ACL. If it were intact, it would only allow my shin to come forward slightly. Instead, it spilled out like milk on the kitchen floor.

He did not speak to me as he jotted some notes down on the chart that would go along with me to the hospital. In fact, no one spoke to me. A mutual respect among athletes for the situation I found myself in. We have an innate sense of knowing when to shut the hell up because words won't make a lick of difference and silence is the only way to properly mourn the loss of a comrade's dream.

At some point, someone reached my parents in the stands to let them know I would be leaving via ambulance right away. They were told to meet me at the hospital, which was good because I didn't want them to see me like that. The pain felt like a living, breathing presence as it stretched its fingers further up and down my leg. Every bone in my body had begun to ache with a force that made my jaw chatter.

Later, I would learn I had also cracked two ribs, chipped a tooth, and suffered a mild concussion on that play.

No parent wants to see his child so close to the edge. I asked the doctor to make sure they were kept away until I could get a shot of morphine, or something else with a kick.

Part of my knee had to heal before the surgery could even happen. I sat around for weeks, as valiant efforts were made to reduce the swelling and get me into the OR. Finally, I had the surgery but I already knew what would happen. Rehab would get me back to my life, but it would never return me to the only place I wanted to be.

I went through the motions even though I was withering away on the inside. Teammates would stop in, telling me about the plays they were tweaking, how every other running back was always a second or two off my time. They played their roles well, talking about how we would rip it up when I got back. We never spoke it aloud, but we all knew. I was out. Game over.

I did try, however, to get back to where I was. I hit the gym harder than ever, building up my strength and endurance, hoping against logic it would help me compensate for the speed I knew I had lost. It didn't. Very early in the season we all could tell I just was not the sure thing I used to be. Plays we used to execute like clockwork began to feel impossible. When timing is everything, I was either early or too late. I bobbled the hand-off, tripped along the outside, and could not fake for shit. It was all falling apart, and I was losing my nerve. I began to anticipate the hit when I should have been focusing on the run.

My parents sat me down one day to have the hard talk. I surprised myself with my honesty. I admitted I felt weak for the first time in my life. They told me they were proud no matter what, but I needed to begin planning for life after football. The conversation felt unnatural for all of us; football was all we had ever known. *It had been my entire life.* Just like that, it was over. We all felt the sting.

Thank God, I had the presence of mind not to cancel my subscription to *Sports Illustrated*. One day I started going through the stack that had piled up, and the tide began to turn. I found an elective photography class for the next semester and jumped in feet first. I asked a ton of questions, made many mistakes. Eventually, I got better, more confident, *excited* about something again. The professor took a strong interest in me, telling me I had a good eye, encouraging me quietly to try it this way, or that way. He had just the right personality for me at the time. He wasn't like any of the mentors I'd known in sports. He wasn't wild with frenetic energy, and he never got in my face. He spoke softly, like you actually had to *listen* to get the subtlety of his message. He did not speak in terms of winning or losing, and skill had nothing to do with physical power. He offered praise only when I deserved it, and when it came I knew I had gotten it just right. He gave me reason again to believe in myself, that not all was completely lost.

He could never have known it at the time, but he may have given me the biggest gift of all. *A purpose.* I felt strong again; for the first time in what felt like forever, something mattered to me.

Several girls came and went during this time. That's what college is for, after all. A few of them made an impression, but most of them were interchangeable. Pretty faces that faded into silly drunken nights, guided by nothing more than youthful energy and urges.

I probably have never been in love in the purest sense of the word. As an adult, only one or two girlfriends have ever lingered long enough to have a toothbrush in my bathroom. The Bridget disaster notwithstanding, we usually part ways as friends, but I am typically the one who insists we part ways.

Thankfully, my sister has already given my parents two grandkids to spoil, because for a while they were breathing down my neck like sloppy St. Bernards. I get it, I really do. Maybe it's just not in the cards for me. Marriage and kids remind me of walking into a dealership looking to buy a Porsche. Somehow, someone throws you a sleek sales pitch and you drive off in a minivan. It's only when it won't fit in your garage that you ask yourself what the fuck just happened.

I find Alicia in my playlist and put my earphones in. An older couple has settled into the seats to my right, but no one is sitting to my left. I close my eyes and listen for her piano groove to start. I get about halfway through the song when I feel a sharp push on my elbow. My iPod is ripped clean from the cord connecting it to my earphones.

What the fuck?

I bolt upright to save it from falling to the floor and smashing into a million pieces but I connect with *flesh* on the way down. I pull my hand back like it's been burned, as does the woman now standing directly above me. She looks up from under the ridiculous baseball hat that covers almost her entire face and tries to offer an apology. She seems to stutter as her eyes lock with mine.

We stop moving. I feel like I've stopped *breathing*.

I sit there frozen in place, staring into the greenest eyes I have ever seen in my entire life.

Chapter 12: Ahmed

My teachers didn't know what to do with me. I was learning at a rate my other classmates could not keep up with. I loved the idea of gaining knowledge. History, languages, math, anything that had a purpose or a place in this world I wanted to know about it.

I jumped from one grade to the next as the school tried to keep me challenged but not overwhelmed. My parents were proud, but never pressured me to be perfect. I never felt that I had anything to prove, learning was easy for me. Once I saw a number or a word, I could summon it forth in my head with nothing more strenuous than a simple thought.

They called me *gifted*. I thought of it more as *cursed*.

I had a vivid imagination, even as a child. My school was on the bottom floor of the hospital. My parents stopped in every day around lunchtime. We would sit together at one of the tables, my father's knees pushed to his chin as he tried to fit his enormous body into the tiny plastic seat of our classroom chairs. My mother would laugh at him, roll her eyes, and say to me, "That's your father, Ahmed. Always the clown."

My friends did not have fathers who would sit in these tiny chairs and they would laugh at him, too.

During this time each day I would tell them about what we had learned, but I would add things. *Strange things.* I would tell them that I saw a man lurking in the hallway just outside our classroom. They would look at each other with concern, then one of them would leave to speak to the teacher who would always assure them there were no men in the hallways and I was never in danger.

Maybe the *feel* of Iraq was affecting my perception. Each day when my parents would take me to the market square to buy food for dinner we would pass dangerous looking men armed with swords, knives, and guns. My mother, under her burka, would whisper sharply at me not to stare, but I could not help myself. My father would hold me firmly by the hand the entire time we were out on the streets. He did not let go until we walked through the front door of our home. He never said anything, but I could feel him tense up during our daily trips to the market.

He did not fit in there, and neither did I. People would look sideways at our white blond hair, ruddy skin, and icy blue eyes. They did not often see our type and we were interesting to them but it was unnerving to attract such attention, especially for my father. I wondered if he wanted to go home. Did he miss his family? Did it feel strange to be living in such a murky world as this?

Although most of the faces I saw each day were nothing like my own, there were a few American doctors working at the Baghdad hospital during those years, and I went to school with their children. My subtle British accent slipped away as I mingled with other people and dialects. Many of them did not stay long, so the friendships I formed at an early age dissolved when my classmates would move on. I was not allowed to be outside by myself, so I did not become friends with the Iraqi children growing up around me.

By sheer will I learned Arabic, and spoke it fluently by the time I was nine years old. I did not know it at the time, but it would serve me well soon enough, keeping me connected to the people I would need to communicate with as an adult.

Our home was sparse and simple, comfortable but not fancy. We would see the presidential palaces from the street and wonder how one family could fill so much space. My parents taught me about Iraq, and its people, but we never once tried to find my mother's family. She had no desire to see them again, or allow them any sort of connection to her husband and son. She never even disclosed her last name to me, as a way to seal off her family for good.

I never really wanted to know them anyway. Her father disgusted me with his cruelty and rage.

There were parts of this strange land that were beautiful. On weekends when my parents were not working, we would travel to the Arch at Ctesiphon. My mother would hold my hand as we craned our necks back to stare at the towering vault that stood a hundred feet tall. She would laugh as she told me it as the only thing taller than my father.

Together, we would wander inside the national museum looking at the collections of Mesopotamian antiquities, including clay tablets and a four-thousand-year-old harp. All of it fascinated me. We would travel to cities named in the Bible, and together we would gaze upon the gnarled old tree that was supposedly Adam's in the Garden of Eden. The beauty of my mother's native land stunned my father, and she had a proud respect for it, but I always thought she showed me these magnificent places as she would any other interesting part of the world. She wanted me to see it for what it was, not because it had a connection to her.

As we traveled across many miles, exploring ancient towns and historic sites my mother would remind me that chemical weapons plants surrounded many of them, along with missile ranges, and bomb shelters. "What mankind can do, Ahmed," she would say. "We create beauty then call for its destruction. This is what happens when God is forgotten, when His power to protect the innocent is lost." I fumbled with the meaning of that for many years. Only later, when the precious Arch was so badly damaged and at risk of collapse, would I understand her words exactly.

Eventually, my mother became director of OB/GYN services at the hospital. She worked high-risk cases and developed a program to help women experiencing the heartache of infertility. Western medicine was far ahead of what Iraq could offer at the time, but my mother was determined to open the door to the possibilities. I think that with each new being she helped bring forth she chipped away at the damage done by her own family. She would tell me of the exact moment when an innocent new life began, how she would watch the tiny lungs fill with air for the first time. Because there was such joy in her life during this time, I do not think she ever fully anticipated the danger we would soon be in. Even though she had seen evil first hand, my mother always tried to close her fist around hope. She never let it go, not even at the very end.

My father focused on general and vascular surgery but saw his fair share of battle wounds from the many conflicts. He didn't like the notion of returning young men to the battlefield, and tried to develop a firm bedside manner that discouraged them from ever coming back to his OR. Deep down he knew if he never saw them again it was because they were probably dead. Many of them had grown into religious zealots by the time they reached their teenaged years, fully committed to either the government or a faction seeking to overthrow it. By the time they got to him, most of them were too far gone.

During this time, I noticed a change in my father. He still had an easy laugh, especially for me, but the lightness in his eyes was fading. Few things in Iraq brought him joy. There was no fishing village to bring me to, no family pub to laugh in, and no English hills to drive through on a lazy Sunday afternoon. His love for my mother never wavered, but he was suffering.

As the years progressed, he began to grow increasingly concerned about the safety of the country. His Kuwaiti boss spoke to him about the growing tension between the neighboring nations; he had begun to fear a backlash. News would come to him from his family back home that was not good. He quietly told my father to consider leaving Iraq temporarily to keep us safe. He was a good honest man and he had grown to care deeply about my parents. My father trusted him. He grew more and more distracted, his brow would furrow with deep concern as he watched me play on the floor of the living room. I was an astute child and asked my father to explain to me what had him so worried. He did, to an extent. He spoke gently to me, but with an urgency that even I could detect.

I would hear my parents discussing this at night, when they thought I was sleeping. My mother resisted his pressure to leave Iraq and return home to England. She was too deep into her work to go. It was the closest thing to an argument I had ever heard them have. By the time I really did fall asleep I was worried, too.

As I reached the age of ten, I was approaching the end of my life as I had known it. My father spent more and more time speaking to his family back home in England. Time was running out, but he and my mother were at odds. She simply refused to leave the hospital and the patients who had grown to trust her. It was a no-win situation for all of us.

My mother would not go. My father would not go without her. So we stayed in Iraq. We stayed until only one of us was left.

Chapter 13: Ella

Stupid carry-on bag.

It slides right off my shoulder and whacks the elbow of the guy behind me. As I turn around to apologize, I see his iPod heading for the floor. I make a quick effort to grab it before it smashes into a zillion pieces. He moves at the exact same time. Our heads come dangerously close to slamming into each other, while my baseball cap dislodges from my ponytail and comes flying forward to cover almost my entire face. Blind now, I reach wildly for the tiny metal box but end up connecting with something else. I grip it quickly, then let go as if I have a fistful of angry bees. We pull our hands back at the same time, and I look up at him with enough force to kick my hat backwards off my forehead.

"I'm...ahhh...so sorry..." I manage to blurt out. I get my first good look at him and I realize he's the same fidgety man I was watching in the terminal. Our faces are just inches apart as I try to stop staring at his lips, his nose, and his eyes.

My God, what does he have to be so angry about? This man is perfect. Good work, Ella. Perfect or not, he was obviously already having a bad day.

"Uhhh, is it broken?" I don't recognize my own voice. "You can have mine."

Duh, why did I say that? I fumble for my bag anyway trying to find my own iPod as a lame peace offering. Was I really going to give him my iPod? Would he take it? I can't find the damn thing anyway, and he's trying to stem the flow of babble streaming out of my mouth.

"Don't worry about it. See, it's fine." He produces his iPod and holds it up for me. I can tell it looks no worse for the wear and he smiles broadly at me. His teeth give me a few more things to stare at. "Are you okay?"

His voice is like the cushion of an oversized couch. Soft, deep, impossibly alluring.

"Oh, um…yeah, I'm fine." I manage to find words again as I hoist the bag away from him and start to turn back to the aisle to find my seat. "I'm just sorry about that. I didn't mean to disturb you, glad your iPod is okay."

He's still smiling at me though I notice his eyes squint as if he's trying to figure out what I look like underneath the lid of my baseball hat. Oh crap, does he recognize me? Is he going to text his buddies that Vice President Sheridan's clumsy daughter almost trashed his iPod?

"Yup, it's all good. Heavy bag though, maybe next time you should leave your crock-pot at home."

Ha, is he laughing with me, or at me? Probably *at me*, I am a joke after all.

"Hey, have we met before? You look familiar somehow, but I just can't place." he trails off, cocking his head to the left as a little tuft of hair comes lose and drops down on his forehead. *God, he's really handsome.*

"No, no I'm sure we haven't. Sorry to have bothered you again." I try to discourage another response, but it's hard to look away. I break our gaze to check my ticket again and realize my seat is directly across the aisle from his.

"I'm just going to sit down now and leave you alone." I try to give him a small grin that signals the end of our clumsy encounter. I can feel the hot breath of passengers huffing and puffing behind me. Without even trying, I manage to draw as much attention to myself as humanly possible. Their annoyance level peaks as I struggle to get my bag and my body into the right seat, demanding from them an extra few precious seconds of patience. I can feel the stress sweat starting to flow in small trickles down my back. I keep my head low and my eyes to myself as the people lined up behind me begin their single file flow to the back of the plane. Many of them shoot me a look of pure disgust for keeping them waiting. The whole incident probably cost them an extra two minutes, but in the uncomfortably tight space of the plane's main aisle, it is an unacceptable inconvenience.

Sorry, I'm so sorry. Please don't tell my mother.

Once I'm settled, I risk a quick glance over at the iPod hottie and I'm glad to see he's gone back to the music he seemed to be enjoying before I blew in like an 18-wheeler on cruise control. I hope he has given up on figuring out why I look familiar to him. In another life, on another flight, maybe we could have exchanged more than just one awkward moment. If I weren't about to embark on a medical odyssey to save my own life, if I weren't so emotionally unavailable, if I weren't *me*, I would really enjoy a few moments of his time that didn't involve the implosion of his iPod.

My full weight now settled into the small plane seat, it hits me like a ton of bricks that I am flat-out exhausted. The roller coaster I have been on for the past several weeks is coming in to the gate and I really want to get off. I feel like I'm losing my mind. I have had conversations with people at work that I have completely forgotten about. I have promised drafts or rewrites on a particular day and then failed to deliver on any of them. I am losing control over my own life and it's terrifying.

To my horror, I feel the hot sting of tears in the back of my eyes. The inevitable migraine starts to kick at my skull like a horse trying to get out of a burning barn. I take the corner of my shirt and try to dab away the mortifying moisture along the sides of my nose.

Dear God, get a grip, Ella.

For the vast majority of us born with fully functioning body parts, we fall into a sort of complacency. We grow into beings who expect each organ, limb, and brain cell to stay the course. I have been leveled by the idea of actually *losing a body part*. It's not as though I give my breasts much thought each day. I don't. However, the concept of removing one of them from my body is settling in like wet cement. My stomach hurts, my head feels fuzzy, and I feel totally let down. I thought my body and I were a team. I took care of it; it took care of me. Together forever.

Well, apparently, nothing lasts forever, not even the stuff we are born with that we assume is built to last. I guess even God's hands forgot to tighten the bolts on a few of us.

Even though I'm being told there is great hope for a cure, I'm painfully aware of all the things working against me right now. Typically, young women who are diagnosed with breast cancer get the really shitty kind, the cancer that digs in its heels and decides to either stick around for awhile, or takes you down right away. We don't yet know which one has come out to play with me. Doctors can tell a lot by the diagnostic tests they order up like deli sandwiches when *the lump* first makes itself known, but they won't know for sure how deep it is, or how far it's spread until they open you up and take a look inside.

Here's how it goes: When you're nothing more than a pile of raw nerves they send you along to the breast center across town. We are told to let our boobs hang loose as we sit in a room with other paranoid women all wearing our open-in-the-front johnnies that feel more like wet t-shirts.

"Go ahead," you want to say. "Take a look. I may not have them much longer anyway."

One by one like ants to a poison picnic, they march you into a room full of white equipment. In one corner sits the computer that will pop up black and white images featuring the guts of your breasts. But directly in front of you, a plastic tray hangs off the arm of a machine that stands almost as tall as the paneled ceiling. You begin to wonder how in the world your boob will fit *on* that tray, or *in* that tray, or possibly...*under that tray?*

God forbid!

Then the woman you have forgotten was even standing there tells you to lift one arm while she literally scoops up your breast with her own hand and places it, pulls it, *pummels it* into that nasty tray.

"Hold still, try not to breathe." "Don't worry," you want to tell her. "I haven't breathed in days."

"And...good. Now the other side." And the other boob gets the scoop treatment, too. Have to make sure we demoralize both breasts, wouldn't be fair to leave one out now, would it?

Next comes the best part of all, the waiting. You watch the technician's face like a hawk, trying to pick up the slightest furrow of her brow that would give you a sign. How 'bout a smile, please give me a smile. Tell me I'm okay. Of course, they are all masters of the stone face, and continue to call you "honey" or "sweetie" regardless of what they are looking at on the screen. The final word has to come from the radiologist, who will pour over the insides of your black and white breasts like syrup over pancakes, looking for that little nugget of junk that could have the potential to kill you.

It is a sickeningly simple way to find cancer. We are told it saves lives. I have yet to see how it has done anything so far but ruin mine.

The beads of sweat down my back seem to be drying up. I push back against the seat and cross my left leg over my right knee. I look out the window at the men in yellow vests scurrying around the sides of the plane, loading luggage. The sun is shining today, skies are clear.

Mornings are good for me right now. When the sun is out, I have hope. Nights are horrible. When I am alone in the dark, the bad thoughts come at me like pelting rain. I cannot escape them.

I worry about what is about to happen to me.

I worry about the drugs I am about to take.

I worry about my family worrying about me.

I worry I won't make it.

Can we go now? As if the crew heard my silent plea, they begin to roam the cabin shutting the overhead compartments and asking us to fasten our seatbelts and turn off our electronic devices. They tell us we will be taxiing to the runway shortly, and we're next in line for takeoff.

The guys loading the luggage slam the belly of the plane shut. The thud makes me jump. I try to relax again and wait for the churn of the engines. Pretty soon we'll be airborne. Pretty soon I will make Lauren cry. Pretty soon I will rock the world of the nation's second in command. No wonder I have a headache.

Chapter 14: Dezi

How do I know this girl? Where have I seen her? Is she a model? Old girlfriend I knew during another time? For the life of me, I cannot figure it out, but sure as shit, *I know her.*

The eyes are mesmerizing, unforgettable, and green like summer grass with tiny gold flecks around the edges. Course, it was clear she was trying to hide them and everything else about her under her baseball hat. She became almost panic-stricken when I asked if we had met before. Is she just some super-important type who loathes the idea of mingling with us common folk?

I look over the aisle at her again. Her hat is back in place, covering almost her entire face. I can make out nicely defined cheekbones, full lips, and a strong chin. Everything else, including those eyes, is concealed beneath the shadow of the brim.

I need this like a hole in the head. I have no business even thinking about trying to work up a conversation with her. She's weird, anyway. A skittish, standoffish, stuttering mess of nerves that I should avoid like the plague. A woman like that is always too much work. She's probably so needy you'd forget how jealous and emotional she can be. I cringe, thinking this is usually about the time most guys would signal the waiter for the check, call her a cab, and delete her number from their cell phones. Sorry, honey, he's just not that into you.

In spite of all the reasons why I shouldn't, I can't help but stare at her. She has put her head back against the seat and closed her eyes. A quick look would tell me she was completely at ease. But as my eyes linger I can see her foot, crossed over her knee, bouncing non-stop. The old Ugg boot she has on looks like it is possessed by some buzzing energy.

She can't sit still. Nervous flier? Her fingers are twined together but they keep moving against each other so firmly she'll give herself blisters. Her mouth is pulled into a set line. As much as motion is flowing through her from the neck down, her face is perfectly still. I watch her pull her shirt down over her wrist to catch some extra fabric then wipe it over the corner of her eye.

Why is she crying? What could be so terrible in her life that she would climb on a plane all alone and begin to cry before we even leave the gate?

Should I care? Absolutely not.

But I do. And I don't know why.

As far as I know, she could be as twisted as Bridget. She could have just slit someone's throat and buried him in the back yard. She could be a raging bitch, with no friends, and a hundred cats. She could have been dumped by a guy because he refused to marry her. She could be pregnant, with six other kids at home, freely adding to our already overpopulated welfare nation.

Or she could have been hurt. By someone. By something.

I put my fingers alongside my temples and try to will my memory to come up with the connection. Where have I seen her? Why do I feel like I know her? What is going on?

Remember, Dezi, remember!

This isn't usually how it happens for me. I don't go rushing in, hell bent on getting to the bottom of a woman's personal problems. This kind of thing usually sends me running for the hills like my hair is on fire. I need female drama like I need a bikini wax.

Not. Like never, ever.

Yet that inexplicable *thing* keeps my eyes locked on her. She doesn't know I'm watching, she probably doesn't even care. I just can't…pull…my…eyes…away.

I feel this strange urge to protect her. Talk to her. Make her smile again. Suddenly, Bridget seems like a lifetime ago. I'm not worried about the senator waiting for me in L.A. In this moment, the strange tormented girl is my only concern.

Hey, don't get me wrong, I'm a guy. Finding women sexy and attractive is what we do. Spotting a potential hook-up at a hundred paces is a skill we learn early and practice often. This is different. It's not that I haven't noticed that her butt is slim and round and packed just right into the back of her jeans. Yeah, I caught the long strand of light brown hair that fell out of her hat when she darted down to grab my iPod. I want to tell her that no matter how hard she's trying to hide right now, I can *see her*. I want to know where she's going. I want to know why she's so upset. I want to know what she had for breakfast.

As my mind spins, *the voice* is silent. I begin to wonder if the powerful vibe I am getting from this person started long before I boarded this plane and had the fortunate pleasure of almost having my iPod destroyed by her swinging shoulder bag. Could it be I was meant to be in this seat on this day at the exact time her world seems to be falling apart?

Fate has burned me before, made me kneel before it in full submission. I have tried to take away its power, to strip away its intent until it is nothing more than a series of events. I have learned to rely on my own intuition, *the voice*, and my gut. It's how I've become successful, how I've shaped my entire life.

So why do I have the distinct feeling that this is entirely out of my control?

Why do I feel like everything is about to change?

I figure that I have the next six hours to wrack my brain. Maybe it will come to me when I'm not trying so hard. I rotate the dial on my iPod to call up something loud, something to distract me, give me a mental break. Just before I put my earphones back in and give in to the music, the aging yet well-put-together woman on my right whispers something she clearly wants me to hear.

I play along. Why not? I'm going to be stuck next to her for awhile, don't need to make any enemies already.

"I'm sorry, I missed that. What did you say?" I ask, giving her my full attention.

"I said you have to be the damn president of the United States to get a plane to leave on time," she quips, thrusting her diamond encrusted watch in my direction. "See, we're already twenty minutes off our departure time. That means my driver will have to circle the arrival area because he won't be allowed to park there and wait. Jesus, it's *such* an inconvenience traveling commercial." Then she leans in real close to me like she's got a major secret. She lowers her voice even more when she tells me "the family jet" wasn't available today.

"Yeah, my jet was already taken today, too. I know what you mean. Enjoy the flight." I turn my head away and slam my earphones in before she can reply. Seriously, lady? Who's the poor asshole stuck funding your spoiled ass?

Just then, my eyes snap open and I reach total clarity. The realization hits me harder than any left tackle ever did. I hit replay in my head and focus on what the uber-rich socialite stuck slumming in first class just spat out.

Have to be the president of the United States…the president…of the United States…the VICE PRESIDENT!

Holy shit, I *do* know the tattered and broken soul who has just stumbled into my lap and into my life! Everybody knows her. You have to be a moron living under a rock *not* to.

Mystery solved, but now there are only more questions.

Now that I know *who* she is, I have to figure out what in the world she's doing here, belted into a flight bound for Los Angeles, wearing ratty old Ugg boots and ripped jeans, and hiding under an old baseball hat begging people not to notice her.

More importantly, why is she so upset?

Talk to me, Ella Sheridan. Tell me your story. I'm right here.

Chapter 15: Ahmed

It felt like the end of the world. All of a sudden there was nothing but chaos, blood, and death. They are the images that haunt me every time I close my eyes. To this day, I see it happening behind my closed lids as if I were still there. I cannot escape it, and sometimes I don't want to. It gives me the resolve to move forward.

My parents told me I would be safe. As a child, I wanted more than anything to believe them. What my eyes saw in the days leading up to the events that would take them away from me, told me that I already knew better. I was not safe at all.

Most of the American doctors had pulled their children from my school and returned home. They were warned, long before the Iraqi people were, of the approaching storm. They had nothing holding them to this place. So they returned home together, safely. The rest of us were not as fortunate.

That last morning my mother brought me to the hospital with her. She was not comfortable leaving me home and my father had been in surgery for hours. The doors of our school had been locked shut. No one was there anymore. I had no other place to go.

My mother knew her most fragile patient would go into labor. She knew it like a higher being had whispered it into her ear. The child would come on that day, and she had to be there, no matter what. The girl was young, sixteen years old, and terrified. She had been gang raped and left on the front steps of the hospital many months before. My father had rushed her into surgery to repair the most obvious wounds, but it was not until several months later that she returned. By then, her family had thrown her from their home, calling her pregnancy a disgrace to their name. She had no one, and yet she was about to become a mother.

She did not labor well. Being so young and not yet fully developed, my mother was worried about her narrow hips and the wild swing of the infant's heartbeat. Hours went by until her screams began to drown out the ratta-tat-tat of gunfire and explosions in the streets.

My mother brought me to her office. She had packed food, water, games and books into a large bag. I had picked through it, noticing there was absolutely nothing in it for her. The only items she thought to pluck from our home that morning were solely meant for me. She asked me to sit under her desk, pushing in her chair until I felt like I was in a cave. She checked on me every half hour, making sure I was sipping water and eating. She told me my father would be down soon to pick me up and take me home. They both thought the next several hours would be safer if we were together at the hospital.

I could hear the exact moment that the young girl gave birth. She had sounded like a wounded animal, throaty, breathy, and barely able to cry anymore. So weak from exertion, she likely prayed for death believing her trauma would never end. As her moans grew more intense once again, I could hear my mother speaking to her. With quiet words of encouragement, the same she spoke to me when I was studying my lessons at our kitchen table, she willed the girl to keep working. I have no doubt in those final moments my mother saved that girl's life.

The wail of an infant ripped through the air. I smiled in the dark space under her desk, imagining the feeling of bringing forth new life with your own hands. She amazed me. My mother kept tiny pictures of all the infants born in her delivery room around the edges of her desktop. She knew all their names. She would tell me how there is no love like the kind a mother feels the moment she sees her newborn for the first time. She felt honored to witness it every single day.

I wondered if she knew how much I loved her. I wondered if I even knew the right words then, at my young age, to make her understand. I wondered if the horror of knowing she would lose me made her regret ever having me in the first place.

I slid out from under the desk and poked my head out of the door, to look down the hall to where the delivery room was. I wanted to see my mother. I wanted to be with her right then, when I was growing more frightened as the light dimmed into darkness. I needed to know what was keeping my father from me, and how much longer I would need to wait. Even though I was always a child who did as I was told, I could not stand the isolation of the office any longer. Against my mother's instructions to stay put, I had left her office and walked down the hall. The few remaining overhead lights threw large sections of the hallway into shadows. I listened for the infant's wails to guide me to the delivery room and to my mother. By then, the girl had grown silent. I did not know what that meant, but I heard scurrying in the delivery room as I approached the door. My mother would not be happy with me if I interrupted her at that critical time so I tried to peek carefully around the corner of the door. Being a growing child not fully in control of my body, I leaned too far into the doorway and lost my balance. I stumbled blindly forward grabbing for the knob on the heavy door to break my fall.

"Ah, Ahmed," she had said to me, completely ignoring my ungraceful entrance into the delivery room. She even seemed to have forgotten that I was supposed to have been in her office right then. Instead, she reached out her hand, "You have arrived just in time to greet a brand new life," she spoke softly to me as she held the swaddled infant in her left arm. She tousled my hair with her right hand, and then lifted my chin so she could look me directly in the eyes.

"Remember this moment, Ahmed. There is danger all around us right now, and lives are being lost. However, there is always hope. You, and this child, are *my* hope. For a future that is different from this. Be strong, my precious son. No matter where you wind up in this world remember what you have seen, today and always."

She gave my nose a soft pinch before returning the child to its young mother still surrounded by attendants. She told me to stand in the corner of the room so that I would not be in the way. Difficult hours were ahead for the young girl; she had lost a good deal of blood and was very weak. Her face was ashen as she tried to lift her head and look for her new son. A nurse firmly pushed her back into the pillow, reminding her not to lift her neck. Blood was still pumping out of her at an alarming rate, prompting my mother to snap her attention back to the girl.

"Ahmed, let's go out in the hallway for a moment. Let your mother work." A nurse had taken me by the hand and led me outside of the delivery room. The young girl was on the edge and none of them wanted me to see her die.

My mother had stayed in a war zone for girls like her, and the babies they delivered. She had sat me down on more than one occasion to explain the commitment in a way she hoped I would understand. She told me that nothing was more important to her than I was, but she had other people who needed her, too. She did this while we were doing other things together. The difficult talks would come when we were finger-painting, or cooking dinner, or doing homework. When she knew my mind was busy and less apt to hold onto her words with the kind of energy that would eventually bring resentment. She wanted me to learn how to distinguish love and responsibility as two separate ideals. One could love another entirely, but still feel responsible for many, many more. It was an internal struggle she fought for a long time.

The nights when a delivery would stretch into the early hours of the next morning, she stayed at the hospital. I could hear her trying to walk quietly into our house before dawn, the footsteps leading immediately to the door of my bedroom. I did not want her to be upset with me for staying up so late, so I would pretend to be sleeping as she crossed the tiny space of the room to lean over my bed.

"My little Yellow Fellow," she would whisper. "Mother missed you so much tonight. I love you." She would brush back my light hair and place a soft kiss on my forehead. "Yellow Fellow" was the nickname she and the nurses at the hospital had given me years before, an affectionate reference to my blond head that stuck out like the morning sun, impossible to miss.

My parents worked very hard to keep their schedules open enough for one of them to be home with me at all times. My father had become deeply worried about my safety in those final days, and had a difficult time leaving me at all. Like my mother, duty called for him, and he always answered it with the utmost respect for the people who needed him at that moment.

He did not come home to us that last night.

The Kuwaiti man who had become like another father to him had been shot through the head while sitting at his desk trying to call his worried family back home. The man had one last chance to tell his wife he loved her before the phone shattered as a stray bullet from the street penetrated the window behind him. My father had worked on the man for hours in the operating room trying to save him, but the bullet had done too much damage. When he realized there was no hope, my father sat by his friend until he slipped away.

There were many more lives hanging in the balance during this time. My father worked almost non-stop, on soldiers, villagers, boys, and old men. Each life was worth saving to him and although he knew the hospital could fall under attack at any moment, his responsibility to his patients kept him focused and present the entire time.

My mother had come to me in the hallway shortly after the nurse brought me out. I was having an apple and she asked me for a bite. Her eyes, always aglow with that peaceful green light I had known my entire life, looked dark and tired. There were rings of exhaustion under them, and her skin had grown pale. She told me it was safe for us to leave, but she wanted to find my father first so we could all go home together. As she said this, I could hear more gunfire outside.

All at once, my mother reacted. She seemed to have an urgent sense that we needed to leave *at that exact moment*. She told the nurses to get the young girl and the baby down to the bottom floor of the hospital for the night. There was nowhere else for them to go. Under normal circumstances, my mother would have been by the girl's bedside the entire night to watch over her delicate condition. That night she was simply a mother with a child of her own to keep safe. She seemed to know instinctively she needed to get me out of there quickly.

She checked the girl's vitals one last time, and gave the nurses a nod to move her. The infant was in a separate bassinette rolled behind his mother's bed. The small group turned down one side of the hallway, while we raced down the other. My mother reached for my hand and held it much more firmly than usual. She whispered to me to keep my head low as we walked down the center of the hallway to avoid the glass of the window if it suddenly shattered. Huge explosions outside that seemed to be inching closer to us had joined sporadic but deafening gunfire. I knew we were going upstairs to find my father, but the hospital had gotten very dark. The elevators were out and the stairway was black as tar. My mother kept her fingers locked on mine as she pulled open the heavy door and we climbed the stairs to the third floor where my father was. My mother kept us moving forward even though we were both fighting pure terror with each step.

Finally, we reached the door in the stairwell of the third floor and raced inside. The hallway was in total darkness, but we could hear voices. My father had his back to us as he leaned in over a patient, speaking clear concise instructions to the frightened young man who had lost his right leg. His steady hands did not falter even as my mother entered the room behind him and spoke his name in a hurried voice.

"Easton, we are here and we need to take Ahmed home now." It was difficult for her to interrupt his work, but her primary concern was my safety.

"Easton, let the nurses stabilize him. We need to get our son out."

"Hiya, Yellow, don't come in my boy, I'm almost done and then we'll head right home." His British accent became more pronounced during times of stress, and his words had risen with a lilt at the end of each syllable. He motioned for my mother to keep me away from the bloody scene, so she backed me out of the room, returning us to the dark hallway.

"Come here, darling," he said to my mother. She told me to stay where I was, and walked back toward him. He said something to her that I could not make out. She looked sadly into his face, and nodded. She kissed his brow, squeezed his arm, and said to him in a soft voice I could barely hear, "I love you more than I could ever imagine. I will see you again Easton, very soon."

My father then stepped away from the table and faced me in the hallway. Covered in the man's blood, he did not reach for me but his eyes held me tighter than his arms ever had.

"Hey, kiddo, I've got to stay here just a while longer, but I'll be right behind you. Stay low my boy, and take care of your momma."

His voice broke only slightly as he spoke what would be his last words to his son.

"Ahmed, I love you."

"I love you too, Daddy."

Goodbye.

My mother and I turned back to the stairwell and climbed back down to the main floor. We were moving so fast my heart was pounding and my legs began to ache. I tried to ask my mother to slow down because I could not keep up. She told me to keep moving, that we needed to get out of the building. Our hands were starting to slide apart because our fingers had become stiff and sweaty by exertion and raw nervous energy.

"Ahmed, we need to keep moving until we see light. Until we see clear air and no smoke. Keep running even if you cannot see me anymore. Keep running, my son; keep running. Promise me you'll keep running *away from here.*" She stopped suddenly and grabbed me by my shoulders. She hugged me fiercely and brushed her lips against my ear. "Ahmed, I love you. You are strong and you are good. You will survive. Keep running!"

Just as she turned away from me, the world turned red. I was thrown back against the concrete wall as our fingers were ripped apart and my mother disappeared. The walls around me collapsed in, the floor buckled, but I could not hear a thing. Everything had gone silent. My head hurt, and I was swallowing what tasted like blood. I tried to move the mounds of debris off my legs, testing them to see if they could still move. My sneakers had been torn off, my right foot was bleeding, but I could move it. My arms were scratched raw, my fingers numb. One by one, I tried to make them bend. I clawed at the dusty rubble over my head until I could breathe again. The air around me smelled like the burning embers of charcoal.

I looked around. I looked up. How was it that I could see the stars in the sky? Where was the roof, where were the walls? The hospital was no longer standing. There were mountains of twisted metal all around me, and I could hear moaning. I dragged my legs free, and knelt on the shards of sharp concrete that had been the floor. They shook when I put my weight on them, trying to stand. I knew I had to move.

Ahmed, keep running. Promise me. I flashed back to my mother. Where was my mother?

My eyes searched wildly for something to tell me she was still there. I searched for her hair, her white lab coat. Anything.

"Mother!" I yelled. I heard nothing. I saw nothing. Then, my eyes found a tangle of dark among the crumbled ruins. I rushed over, knelt in front of my mother's body. I brushed aside the dust on her head, on her face, on her hands. I spoke in a whisper because my voice was gone.

"Mother, I'm here. Come on, get up, we need to find Father."

Why wasn't she moving? Couldn't she hear me? Her head rolled to the side, and I felt a rise of hope that she would get up, take my hand again and bring me home. She did not move again after that. Instead, I saw her eyes were open and they were staring. Not at me. Not at anything. She was gone.

I reached over, and with two fingers, I closed the lids forever. Her beautiful green gaze, finally at peace. I reached for her hand, pulled it into my small fist and then brought it to my lips. I kissed her hands; kissed her cheek. I put her hands back down and I told her I would honor her wish. I would run. I would run away from there, and I would survive.

As I stood up, I noticed movement out of the corner of my eye. The air was hazy and I could not see who it was but I could tell it was a man, and he was calling out to me.

"Ahmed, come with me if you want to live." I had wondered how he knew my name. As I walked closer to him, and the smoke cleared, I recognized the dark face as the one that had haunted my dreams at night. His was the face of the man in the hallway of my school. The face I thought I had imagined.

I turned and ran. Like my mother told me to. I tried to be strong and good and do as I was told. I tried to survive.

The man caught up with me quickly. He did not speak again as he folded me under his arm and charged out of the rubble. He ran until the air was clear and the moaning all around us had stopped. We had survived, though I did not know what he wanted with me.

"Ahmed, you are safe now. Don't you recognize me?" he had said, his voice husky from physical exertion. I had recognized him, but I was fearful of him. I told him I had seen him outside my school door.

"Yes," he told me, "I am the hospital custodian. The building has been destroyed, there is nothing left. Your parents are dead. I will keep you safe. Do not be frightened, Ahmed, I will protect you."

Your parents are dead.

His words felt like rocks pelted at my heart. I looked at this man, who had seemed like a monster to me, and began to cry. The salt of my tears made the raw scratches on my face burn. Everything hurt, from the inside out.

"I have to keep running," I told him, "my mother told me to run until the air was clear and the smoke was gone. Please, I have to go."

"Okay, then," he said to me, "we will run, but we will go together. I will bring you to a place where you will be taken care of. Do you trust me, Ahmed?"

I didn't really, but I went with the man anyway, because I had nowhere else to go. As I looked around at the death and destruction that had ripped my family away, I decided I would never trust anyone again. It hurt too much.

"Please," I said, "wait." The man reached for me again to force me to move away.

I held my ground. I pushed his hand away as I darted back, trying to find the place in that wasteland where I had left my mother's body. I moved over shrapnel sharp enough to cut clean through my tendons, bending down to search for the one thing I knew was still there. I could not let it be destroyed; it had been special to her. It was the first gift she had ever received, and she had wanted to give it to me one day.

I found her, gently moved her hair aside, then rolled her head back enough to reach my small hand behind her neck. I fumbled with the clasp until, finally, the tiny hook let go and the necklace slid off.

The golden bird with spread wings had been covered in ash and flecks of my mother's blood. I clutched it inside my fist to keep it safe. The bird has stayed with me every day since. The only piece of my mother's life I have left.

As I told the man I was ready to go, I did not cry anymore. The tears had dried up, but something dark had seeped into my soul that day.

It has simmered there ever since.

Chapter 16: Ella

Do I tell her right away, as soon as she walks in the door tonight? Do I whisper it when she rushes over to throw her arms around me? Do I break the news over a bottle of wine, when we're both a little numb? Really, how *do* you trample over your best friend's heart? With slippers, or steel cleats? Don't they both end up leaving gaping holes anyway?

She'll want to be strong for me. She'll offer to fly back with me to ride shotgun on my journey through the cancer ward. I will tell her no. She'll put up a fight, but in the end we'll both know she can't leave L.A. She's in too deep there, her job is too demanding and she is honest enough to admit both. She'll be pissed at me for not telling my family, at first. Then she'll understand. We'll both laugh at the idea of Kelby feeding me ice chips when I'm all strung out on chemo, or my mother sponging specks of my puke from her Chanel suit.

Maybe I'll be one of the fortunate few who don't suffer the excruciating side effects of chemo. Maybe instead of becoming a walking skeleton I'll blow up like a house.

"Gee, Ella, one too many trips through the drive-thru?" someone will inevitably ask, because their mouths will speak before their tact can catch up.

"No, thanks for noticing, but it's actually the steroids I'm taking right now. They just might save my life, or perhaps make me so frigging fat my heart will explode."

At least we will laugh. Lauren always makes me laugh. Here is a girl who has built a life on a foundation with a dozen cracks in it. Never cruel but always honest, you either love her or hate her. There are plenty on each team. Kelby and Lauren do not get along *at all*. They are cordial but cool. Lauren thinks most of Kelby's life is ridiculously self-serving. Kelby resents Lauren for not giving her enough attention. Kass, on the other hand, adores Lauren. If it didn't horrify me to think of the two of them getting busy, I'd say they were perfect for each other. Lauren's hot passion for life combined with

Kass's good-natured acceptance of just about everything. They would make good-looking babies who could either light up the stage, or Hail Mary their way down the field. They would be blessed with enough talent for an entire city block. They'd also be half Sheridan, and I wouldn't be so quick to wish all this complicated circuitry on anyone.

I have been out to see Lauren a few times over the past year. I dare say it is the one thing I do that makes my parents wild, especially my mother.

"Why, Ella?" she asks me, her clenched hands kept firmly beside both hips because showing outward emotion is not an option. "Why do you feel the need to defy us like this? It is *quite* immature and irresponsible."

What I really want is to blurt out the truth. Tell her it's because her world is too demanding, and I'm a grown woman, and no one gives a shit anyway that I'm sitting next to them on a packed flight to L.A.

My mother doesn't seem to realize the nature of the world today. She lives in political dreamland, where everyone roams the hallowed halls of the Capitol with wide eyes, full hearts, and good intentions. Somewhere along the way they become so completely disconnected they actually believe their own slogans. *Puh-leeze!* Look around. *No one* wants to get involved anymore. Strangers don't even make eye contact unless unforeseen circumstances force them to acknowledge the human presence an arm's length away.

So there you have it, Mom, the short answer to your rhetorical and annoyingly repetitive question of why I defy you the way I do. Don't ask me for the long version. That one might get personal.

Yet the expectations remain firmly in place. Most of the time, we march in line like the good soldiers we are. Except today. Today I am going AWOL to *take care of me.*

My mother will be in meetings all morning, so it's safe to assume, given the time change, that I have until early evening before she gets word that I've sprung myself from the big house again. Her first assistant Marjorie will notify her when my credit card purchase surfaces as an alert. Marjorie owes me nothing, but I think she feels a sense of sympathy for us as we're being tracked as fiercely as big game on an African safari. Don't get me wrong, though. She will turn me in. She always does.

Because *it's her job* to blow my cover.

Thanks again, Marjorie, you win. You always win.

I'm not even sure my father is around right now. He doesn't always tell us when he travels on business. He's also been known to take off on a Saturday night to watch one of Kass's games in person the next day. Sometimes an alert cameraman will find him in the owner's box, sipping a beer with his sleeves rolled up to his elbows. He is forever the football hero and once someone clues him in that he is on TV, he will give a little wave, a big grin, and thumbs up.

Hello, my fellow Americans.

There's always the possibility that Kelby may beat Marjorie to the punch. Kelby doesn't do well with secrets, especially ones that suggest to her I'm getting away with something she wouldn't be able to. I can hear her now: *"It's not fair, Mom. What makes Ella so special?"*

Nothing, Kelby. Nothing at all. I am anything but special.

We're rounding the final corner before the straight stretch of the runway. The pilot revs the engines one last time to make sure they are ready for takeoff. If I weren't painfully aware that three-quarters of all fiery crashes occur during takeoff or landing, I would be able to enjoy the sheer wonder of feeling us lift off the ground and shoot straight into the clear blue yonder. Instead, I sit here, all tense and shaky. I look around the cabin and notice most eyes are on newspapers, books or magazines. Doesn't anyone else worry we could go down? Just like it is designed to, the plane lifts gently off the end of the runway and we begin our ascent. Skies are clear so I can watch the cars, people, and buildings below quickly becoming tiny specks. It's a smooth ride up. No clouds to shake us around, just nice clean air. Maybe that's another good sign. No turbulence, at least for the next six hours.

I think of that old movie, *"Airplane." Don't call me Shirley,* and the shit hitting the fan. Only this time, when the shit does fly the splat will land squarely on me.

Take that, Ella. Yeah, real life is *so not funny.*

I grip the armrests on a tiny bump. Total cliché, I know, but I am a white knuckler, especially during takeoff when the engines sound like they are about to spontaneously combust and the clouds rattle the wings like wind chimes. And of course, I wait. I wait with frantic anticipation to hear from the pilot that we're doing okay up here.

I take what I hope will be a deep, calming breath. Instead, the pull of airplane air only reminds me how much my stomach hurts, and how badly my eyes sting. I didn't bother with makeup today so I pry one hand loose to rub them slightly, trying to take away the burn. I have a whole drawer full of fancy creams and powders in the bathroom of my apartment. Most of them are Kelby's castoffs. She has more expensive makeup than anyone I know, even Lauren. Kelby is actually most alluring when her face is clean and her eyes are honest. But her face is *never clean.* Kelby is always camera ready.

I don't even remember if I bothered to pack any makeup at all. I mean really, what would be the good in trying? Would smoky eyes and bee-stung lips convince my little cancer cluster to throw in the towel? Who gives a shit if my face is red, there is a zit on my chin, and my eyes are sinking into black holes of despair?

My mother would, that's who. What I have going on right now is unacceptable. My father would lower his head until his chin touched his neck and chuckle at me. "Going for a particular look, Ella?" he would ask me, more in support of my mother than out of real concern for my faltering sense of what is chic. At least he'd try to keep the fashion police from hauling me away to makeover hell. My mother, on the other hand, would personally hand me over to be cuffed.

We've done this before. It reads like a playbill. Act I: Important Sheridan event and Ella blows it by looking like a schlub. I get the look that travels slowly from the wisps of hair that just won't lie flat, to the belt that doesn't quite match, to the shoes that everyone knows should've been four-inch pumps instead of *three.* Then, my mother lowers her glasses so half her eyeball is behind the lens, and the other half is aimed at me like a laser beam. I'll tell you this much, *looks can kill*, and I'm always dead long before intermission. Kelby shows up looking like a supermodel, while Kass could pull off a paper bag if he had to. Then there's me. Taller than my sister, with long arms and legs, I just stick out, and not in a good way. The White House photographer is a good-natured man who always gives me a wink as he pushes me to the back row for official event photos. Almost as tall as my father and brother, I am awkward and uncomfortable. I am like the punch line of that old game we played in grade school, *What-In-This-Picture-Doesn't-Belong-Here?*

Me. That would be me. I don't belong there. I never have.

Both Kelby and Kass are dynamic personalities who get a good amount of press. Although I suppose there's an interest in me, too, it's not anywhere near the level of what the rest of my family gets. Kelby is on the cover of magazines often. Her lovely face smiles out at me as I grab a newspaper at the stand outside my office. Kass is busy with his team for a good chunk of the year, but in the off-season, he helps my father with his charity, spending a lot of time with the kids.

Kass will make a great father someday, as long as he gets his insatiable appetite for slutty women in check first.

I have never given an interview. I have never sat for a solo photo shoot. It's not like I'm trying to be mysterious or elusive, it really isn't. I just don't think there's all that much to talk about. Sure, I could tell you about growing up with the vice president, or the football icon, but that's not really my story to tell. I have my own perspective of course, but I had nothing to do with their successes. I always politely decline the requests, and forward them to my mother's press office to be filed away.

For some reason my parents give me a wide berth on this. There is never any pressure to put myself out there, except for official White House events when family is not only invited, but also expected to be there. I wonder if deep down they know the truth. I am boring; I don't have anything interesting to say. I am not a celebu-tard (sorry, Kelby) or a professional athlete, or much of anything at all. I'm not even the married Sheridan daughter with the cute kids who add that sweet mystical quality to the family snapshot.

I'm not a *total* loser. I have a job. I have an apartment. I make my own money and my own decisions. I have a few friends, and feel like I can trust *some* of them. I have had boyfriends who were good, intelligent, and interested. They always leave for the same reason. I don't blame them. Before *they* can think I'm important enough, *I* have to think I'm important enough.

I guess I'm just not there yet.

Maybe this whole cancer experience will change me. I will have no choice but to share it. With my family, with my friends, and with the nation, which I suppose in the interest of full disclosure, deserves to know what is happening in the vice president's personal life. Just in case the day ever comes when she could have her finger on the button, the world should feel safe in knowing that my little crisis won't make my mother's hand twitchy.

I mean, who really likes who they are anyway? Aren't there always a few things you would change if you could? I don't mean physically, although I understand why people go there. As long as it's subtle, of course. *Hello, Priscilla Presley, don't you know how good you had it? Why mess with perfection?* I mean internal changes. The big ones, the really personal ones. When you take a good hard look at yourself and figure out what isn't working for you. Too controlling? Don't stand up for yourself? Depressed? Why?

Maybe after all this is over and I'm standing before God ready to walk through the pearly gates, I will remember this time when I was forced to make some changes. When I looked at the world I had created for myself and decided to shift it around a little like the furniture in the living room. Move this, reconfigure that, and make it all work *better*. Maybe one day I will allow someone to care for me, take out the garbage, and change the oil in my car. But can I let go, and *share*? Can I take, and not always worry about the give? Can I love without trying to understand all the reasons I don't deserve it right back?

Cancer makes life heavy. It forces you to dig around and address the potholes that have been ripping the wheels off for too long.

I know I have a lot of work to do. My potholes are like bottomless pits.

My eyes move to the right. The iPod guy is lying back on the seat with his eyes closed and his face calm. How I wish I were like that. Can I have what he's having? A little shot of peace with my Diet Coke. I study him more closely. Excessively good looking not to be attached. I scan his left hand. Nothing. No ring, no tattoo (because you never know these days); his finger is bare. The younger set is into all sorts of new and exciting ways to celebrate their never-ending love and devotion. Course, it gets tricky when the eternal flame that is emblazoned on your flesh packs up and moves out. His ring finger is completely smooth, not even a wrinkle of disturbed flesh that would suggest he is prone to taking it off when the mood grabs him, or *someone* grabs him.

His hands are big, with chunky veins running up his wrists. He has them placed on each knee, because his legs are way too long to fully stretch out in the small space between his chair and the one directly in front of him. Even in first class, he fills his entire space.

He is probably used to having any woman he wants, probably never suffered through a blind date in his entire life. I picture him flying into L.A. to meet up with the swimsuit model he's casually seeing these days.

He is stylish in that can't-be-bothered sort of way. Jeans are neat and even pleated down the leg, but they're still jeans. Leather shoes are scuffed along the edges, but I can tell they're not cheap. His hair has a touch of gel to hold most of it in place, but he is totally unconcerned with the few pieces that are astray. He doesn't strike me as a salon guy. Instead, I picture him shooting the shit at the barbershop, with the old guys who've been coming around for decades.

"Hey, fellas, how are the grandkids?" he would ask. The graying, balding, and paunchy regulars would take turns gushing with pride about how little Josephine can ride a two-wheeled bike now, Mikey is the starting pitcher on his little league team, and Nicholas just made the honor roll.

He'd smile back at them, and he'd mean it. He is real; I can just feel it.

And that matters, how? In reality, I am not in his league. I'm the girl stuck way up in the nosebleed seats with all the other pathetically unavailable and perpetually single people. Maybe I'd get a passing glance when he recognized me but it would only take a few minutes of conversation before he'd give me a long sad look and ask if *my sister* would be joining us anytime soon. Who wants the dull sister, when you can have the hot sexy one instead? Kelby would be all over this guy. Why not? He's just as perfect as she is.

That's why I am completely mortified when he suddenly opens his eyes and looks straight at me. There is no worse feeling than getting caught staring at someone and I am beyond embarrassed. I want to slink away in shame, but where can I go? We're stuck here, together, for the next six hours. Do I apologize, do I ignore him, do I smile and try to play it off that I'm actually a really cool chick and not a complete dork…with cancer?

Turns out, I don't have to do anything at all. Because for some reason I can't begin to explain, he smiles.

At me.

"Hi," he says. He pulls one of his bear paws off his knee and reaches across the aisle. "I'm Dezi." His hand is warm and surprisingly gentle as I put my own into the middle of it. His fingers close around mine again. Gone is the jolt I had before. This time it feels strangely like home.

"Nice to meet you. I'm Ella." It doesn't even register to use the silly name that is on my ticket. He could be looking to bust my story wide open, alert the world that I'm sitting here looking like a bag lady. My mother would be so proud.

I don't care. I cannot lie to this man.

"I know," he says in a soft voice. "I know exactly who you are."

Jennifer Vaughn

Chapter 17: Dezi

I never get nervous talking to a woman. I never *don't know* what to say. I've sat here for way too long wondering how I could possibly strike up a conversation with her.

Obviously, something is wrong. She is gripping the armrests so tightly her hands are shaking. Her entire body seems like it's caught in a force field of stress.

Hers is a great American story. The Sheridan family is quite awesome, really. They are all unspeakably good-looking, talented and successful. When they take a picture, they really take a picture. You don't know which one to stare at first. The mother is strong, straight, and extremely proper with good bones and a slim, well-defined face. The father is taller and thicker. Known, of course, for his years in the NFL, he is also cool for other reasons, like his squeaky-clean record. A quality, stand up man that I have admired for years. The sister, a total hottie, beautiful face, good body, great smile. The brother is a funny, easy-going kid who can spiral a football down the field with the best of them.

They are the perfect family, or they have us all fooled.

Ella is the one who seems to avoid the spotlight at all costs. She is always in the back row of the picture, standing next to her father and brother. She resembles her sister, but has her own look entirely. Not quite as blonde, a bit taller, and less curvy. She reminds me of a volleyball player, strong back, long arms and legs.

I can't remember if I've even heard her speak before. She never gives interviews, and far as I know, has a regular job like the rest of us. I don't think she's married or has kids, but she could be in her late twenties by now.

I wonder again what she is doing *here*. Maybe I have it wrong, but aren't they supposed to have their own plane or something? Can't they just call their people, and tell them to gas up the jet? There should be *some* perks for being the vice president's kid.

The official photographs released first by Mel Sheridan's campaign, then the office of the White House have been beautiful. I know who their photographer is, and he is one of the best. Completely at ease, he floats around the stage or the front row just below the podium snapping away with a fluidity that I find fascinating. Too many photographers wind up planted on a platform, looking for the ideal way to catch a moving object while their feet are stuck firmly in place. Problem is, if the target is moving, you have to be moving, too. Some of my best work comes when I'm upside down and twisted backwards, firing off my shots at someone doing the same thing.

I have taken a couple of cues from his work through the years. He is a master of the moment. His field of vision is always set perfectly, and his eye for color is spot on. Instead of insisting on bold and bright like most photographers would if they were trying to make a statement, he goes with earth tones and just a *splash* of color. It works well. The golden good looks of the vice president catch your gaze instead of a garish snap of red or blue that is too over the top.

With as much talent as he seems to have, there is one thing I have never understood. Why, when the second family is positioned for one of those photos that will eventually be released for White House purposes, is Ella always stuck in the back like the ugly stepsister? She is so tall and graceful I would flank her on the side, leaning slightly in, so your eye travels the entire length of her body. Her presence is powerful, yet subtle enough not to disturb the flow of the family dynamic. Kelby is *always* seated next to her mother, long legs crossed slightly in front of her, eyes locked on the lens, smile ironed on. Kass is *always* next to his father, though as far as setting the middle of your shot, you couldn't ask for a more perfect twosome. But hanging off the side, almost like a wilted limb that needs to be trimmed from the old oak tree, is Ella. Half her body tucked behind either her father or brother, she is never fully represented. Why would you waste her?

I wonder if that's how *she* prefers it to be. Is she lost in this big life of hers? Overwhelmed? What is really going on here that we don't know about?

I don't want to come on too strong. The door opened a crack when we found ourselves looking right at each other. Do you ignore that kind of moment? No. But how do I move in? That's the real challenge because she is not the typical stranger you might meet on a long plane trip. The pretty girls you spend a few hours making small talk with, flirting, touching maybe, but with no intention of ever seeing each other again. You deplane with a smile and a nice memory but quickly resume the life you already had going on.

This needs to be different.

I don't want to make her think I'm some rabid fan who has her picture hanging over my bed. She's probably got too many of those types as it is. Her hand feels warm, and solid in mine. Like you *know* it's there. I have a hard time letting go, and I let my fingers trail along the inside of her palm as we each pull back.

"I know who you are," I tell her again, softly. I get the whole incognito thing so I don't want to blow her cover here. "It's a real pleasure to meet you. I voted for your mother, you must be so proud of her." I have no idea if this is a good way to try to work up a conversation, but I figure it's safe and at the very least, forces her to respond.

Her lips pull up at the corners, but she doesn't show any teeth so I can already tell it's not her *real* smile, it's the one she uses for people like me who probably come up to her all the time with inane, gushing comments.

Like the one I just threw out. Off to a great start here, Dez.

"Thanks, she'll be happy to hear that. I don't think I've ever known anyone named Dezi, it's...interesting." Then to my complete surprise, the smile opens wider and *it is breathtaking*. She lifts her face from the chin up, trying to make eye contact with me while keeping her hat in place. Up close, her eyes are stunning. The green is even deeper, but they are warm and kind and squint up just a little bit around the edges when the smile is genuine.

My God, that photographer is missing all of this. My camera would find you, Ella.

I want to keep this light and easy, keep her talking.

"Yeah, it's unique I suppose. I think my parents wanted to make a statement. There were sixty Michaels in my graduating class, only one Dezi. It just about guaranteed that I got the right diploma handed to me, but there was no one to hide behind when I messed up." I laugh, hoping it doesn't sound awkward, like I am trying too hard. *Whoa, this is strange.* I am toeing a line I have never had to walk before. Talking to a woman is like a sixth sense, I've been good at it my whole life. So why do I suddenly feel like an eighth grade boy with a face full of zits and food caught in my braces? Why are there stirrings in my stomach that feel suspiciously like nervous butterflies? What the fuck is happening here? I stay the course, because I know if I do, it will be worth it in the end. *She* will be worth it. She smiles right back, and it feels so good.

"That's funny. We have something in common. I was the only Ella in my graduating class. It's actually a family name. My mother's grandmother was Ella. I'm named after her." We have not broken eye contact once, until now. I look down only because I feel like I'm getting dangerously close to losing myself in the green pools.

Stay with me here, Dez.

"I think it's beautiful. I can also say I have not known a single Ella in my life, either. Until today." I pause, hoping to put the proper emphasis on those last two words. Does she get what I'm trying to say? Do I even know what I'm trying to say? The plane bounces on an air pocket and she rips her hand back and clutches the armrest again.

"I'm thinking you don't like to fly, huh?" I ask her, then push on when she doesn't answer right away. "My sister is like that, she will avoid a plane trip at all costs, except if it means piling her kids into the car for an extended road trip. That is a much worse fate."

"No, flying doesn't work for me, either. Not so much at all," she says, trying to smile but failing miserably.

"Should I keep talking, to distract you? Or…something?" I kick around offering to just shut the hell up and let her do whatever she needs to do to chill, but I resist. I don't *want* to leave her alone, and I hope she doesn't want me to either.

"No, no I'm okay. It's a really embarrassing thing to admit, but I will be better once I hear the pilot tell us to sit back, relax, and enjoy the flight." She exhales loudly, like she's resigned to the fact that her wiring is off. It's almost like she considers this minor phobia that half of the flying public shares right along with her, a personal defect.

She goes on, trying to make me understand, "It's weird, I know, immature, stupid. Most people tune out everything the pilot says. Not me. I need to know the pilot is good up there, so that I can be good back here. Pretty lame, huh?" She bows her head, chin down again, eyes looking away from me now. I wonder if she's looking for some kind of confirmation from me that I think she's pathetic. Jesus Christ, who could ever tell this woman that she was pathetic?

Or put her in the back of the family photo.

It all begins to make sense. Hiding under her hat, not a stitch of makeup on her face, it's all an exhausting effort to fade into darkness. I've known her for fifteen minutes and I can already see huge cracks in her arsenal. This woman has been hurt, beaten down, and completely stripped of self-confidence. This must be what comes from being disregarded so often you think you need a perfect stranger to remind you how useless you actually are.

How sad. How utterly tragic.

"No," I tell her trying to speak gently but firmly. If I didn't think she'd smack me I would have reached out and taken her by the shoulders so I had her full attention. "It's not lame at all. My sister is *worse* than you are. She won't even get on a plane unless her entire family is with her. Kind of like, if she goes down they all go down with her."

I want to make her laugh, to let her know she is *hardly* the only one who gets jittery.

"And, to make it worse our grandfather was a pilot! He would tell her all the time how safe flying is, how she's more likely to get eaten by a shark than die in a plane crash. Of course that backfired when she decided she wouldn't swim in the ocean anymore. Kind of ruined our beach vacations for a few years." I look for an opening again. She dangles a hook with a subtle lift of her head. As she begins to smile, I notice a slight dimple in her left cheek. I think then that I could watch her every hour of every day for the next hundred years and still find things that amaze me.

Huh? Who am I? What have I done with Dezi? This new guy is as soft as a decaying peach.

"I know, it's ridiculous. I can apply logic till the cows come home, but I still do this every time. I'm sorry, I feel like I'm taking you away from your music." She motions with her head to the iPod that is sitting on my lap. With a tantalizing spark of sarcasm she says, "It would have been *so fabulous* if I had smashed that up before we even took off. I'm a bit of a klutz, as you probably noticed."

There she goes again, offering up her shortcomings on a silver platter. Here are all the reasons why I suck.

"But you didn't, remember? I caught it, crisis averted, no harm no foul." We are looking at each other, taking all of this in. She has no real reason to keep talking. We could easily end it right here, with a smile and a polite "nice to have met you have a good day." I could throw my earphones back in and chalk it all up to an interesting encounter.

Then wonder what could have been for the rest of my life.

Fuck it, here I go.

"Ella, can I say something that may sound a little strange right now?" I just have to know. Am I imagining this or is something happening here?

"No, I have never seen Monica Lewinsky's blue dress," she deadpans.

She's funny, too.

"Ha! Yeah ummm, good to know, but I...ah..." I am a stuttering fool now. I feel like I'm in adolescent hell, trying to kiss the prom queen.

"Dezi, what's wrong? It's okay, you can tell me."

I know that she means it. I *can* tell her. She is looking at me with a touch of concern that I find endearing. I pray that there is wisdom and purpose to be found in serendipity and circumstance, and I try it again.

"All right, although I may be making a complete ass out of myself. Stop me if I'm going off the reservation, okay?" She nods, takes the pointer finger of her right hand and makes two crosses over her chest.

"Cross my heart. I promise to tell you if you are an ass." Her lips pull back to mock my suddenly sober tone. I feel a rush of adrenaline, as if I'm getting off the chair lift and the trail ahead of me is a double black diamond. I point my skis straight down, and push off.

"Ella, I am a photographer on my way to Los Angeles for a pretty important shoot. I have a ditzy girl hot on my trail, even though I've broken up with her every which way I know how to. I have never been married, and I have never wanted to be. I live on the East Side, and eat Sunday dinner at my parents' house in Jersey twice a month. I know who you are, but I have no idea *who you are*. And, I guess what I'm trying to say here is…I'd like to try to find out."

My skis bounce on the ice, I feel like I just took a sharp turn on dull edges. Exhilarated and shaky, I am totally off balance. Silence. I get silence, followed by several quick blinks of her eyes.

"So," she says finally. "Is your mother a good cook?" There is a different look to her smile this time. It is pure, and sweet, and so goddamn sexy it takes my breath away.

"Yeah, she's the best." My voice is so low I'm not sure if she can hear me.

Just then, we both seem to notice the empty seat next to her.

Chapter 18: Ahmed

The man was well-intentioned. He kept me alive when there was no one else who wanted to. He took me to his home several miles away where he cleaned my wounds and made sure I ate and slept. I was dizzy with grief and my body had been battered, bruised and ripped open by flying debris. My feet were raw and bloody, with tiny rocks embedded in my soles. My shoes were somewhere in the rubble of the hospital. I had nothing.

The man stitched several of my widest gashes closed with a small sewing needle and black thread. I remember being too traumatized to even flinch. We stayed inside for many days, with no electricity and rotting food in his kitchen. He had a battery-powered radio but the reports were all state controlled, and gave us no real sense of what was happening. Even in the distance, we could hear explosions, some of them close enough to shatter the windows of the house until they were nothing more than shards of glass attached to the wooden frame. Animals scurried about through the streets, displaced from their homes, hungry and lost. We saw no one.

I began to wonder if we were the only ones alive.

I had no real desire to survive at first. I ate only when I felt as though I would collapse if I didn't, and sleep was never restful. I saw my mother's death over and over again. I saw her eyes, her hair streaked with the blood that had seeped into the ground and turned it black. I saw it all in such detail I would shake myself awake because I could no longer bear it in my dreams. I heard her words in my head, as if she were standing directly behind me.

I thought of my father, so committed to saving the life in front of him he probably never heard the bomb hit. I imagine that he died with a scalpel in his fingers, and a sense of deep disappointment that his mission of mercy on this earth was interrupted. Both he and my mother had so much more work to do. They had dreams for me, and hopes, and high expectations.

Did any of it matter anymore? I struggle with that even now. I would lie awake on the man's couch with a blanket pulled over my head to shut out the vile noises outside. I considered walking deep into the desert one night, and never returning. Who would miss me?

It became a horrid place. The land was charred, buildings had fallen in ruins, and the streets were filled with the dead. Bodies sat in their own gore, rotting into the sand and stones beneath them. They were the sights and sounds of a child's worst nightmare and yet no matter how tightly I squeezed my eyes shut, they never went away.

I wondered if my grandparents in England had gotten any kind of notice of my parents' deaths. Did anyone remove them from the collapsed hospital? Were they among the bodies left with no blessing, no burial, granted no respectful passage into the next world? This thought haunted me most of all. To think of those beautiful people picked apart and eaten by feral dogs hungry for flesh and bone.

Many days and nights passed. Slowly, life began to return to the city. Merchants returned to the market square but few people had any money to buy things. Americans roamed around with the most enormous rifles I had ever seen. They looked at me with curiosity and familiarity. I did not look like the other Iraqi boys they had encountered there. Some of them even spoke to me, but I pretended not to understand them until they simply stopped trying. I had nothing to say to them.

My parents had explained this war to me. It made sense to me when they said the Americans had come to take evil away. They told me that all boys and girls should be able to go to school, that all parents should be allowed to work and contribute, and everyone deserved to be treated equally. They believed in the effort to liberate the people, but I don't think they had a clue what would happen once it started.

Food was scarce, clean water hard to come by. The man's family lived in a small town outside the city. He had asked me one day if I would like to go home with him. He explained that there were other children there who might help make me feel less sad. I did not believe he would have let me stay by myself in his little apartment, but I figured that was his way of trying to grant me some independence. Although there were no ties between us, I went with him. I look back on this as one of the most important decisions of my life.

The man did not speak all that much as we walked along the scorched desert sand en route to his family home, but I did know a few things about his life. He was an honorable man who had been working at the hospital to send his son to school. He stayed in the city for work, but missed his home terribly. He told me I reminded him of his own boy, not in appearance of course, but in intellect. He said he would watch me sometimes from the hallway, amazed by my focus and calm demeanor. His son was to be a scholar, born with a knowing mind that would take him out of this country.

The man did not like the war, but he also did not like his country's rulers. He told me they were savages. Years before, his own brother had been an elite athlete. One night, he was murdered. I had listened intently as the man told me what happened. He tended to speak quietly when the topic was of importance to him, so I had to lean in close. The man's brother was a rugby player, one of the best on the national team. One particular season, the team lost several times. Because his brother had been the captain at the time, he was singled out for punishment. Men came to their home once nightfall had darkened the sky, kicked open the door, grabbed his brother out of bed and dragged him outside. As the family watched, the men threw what looked like water on his brother until he was dripping wet. Only it was not water at all. It was acid. Mere seconds after it settled on his brother's skin the screaming began. The man told me he could do nothing but watch as his brother's skin began to peel back from his muscles and his ferocious cries faded into low moans. His mother fainted on the spot, while his sister covered her face with her hands and sobbed. His father, however, remained rooted in place, expressionless as he watched his son die. When the moaning finally stopped, his father turned and walked back into their house. He never spoke of that night again.

I must have had a strange look upon my face at that point, because the man stopped walking and looked down at me. It was not his father's fault, he had explained. He had loved his family, but had a deep respect for his country. He had known what would happen when powerful men became disappointed. With great honor came great sacrifice, even if that meant your own flesh and blood.

As our heads hung low, we resumed our journey. I did not know what to say, even though I felt sad for this man and his brother. His story reminded me of the ones my mother had told me of her own father. It made my throat ache with grief as I thought of my parents again. My father would have laid down his own life before he would ever let another man harm me.

I had known a much different kind of love. That was over now.

We walked on, until we saw the light of a fire getting closer. A tiny house appeared in the distance, dark except for the orange flames tangling like vines into the night sky.

"Ahmed, it is quite late. I will make you something to eat and then you should try to rest. It has been a long journey and I am sure you are tired." The man never touched me, except that first day when he gripped my arms tightly to pull me from the rubble. Maybe it was the emotion of returning home that had him reaching for me all of a sudden to place his arm around my shoulders. I had ducked away, not ready to accept even the slightest touch of another man's hand. I did not mean to insult this man, because he had shown me nothing but kindness, but he pulled away quickly.

"I am sorry, I did not mean to frighten you," he said softly.

"I know," I told him. I followed him silently to the front door. He didn't want to alarm anyone inside, so he knocked softly and spoke someone's name out loud. After some scurrying noises inside, the door swung open and a woman threw herself at him. He hugged her tightly, praising the heavens that she was safe. He spoke so quickly I could not follow. Apparently, he asked about others because I could recognize names. As he smiled and nodded back at her, it struck me. I remembered him clearly. I realized then that the face that seemed to be watching me from the hallway always had a smile on it. He was smiling at me because he was thinking about his own son, and missing him.

How ridiculous I had been to fear him.

The woman had wrapped her burka around her head so I could only see her dark eyes as she knelt in front of me. She asked me if I wanted something to eat or drink. She did not reach for me, but her voice was soft and it reminded me of my mother's. She stood up and walked over to the kitchen. I pulled out a wooden chair next to the table, and without even asking for permission, sank into it. My body was so very weary, my heart heavy as a rock. I folded my arms, locking each hand into the opposite elbow and laid my head between them. I do not remember the woman coming back from the kitchen, nor do I remember her leading me to a soft bed in the back room. The next thing I can recall was waking up to half a dozen small faces staring at me with huge curious eyes. The tallest one spoke to them sharply and they scurried away. He resembled the man a great deal. I assumed he was the son who would be going to university soon.

He spoke to me then, in English.

"Hello there." His voice was deeper than I had expected it to be. "Welcome to our home, thank you for keeping my father safe." I was not sure if he was being serious just then, or was trying to make me feel important.

"My name is Malik, I am fourteen. I will be going away to university soon. Have you gone to school?" he asked, with raised eyebrows. I told him that I had been in school at the hospital. We talked about what I had been studying, how I had learned Arabic. Although I knew my fair complexion must have startled him, Malik never asked me about it in those early days. Only later, did we speak at length about my parents. He never breathed a word of it to anyone. It would turn out to be his only redeeming quality at the end.

He was a brilliant boy. He was able to rig radios and television sets with old batteries, wires and cables so they all ran off the same power source. Their house became a meeting place for the entire village for news of the invasion. They would sit, shoulder to shoulder, watching the reports quietly together.

Malik's mind was always working, spinning new thoughts into ideas. He would use a stick to draw math equations in the sand, explaining how the numbers could design pathways for the flow of electricity, or set the trajectory of a missile from a military tank. He told me he was going to be a scientist. He asked me what I wanted to be. I told him I didn't know, because I wasn't entirely sure I would live that long. There I was, a child among strangers. What right did I even have to expect that I would grow into adulthood?

Malik and I became inseparable. I followed him everywhere, craning my neck to hear him mumbling into the dirt during one of his lengthy number conversions. Soon enough, I could finish them off in my head long before he did. His father would watch us from a distance, with a look of concern on his face. I did not know what was troubling the man, until one night when he approached me while I was lying in bed.

"Ahmed, are you still awake?" he whispered, so as not to wake anyone else.

"Yes, I am. What is it?" I asked softly. Although I did not love this man, nor would I ever feel that sense of adoration that I had known for my parents, I was genuinely fond of him and appreciative of his generosity.

"I am worried for you here, Ahmed," he began. "I was right about you. You are gifted with the kind of intelligence that will be stifled if you do not get out. My wife and I have very little money, and what we do have will be used to send Malik to school. I have nothing to offer you."

I was not surprised or insulted by his honesty. I never expected anything from him anyway, so I tried to put his worried mind at ease.

"I know that, and it's all right. If it is acceptable to you and your family, can I stay here for just a while longer, until I am old enough to travel by myself? I promise you I will find a way to get out." I had no plan, of course, but this man had already done more for me than most would have. He did not owe me a thing.

"Of course, my boy. You may stay forever if you choose. But we are not your family, nor should you be satisfied with this kind of life. You need to experience the world, and use your gifts, and meet a woman and have your own children one day. Your parents would have wanted that for you, Ahmed, and I do, too." The man's eyes were moist as he took one finger and ran it down the bridge of my nose. That time I did not pull back from his touch. Instead, I smiled.

"Thank you," I said.

"Good night, Ahmed."

With that, he left the room, shutting the wooden door behind him. Finally, the house grew quiet, but I could not sleep that night. I shoved the covers back and tiptoed to the door, opening it a crack to see if anyone was still awake. The room was empty. I quietly walked to the television set. Malik had shown me how to connect two wires to turn it on, and how to connect several more to receive a signal. After a couple minutes, the set warmed up and the images slowly appeared on the screen. Images I had grown disturbingly numb to, images of war and rubble and death on the streets of Iraq.

The only channel that was available was a Kuwaiti station. As the television warmed up, the colors grew brighter and more distinct. There was a woman at the front of a room. She was lovely, with smooth blonde hair, elegant clothing, and a clear confident voice. I had seen her before on TV, but only in passing when the adults had gathered for the news. I had not listened to her until now. The podium was thick and tall; I could only see her from the waist up. She was pointing to different people in the crowd, who stood up and asked questions one by one. It was all about the war, and the death count, which had been described as being very low. That confused me. The loss of life that we had seen was staggering. Did they not know of the suffering? Had they not seen the children decapitated by flying metal as sharp as a sword? Were they not aware that their bombs had wiped out entire families? Mothers, fathers, and children who had done nothing to deserve such a brutal assault. How could they not know what was happening?

I continued to watch the woman, growing increasingly upset that she seemed so ignorant of the scope of devastation. She showed no respect for our loss, offered no apology for what had been taken from us. She spoke in terms I was not familiar with at the time, missile strikes, targets hit, advancing positions. I made a mental note to ask Malik what all of that meant.

One man stood up, asking about reports of dead Iraqis lying in the streets of Baghdad.

Finally, I thought. Finally, she would know the truth. She looked at him, then into the camera. I felt like she was speaking directly to me.

"This is war, and in times of war there will be casualties. We consider the losses unfortunate, but they will not alter our pursuit of justice and freedom for the people of Iraq. We cannot and will not be deterred by collateral damage."

Collateral damage. My parents meant nothing more to her than that?

After taking a final question, she smiled and waved, signaling an end to the discussion. She leaned in closely to the man standing just behind her right shoulder. He spoke into her ear, and they both broke into broad grins.

Then, she laughed. The sound shot into my head like a bullet. Who was this woman, with her booming voice, fancy words and callous disregard for human life? Had she never known loss? Did she have any idea what her "successful mission" had done to my family? To the infant who was born right before the hospital collapsed. To the doctors and nurses who were trying to save lives even as their risked their own.

Did she not realize everything that had collapsed into dust and dirt?

My whole life.

My lips pulled back as I felt rage ripple up from my stomach, behind my lungs, and into the back of my throat.

Who was this awful woman celebrating the death of my family?

I wanted to learn everything I could about her.

Then I wanted to destroy her.

Chapter 19: Ella

Immediate red flags. *I know who you are.* Simple enough phrase that is usually the kiss of death as far as I'm concerned. I am not one to buy a line from a man. I am polite, but aloof, and they usually go away once they feel sufficiently ignored. Now I'm wondering how I keep *this* man from leaving, ever.

Sure, it's probably not a good thing he knows who I am, and even worse that I want to know exactly who he is, too. I want to talk, listen, and make silly plans. I want to know about his work, and his sister who sounds an awful lot like me. I want to sit down for dinner with his parents in their upper middle class Jersey home. I want to see his old school pictures, meet his friends, and stash his favorite beer in my fridge for the times when he just pops by.

Or not.

How about I do the right thing and spare him. From me. From my family. From my cancer. Let this poor man go and have a good life for himself. I hate the moments when I remember who I am. Sticking around me would be like getting a wad of gum in your hair. Pretty soon it's a tangled mess, you need scissors, and you wind up with an unfortunate row of bangs. Sorry, buddy, no one past fourth grade should have to deal with bangs.

I have no business playing into this, and yet he mesmerizes me. So much of my life has been like putting money on the designated hitter. My guy's always got a great swing, but it's just a smoke screen. Pretty soon, he's in slumpsville and I'm stuck paying off his exorbitant contract, and the lease on his Lamborghini. None of my DH's ever come through, why should I think it will be any different this time? One can only expect the benefit of the doubt for so long, and I have too many doubts for anyone's benefit.

As logic barks at me louder than a southern Baptist preacher on a Sunday morning, I shock myself when I feel my eyes slide over to the seat next to me. I've just noticed it's empty; he notices right along with me. We look at each other and can't help but laugh. The preacher goes quiet on me; I can hear him leaving. I don't think he's coming back.

"Do you think you would mind if I joined you here?" he asks, motioning to the open space with his hand. I absently notice that I have released my death grip on the armrests and my foot has stopped shaking on my knee. I don't even know how long we've been airborne. Could it be that I've even missed the pilot's memo of good will from the cockpit? Really, am I that caught up here?

"No, I wouldn't mind. And no to the other thing, too." I feel sixteen again, leaning in for that first kiss on my parents' front porch.

"Come again?" he says with a crooked, confused grin.

"The answer is no. You did not go off the reservation, not even a little bit."

The grin opens wider into a full-blown smile. His laugh is honest and heartfelt, and makes me laugh right back. I am actually laughing again. Imagine that! One thing I didn't think I would need on this trip was my sense of humor. I thought I had left that back in New York.

I move my bag off the seat as he turns back to his row to collect his own stuff. There's a haughty looking older woman who seems to take a personal affront to his sudden departure. Who can blame her, she thought she had six hours with him. Sorry, lady, the good ones never stick around too long.

I usually have a playbook that I haul out when it comes to men: Ella's Rules Of Engagement. It tells me how much I reveal, how deep I should go, how quickly I pull back again. I think of my life, and the circumstances that have kept me under this strictly enforced solitary confinement. Obviously, the other side has seen my playbook because they know how to beat me every time. I try something new. I shut down all the usual things that I start to tick off in my head in the moments after I meet someone new. Is he successful enough? Can he make small talk with world leaders? Will he hit on Kelby? None of that applies anymore. Dezi is different, and let's face it, *I'm* different right now, too. I'm nervous and afraid and sick with something that could have every intention of sending me on to my final resting place in short order.

What an absolutely perfect time to start a relationship, when one of us might not be here to see it through.

"Do you want to slide over, or should I take the window?" He has returned with a leather jacket draped over his arm. He reaches up to tuck it into the overhead bin. My eyes are level with his waist as his shirt pulls slightly upward, over his belt buckle, revealing taut muscles and faint hair. I almost gasp aloud like a neglected housewife with a front row seat at the Chippendale Review.

"Ah, how 'bout I move over to the window. Unless you prefer it?" I start to get up, then pause with my ass half way between up and down. He notices. I can see his eyes glance back before returning to my face. *Thank God for those extra squats.* Those, along with a total lack of appetite lately, have done a nice job trimming away any junk in my trunk. At least I'll be a skinny bitch when I go.

We shuffle around each other, our knees touch, and it feels like a caterpillar is crawling under my jeans. Soft, ticklish movement that is as gentle as an April rain shower. He is huge, but moves by me with a certain grace, completely aware of where each body part is at every moment.

He is what Sade sings about, a smooth operator. He is also an athlete, I think. He bulges in all the same places that Kass does, and my father used to. I'll bet he was a total player in his day, but didn't he say he's a photographer now, with some big job waiting for him? How does that happen? Most of the ball players I know couldn't snap a good shot if their lives depended on it. That's what the trophy wife is for, as long as she's lucid enough to press the right button on the camera. Believe me, not all of them are.

His whole persona is at odds with that river of information that poured out. He does not strike me as the wear-your-heart-on-your-sleeve kind of person. No, he is the play-it-cool, see-you-when-I-see-you type. He even admitted that he has his hands full with someone else right now. The last thing I want to be is the "other woman," who clearly doesn't have the winning hand to beat the house.

"You left me for her?" she would say, and she'd have every reason to be outraged. No one leaves anyone for me.

My head swimming in doubt, I am suddenly rethinking this whole thing. What am I doing? This is not real. As far as I know, this could be a big ploy to see how far he can get with the vice president's daughter. Then sell the sordid details to the highest bidder.

Oh Ella, you stupid girl. Oops, I did it again.

He must sense I have Britney Spears on the brain, because he reaches over and puts his hand over mine. His big, strong fingers cover mine so completely I can't even see them anymore. But I can feel everything. It feels safe.

Stop it!

"Ella," he says. Who says my name like that? His voice feels like one of those hotel bathrobes: thick, warm, impossibly soft and cozy. No wonder so many people tuck them into their suitcases. Who wouldn't want to stay wrapped up in this forever?

"I don't want to make you nervous. I can move back to my own seat. You seem like you're getting upset." He is direct with me and I know he expects an answer. No pulling punches here.

"Dezi," I begin, and then falter. Like usual. My hands start to flutter and my throat feels dry. Where are the flight attendants? I could use a little liquid here, stat! I try again to make this make sense. I have no funny lines ready to roll, I can't fake it and I don't want to.

"I guess I'm just a little leery." I am dying, Dezi, or at least I could be, and I am all closed off like a road under construction. There is no detour and you could end up in a ditch with your tires blown out. I try to give him an easy out. "Is this about my mother, or my sister? Because if it is, that's okay. I can get you an autograph, or whatever, but you don't have to pretend to chat me up for the next six hours when that's all you're after in the first place. I can take your address and pass it along to my moth..."

He cuts me off as sharply as an ice pick.

"Is *that* what you think?" he says, his voice low and angry and I *hate* the thought that I have just upset him. It feels almost like a twinge in my gut. Great work, Ella, thought we burned the playbook already.

"You think I want an autograph…from your mother?" He almost chokes on that last part. I am afraid to answer; there is no answer. I'm sorry, Dezi. I'm a jaded asshole, but you just don't know what it's like to be…ME!

I don't have to say anything, because all of the sudden that flash of anger is wiped clean and he breaks into an ear-splitting grin. Then he guffaws at me.

"Oh, Ella," he reels it back to a mild chuckle. "I told you I *voted* for her. Technically, that means I've gotten everything out of her I want." His hand stays on mine. I can't move. I can feel my heart speeding up. I am on a treadmill sprinting at eight miles per hour.

"This is most definitely all about you. And me. And this strange feeling I've had this entire day. Ella, I think we were supposed to meet today. I'm sorry if this sounds weird to you, because it sounds weird to me, too. But if I'm not straight up with you about all these feelings rushing around right now I'd be lying to myself. And to you."

He pauses, breathes in through his nose and covers my hand again with his other one. "Can I stay, please? I promise not to break into song, or hump your leg, but I would really like to talk. I promise, if you tell me to go away, I will. But I believe I would regret it for the rest of my life. And Ella, I'm hoping you would, too."

I stare at him, fumbling to organize the thoughts racing through my head. It feels like a parallel universe. Somehow I have fallen into the life someone else has the pleasure of living. The girl who is healthy and witty and has every right to meet the man of her dreams on a plane.

No, no, no! I belong on the flip side, loaded up with despair and grim expectations and stumbling blindly into the path of a serial killer with a nice smile. Ella, meet Jeffrey Dahmer. He would like to take you to dinner, or *have you* at dinner. See how it goes.

Somewhere in the distance, I hear the flight attendants starting to unbuckle their shoulder harnesses. The snap of metal is a good sign; soon the drink carts will roll and I can order up a shot of courage. Dezi's eyes are still locked on mine, waiting for me to say something. Where do I begin? This is not the typical boy meets girl and lives happily ever after unfolding here. Who meets her Prince Charming at a time in her life when the frog would be a better fit? As much as I want to lose myself in his story of fate and crossed paths, I am careful to remember that he has a life, possibly even a great one. From what I can tell, this man has parents who love him, and a sister who has filled him with happy memories. He has a job and a schedule to keep. Forget destiny and all that; I need to ask myself what I could possibly offer him, I mean, *really*? I don't even know if I'll be alive very long. Even if I do make it out of round one, who's to say I won't be called back to the ring for the championship bout. Only next time it'll be with the heavyweight title holder who has a crushing right hook. Then what? And what do I say when the doctor warns us I can't have kids because the rush of hormones could cook up another warm batch of cancer cells?

Sorry, Dezi. You would have made a great father, but then you met me. Yeah, that would be a fulfilling way for him to go through life. One miserable letdown after another. True love, huh? Destiny? Sounds more like cruel and unusual punishment.

"Ella, tell me. What is going through your head right now?" He emphasizes the *right now*. If he only knew how complicated things could get. Here he is asking me to do the one thing that feels about as natural as having a pet shark in your bathtub.

"Talk to me, tell me. Come on, even if you are boring as hell I can't go anywhere. Consider me your own private captive audience. So, spill it."

God, he's persistent and I am so tired of being strong, and alone. I wonder how it might feel to lay my head on his shoulder and just *let go*.

For the first time in my life, I tell myself to shut the hell up. I decide to give him exactly what he's asking for. My story.

Chapter 20: Dezi

She has been talking now for over a half hour. I don't interrupt even though I have a ton of questions to ask. I let her go on, because I think if I stop her, she'll pull back again and I'll lose her. I have known her for as long as it takes to cook dinner and yet I feel like she's a part of me.

She is nothing like I expected and yet she is everything I had hoped for, and so much more. She is strong, sweet, and kind. She is deeply proud of her family yet wants to make her own way. The fancy trappings of her extraordinary life are missing. She is simple and entirely genuine. As she divulges one private fact after another, I feel myself falling deeper. I want her to trust me. I want her to know that no matter what happens when we land, I will be there when she needs me to be.

I'm in Ella.

She tells me about Lauren, and I remember a photo shoot I did a few years back with the cast of the show. We both get a laugh out of that one. "It's a small world," she says, with a sweet grin that tells me a good deal about their relationship. Friends, I think, that will be together for life. It is a surprisingly heady feeling, to be allowed into someone's life and entrusted with her secrets. Her smile slips away and she gets serious again. There is more to tell. Instinct tells me to keep my mouth shut and let her work through this on her own. I get the sense she is on the cliff, having one of those Thelma and Louise moments when she has to decide if she should floor the accelerator or back the hell up. I hold my gaze, trying to give her strength by nodding just a bit to tell her I am still right here. Her voice shakes a little, and she suddenly loses her train of thought and bursts out with the most obvious question of all.

"Why, Dezi? Why are you here right now?"

The answer is simple, and yet it surprises even me because it's right there, like instant recall. I don't have to reach for it, it just appears.

"Because I can't imagine *not* being here. With you. I'm not a perfect guy, Ella. I can be an asshole sometimes and I've been way too focused on myself for a long time. I never thought there was something missing, until you stumbled in and almost crushed my iPod."

We both laugh, and she nods her head like, "*Yup, that's what I do.*"

"I know you've got a crazy life, and I can't even imagine the pressure of being you. I have this feeling that you're not quite sure what to do with yourself, and something is really, really wrong right now. Yeah, you have a job and your mother is the frigging vice president, and you go to important events, and cool places and that's good and all, but what else do you have, Ella? What else is there? Or really, you should be asking yourself what *isn't* there. What's missing for you? I think it's the same thing missing for me. So…I guess *that's* why I'm here. And I really want to know what you're so upset about. If you trust me enough to tell me, I would like to help if I can." I would bench press a cow if it would make her tears stop.

I never knew what it felt like to care like this, to hang on a woman's every word. Even if it did hit me as fast as a lightning bolt through the head, it's *happening*. Sure, there are some fabulous people in my life, and I love them and appreciate them, but let's face it, I could go on and prosper even if they didn't. My first and only concern until now has been me. My career, my knee, my important shoot, my future.

I feel like I'm suddenly in on the big secret. *This* is the reason you get a call from your buddy at midnight, when he's all juiced up with joy on the other end of the line telling you, *she said yes! This* is why guys who tape up broken bones without a flinch to rejoin the action on the field, break down in tears when they hear their baby's first cry.

This is what it feels like to fall in love. Jesus Christ, this is bizarre!

She looks at me like I'm speaking in a foreign tongue. Hell, maybe I *am*. I wonder if I could be arrested, charged with being a sentimental freak who is bordering on harassing the daughter of a public official.

How do you plead? Guilty, Your Honor.

"Wow," she whispers. "Who are you?"

Well, jury is still out on that one. All the evidence would point to the fact that at this moment I don't know who the fuck I am. Here is who I'm usually *not*, though. I am not the guy who believes in love at first sight. Lust maybe, but I can work that out of my system quite easily, thank you very much. I never stay for good, and I never want to. I am not the guy who can sit through a chick flick any longer that the time it takes me to eat the buttery first layer off my tub of popcorn. I am also not the guy who expects life's greatest pleasures to plop down in his lap as if they were being delivered by God's own hand.

Like you just did.

So to answer your question, Ella, I used to know exactly who I am. Now I have no idea.

I tell her as much, but I do so in a way that I hope is self-deprecating enough to entice her to stick around for a while to figure it out.

Thankfully, she does, for now.

She is ready to talk again. I hear all about her sister and her brother. I can tell she has a soft spot for him because she gets this cute little grin on her face when she tells me about him. The sister, though, sounds like a lot of work. Ella must notice my expression changing because she is quick to tell me she's not *that* bad. I begin to wonder how family dinners work at the Sheridan house. Everyone sitting around the table telling spectacular stories about their spectacular lives. In this crowd, there is no room for average, or even *above* average. You had better bring it or get ready to push in your chair and ask to be excused.

She must feel like Alice in Wonderland. Her mother talking about having tea with the Queen of England, as her brother chimes in about next week's game and how cool it is to play on Monday nights. *Monday nights!* Then her father pulls out his own Monday Night Football stories and her sister starts talking about being on the cover of *Vogue*. Again. That would be when Ella starts to shrink; becoming so small and insignificant no one can hear her screams. Everyone else just keeps growing larger and larger until they bust out of the roof with their giant egos and amazing achievements. Like King Kong on the Empire State Building, poor little Ella is stuck in a furry grip that is squeezing the life right out of her.

Jesus, no wonder she is sitting here with tears rolling down her face. Her life is like an Olympic qualifying heat, every fucking day. No one can be fabulous all the time. She doesn't look like she has the heart to even leave the locker room anymore.

In spite of all that, she loves them, and I get the feeling that it's a real kind of love. The stories she shares with me are the ones that are simple and sweet. Like how her father still gives her money on the sly whenever she sees him. How her mother keeps a picture of her from the second grade when she had no front teeth, tucked into her wallet. How her brother always calls her after a game even if he loses, just to say good night. She sighs loudly when she explains how sometimes she wishes her sister would just go away. Not for good, she assures me. Just for a while, to get some perspective. She tells me Kelby needs a good dose of real world experience.

I think Kelby and Bridget would get along nicely. Right up until the moment they kill each other.

I remember the advice my old man gave me when I was going on my first date. The key to understanding women, he had said, was to *listen to them*. He didn't elaborate on that, and I watched his face for a long time waiting for more. That was all I got. Turns out, he knew exactly what he was talking about but the rest was for me to figure out on my own.

Now, I get it. Sometimes listening is much more important than talking.

I could listen to her forever.

I shift in the seat to rotate my body more toward hers. She is now cross-legged with her hands folded in her lap. She plays with the frayed edges of her shirt, keeping her fingers busy as she speaks. Her voice is lovely. It is neither deep nor too highly pitched. It floats perfectly between the two extremes. It has absolutely no accent, and the kind of cadence that could lull you into a peaceful slumber. But I am anything but tired. I am energized and focused. I feel like I'm hovering over a puzzle with a million tiny pieces. The border is almost in place, but there's still a long way to go before a clear picture emerges in the middle.

I begin to think she's talking *around* something, holding back a crucial element of her life that would help me understand why she's here. My imagination is wild, spinning one possible scenario after another. Like an investigator at a crime scene, I weigh the evidence and look for clues. No smoking gun or bloody knife, but obviously something is troubling her and I think it's big.

So what is it? Start with what you know, Dezi.

I know she is not the kind of girl who gets all worked up when her jeans won't zip or because some guy doesn't call when he says he will. No, it's nothing frivolous or trite. I can't say for sure, but I don't think she's told anybody about it. If that's true, then she is sitting on something that is life-changing and sad, and it's scaring her. I figure that it's not the kind of information she can drop on her mother or her father because if she had I don't think she'd be here, hiding under messy clothes and a baseball hat. I know that her sister seems too vapid to care, and I don't think she wants to burden her brother.

As I nudge my way carefully into her world I think I can say with some sense of certainty that this trip is not meant to catch a few rays of California sunshine. I *would* say, however, that somehow Lauren is pivotal in what's going on. Is she upset with Lauren? No. She loves Lauren. I can tell just by how her face softens when she talks about her. I wonder if Lauren is in trouble. Is Ella flying in to save the day? No, that doesn't make sense either. This is definitely about her, and she *hates* that. It doesn't come naturally to her to open up. I will catch her looking over at me as she's speaking, like she's trying to make sure I haven't drifted off mid-sentence.

Doesn't anyone ever listen to you, Ella? Doesn't anybody else care?

She is moving on to safer ground now, taking me back to her job and asking me where my office is. We talk about restaurants,

Jennifer Vaughn

museums and landmarks, but I want to get her back to what's really going on. She is crafty, though, very smooth at shifting the direction of the conversation away from herself. Years of practice, perhaps? She reminds me of a Ouija board, spelling things out one letter at a time.

She asks me if I played in high school, college, or both, catching me completely off guard with this. Very perceptive, Ella. How did I tip you off?

"How did you know I played?"

"Duh," she jokes. She's been around it her whole life. She tells me that growing up with two football players in the house gave her a pretty good eye.

"Running back?" she asks. Yeah, I tell her. She digs around some more, curious about what happened along the way. Did I ever consider going pro? We toss around a few names that we both recognize, coaches and players who have crossed our paths at some point. She is like a guy when it comes to this world, the conversation flows easily and comfortably. We can talk stats, positions and plays, and she becomes extremely sympathetic when I tell her about the hit that took me out for good. I keep it simple and positive, like it was all meant to be because I found something else that became just as important to me. I don't want to tell her that I was mired in my own misery for awhile, feeling sorry for myself. Strangely, I don't want to disappoint her.

"I've seen it happen to the best of them, Dezi. Sometimes they never get back up, though. You are obviously smart enough to have figured out how to move on. Many of them get buried by an injury and are never the same. That's sad."

"Yeah, it was sad for awhile. But, hey, that's life, right?" I ask her to tell me more about her work. Bring it back to her, keep it in the present, and build her trust. She looks at me like she gets what I'm trying to do. Suddenly, she doesn't want to play anymore.

Shit!

She is like a ping-pong match. Just when I think I'm going to make it over the net she paddles the ball right off the table. Why can't she just let me in?

"I'm not as interesting as you think I am, Dezi," she says in a tone that is a mix of sarcastic and sullen. "It's not as good as the pictures make it out to be. In fact, I would hesitate to say I am even worth your time. "

Ouch. It is an absurd statement. I flat out refuse to let her backpedal her way right out of my life. Not so fast, Ella.

"Can you let me decide that, please? I was really enjoying our conversation and to be honest, my fantasy football lineup for this weekend looks lame. I could use some expert advice here, care to weigh in on who I should start? There's this one QB having a great season, and I hear his sister's kinda cool, too." I try to go for a bit of comic relief, thinking I can bring her back with that. She does laugh at me, but as she crinkles her nose, she looks like she's trying to decide what the fuck I want from her, because someone always wants something from her. In the kind of life Ella seems stuck in, nothing is free.

While we're still talking football, I ask some questions about Kass for real because I think she could go on about him for hours. She tells me how when they were young he would rush home after school to hurl a football through an old tire their father had hung from a tree in their backyard. She told me when he got to high school there was so much pressure on him to be perfect, or at least as good as his father was. That bothered her; I could tell she didn't think it was fair. Somehow, Kass always came through. She tells me he plays because he wants to, because he loves it so much he can't imagine doing anything else.

Yeah, I know the feeling.

She tells me during high school, Kass would routinely find one player on his team who didn't have the greatest home life going for him. Maybe his dad was a drunk or his mother didn't give a shit about him, whatever. Day in and day out Kass would focus on that one kid, throwing to him over and over again, running the same play until he could guarantee that boy knew it like the back of his hand. Then under the lights with the crowd screaming and the flashbulbs popping, Kass would fire in the perfect spiral that was neither too low nor too fast, but just right. The kid would be the hero. Kass would have given him a moment he would never forget, for no other reason than just because he could.

Ella beams with pride as she tells me there is so much about her brother that no one can see. I ask if he has a girlfriend. Ella rolls her eyes and tells me he has *too many* of those. I ask about Kelby, whether she is seeing anyone. Ella explains something about a boyfriend that probably won't last very long. We dance around the whole dating thing like we're hobbling over hot coals. I step in; she steps out. Finally, I decide to jump right into the fire.

"So, Ella," I say softly, as I reposition myself so that my head is back against the headrest. Out of the corner of my eye, I can see the flight attendants starting to move around. "Are you going to make me come out and say it, or can you sense where I'm going with this line of questioning?"

Moment of truth. I lay my palms down flat on the tops of my knees because they're starting to feel way too hot. My shirt feels like it's made of cactus skin, and there are beads of sweat breaking out along my forehead.

Way to keep it together, Dez. She takes her sweet time. Everything is being weighed, studied. There are very few natural responses with this girl. I start to worry that she's trying to come up with the best way to let me down gently. Don't do it, Ella. Give us a chance.

Then she folds her hands again, like she's reached some internal peace with the answer she's about to give me.

"Actually, Dezi, before I answer that there's something I should tell you."

Okay, I think. Lay it on me. Tell me everything you need to, Ella, but I can promise you it won't change a thing. She starts to tell me, and the trust she is placing in me right now feels as fragile as a baby bird. Then her story stops as quickly as it starts. Because before long, all hell breaks loose.

Chapter 21: Ahmed

I stayed with the man and his family for several years. Malik left to go to university but came home every summer and taught me all that he had learned. Our lessons in the dirt continued with the numbers growing more intricate and elaborate. My mind would soak it in like a sponge until I could scratch out the same answers he got in almost the same time. Malik insisted I memorize formulas and applications. He even had me commit to memory the five main points of atomic theory. He would quiz me every night before we fell asleep. We would discuss elements and particles, compounds and electrons. We were technically still children, and yet we chatted for hours about impossibly convoluted numbers and theories that seemed almost simple and fundamental. My brain was able to grasp it all like there was a handle attached.

Time passed with regularity, of course, but I lost track of dates and their significance. The people of the village were not concerned with birthdays or holidays, so I could not say with any real certainty how old I was when I finally left for good. I had become very tall, and strong, with the face of a man. There were few mirrors around, so I did not study my reflection very often. I suspect I resembled my father in many ways because my hair had grown only slightly darker with age and my skin turned a ruddy brown in the desert sun.

For a time, children of the village returned to a school the elders had set up in a nearby building. I enjoyed this tremendously, because learning new things kept my mind busy and focused. I realized there was a lot I needed to know before I could safely leave. Most of the books had been destroyed, so we relied on stories from the elders and we discussed the television reports we watched on the set Malik had rigged for the house. It was rudimentary and raw, but I developed many skills during this time. I could speak Arabic without the hint of an accent, yet switch to English instantaneously. Most of the villagers spoke only Arabic, so I taught them a few words so they could communicate with the soldiers who passed through every so often.

There were also dangerous men who roamed at will through the desert at this time. Eventually, for their own safety, the children were not allowed to leave the village and the school shut down. We began to see little boys accompanying the men, often armed with weapons. The sight was jarring; boys not yet old enough to shave, carrying pistols, machine guns, sometimes even rocket-propelled grenade launchers that were larger than they were. We learned of kidnappings, and of children disappearing right from their own front yards.

I did not know it then, but there was a trend developing during this time. A style of recruitment so vile and repugnant it defied human nature. I grew to detest these men, with their black hearts filled with vengeance and hate. They wanted to destroy without discretion, harm beings that had done no harm of their own. I considered that cowardly and insensitive.

To seek revenge when it was deserved, however, was reasonable and just.

When it became time for me to leave, the man handed me an unexpected gift. Inside a small box was a tightly rolled wad of cash. I shook his hand firmly and leaned in to clasp my arm around his back. I thanked him for pulling me out of the hospital that day, for saving my life. I had developed a deep affection for him and his village. Although I knew I would never see them again, I did not regret my time here. The man told me to have a good honorable life, and to find success and happiness. He then pulled out a small shiny pistol, and thrust it into my hands, telling me it was not dishonorable to defend one's own life. He knew I would be traveling alone and he wanted me to have some protection. He was also aware of what was lurking in the shadows once the sun set along the desert sand.

The man also asked me for a favor. He knew that Malik and I had talked of meeting up one day, and he asked if I could watch over him. He did not entirely trust his son had pure intentions anymore. He worried he was being influenced by the same groups that prowled the villages looking for the next generation of radicals. I could not say what was appealing to Malik during this time, but it was common for young Iraqi males to take up with these types. His father noticed that each time Malik returned home he spoke more often of the nihilist discussions he was having with underground revolutionists. The elders of the village would hear rumblings of Malik's activities. At the time, they did not know how, from his school on the East Coast, he was able to maintain the connections that stretched all the way back to the tunnels and caves of this land.

I did not intend to discourage Malik as his father has requested. In fact, as misguided and imprudent as they were, these shameful legionnaires might be of use to me one day. I knew they had access to things I did not. Because the man was worried, and had given freely to me for many years, I promised him I would check on Malik. It was not a lie I felt good about, but it was not to be helped.

Once the sandstorm season had passed that year I walked out of the village not completely sure of where I would go, but ready to begin my life. I wished it could be as simple as the man had said, but I was not setting out on my own to find happiness and success. It would only be through knowledge and dedication, steadfastness and wit that I would arrive fully prepared at the end. To get there, I had a lot of work to do.

I needed to give myself a name, establish a fluid and untraceable, yet non-threatening existence. I had to make money. The tiny roll of bills the man had saved for me would not last very long. I traveled mostly during the day by foot, trying to avoid the occasional rush of rain that would come without warning. The desert became like thick mud under the pounding water, and it got dangerous. I set up a tent at night to sleep, but only after walking until I felt sheer exhaustion set in. The hours of darkness were extremely tenuous, unpredictable ones. Winds would whip the sand and grit along the sides of my tent, making sharp metallic noises that would cover up the sound of approaching footsteps. I slept with one eye open, gun on my lap, teaching my body to rest itself while at the same time staying alert enough to react swiftly to a threat.

I would hear from men I met along the route that opportunities for work in Kuwait were robust. Unlike Iraq where poverty kept many people from being able to rebuild, the cities to the south were bustling. There had been a shift in attitude toward Americans and their products. The country was now more willing to welcome innovation and partnership, especially in areas requiring advanced technology. The United States was working to help Kuwait regain its critical role as a trans-shipment point in the region. If I could infiltrate this process, I could develop contacts that would be vital to my future. By the time I had no money left, and the leather of my boots had worn through, I arrived at one of the smaller ports being used primarily for the export of oil products. Finding work was my top priority, and relatively simple given I already spoke clean English and looked as though I were an American contractor. The intense sun had given my face early lines around my eyes. They worked in my favor, adding age and credibility. I needed both.

I was ready to immerse myself in the culture and personality of this new place. I attended as many *diwaniahs* as I could. These traditional gatherings for men became the perfect place to discuss work opportunities, make contacts, and more importantly, open a dialogue about America and its government. I was meeting men who had traveled from the United States for financial gain here. Even though I offered no information about myself, they spoke to me as if I was one of them. It was a valuable lesson for me. I was learning how to shape my personality depending on the crowd I was with. Fitting in with the Americans was integral in acquiring the knowledge and skills that would bring me to the woman I had seen on the television all those years ago. Every move I made now was to get to her.

During one of these evening *diwaniahs* I met the owner of a small shrimp operation on the shore of the Gulf waters. He had enough of an entrepreneurial spirit to see that if he could get into this rapidly expanding industry he could root himself in as a principal fleet. Although I had no interest in his work initially, he mentioned to me his growing need for security. Pirates were trolling the waters, looking for vessels to raid and catches to steal. He asked if I had any experience in designing an alert system that would give his captains enough advance warning to change route or at least prepare for an encounter. Although I was ready to do whatever labor necessary to earn money, this was perfect. It would give me access to technology I had not yet seen, and the men who were already working with it.

The job turned out to be fascinating. The owner had lined up some extremely bright minds to handle his security needs. I became part of this small group, spending many months simply listening and learning from the others, especially the Americans. They were all much older than I was, and educated at universities all over the world. They had specialties that varied from microbiology to nuclear physics, and something I had not yet heard of. Even though at the time it was in its infancy, the use of computers was just beginning to build its almost mystical appeal. My colleagues were among the first to use its capabilities to design first-rate security systems.

It did not take me long to become a contributing member of the group, given my abilities with numbers and equations. We began to discuss the next generation of technology, things that were only being used by a select few. It was heady and intense, and although I would not call us friends, we grew comfortable with each other in a way that I suspect friends do, although I never trusted them completely.

They knew me as Brian. I never divulged my real identity to any of them, and even procured temporary documents with this new name for their records. They thought I was either American or British because I could speak with a twinge of an accent if I so wished. I never confirmed either. They knew I was young, and told me that I should leave Kuwait to attend school. Eventually, I did, but only after I had gleaned all that I could from them in terms of knowledge and experience. I extended my hand to as many people as I could, hoping to learn something from each one of them. One day, I met a man whose father had taught him about aviation. That was a new subject to me and I was intrigued. I asked many questions. As it turns out, the older man would be very useful to me in short order.

When I left Kuwait, our security system was patented, and being used all across the Middle East. The man who had hired us was thrilled with our product. He was fair and honest and sent me away with his thanks and a decent wage for my time.

Although I knew Malik was waiting for me on the East Coast of the United States, I began my formal education in California. I was in sporadic contact with him by then, but we began communicating more often by using developing software. I now understood how he was able to maintain contact with the men in the caves of the desert. They had surprisingly modern equipment and intelligent minds. Malik still had a fondness for me that was separate from the dark liaisons he maintained. I used that to advance my own agenda.

Malik knew I would not have had the funds to pay entirely for my education, and no way to prove my identity, so he helped me design a new one. With his help, "Brian" was reborn as Seth Baxter, a citizen of California whose parents had died long ago. My school records as they appeared in the system were those of a 4.0 student with flawless scores on performance tests. Malik told me any university would make room for me, but only a few would offer financial help. I was to begin in California where, as a resident, I could attend for free.

I studied everything I could. I took courses that ranged from astrophysics and statistics, to American history and writing. I learned even more about computers, how they were being used in everyday business and communication. America was riding a technological wave and I was determined to stay on top of it. It did not take long for my professors to notice my skills and take me aside to discuss my future. They saw in me what my teachers did back in the basement of the hospital. Despite the fact that they would not understand what I was pursuing, I appreciated their knowledge and I took from them everything I needed to move on.

The American culture and its youth were befuddling to me. They were so unlike the young men I had worked alongside in Kuwait. They waited a long time to marry and have children, so there was no urgency to find work or make money. Instead, they *lingered.* There was a sense of entitlement among them that I could not understand. I found their materialistic desires and urges significantly unappealing, so I made acquaintances only if I thought they would benefit me in some way. I avoided women on a personal level, although I did begin to enjoy their company in a physical way. I became aware of them watching me, courting me, and it was never difficult to find a woman with whom I could spend a few hours.

For many years, I would study late into the night, toiling over my keyboard, analyzing data. I avoided sleep because that was when my parents came to me. As much as I was living my life in their honor, they made me weak. They stirred inside me emotions I did not care to feel. They reminded me of a love I had known, and the bitterness I felt when it was ripped away. It took me a very long time to be able to look at the California grass without thinking of the day I closed my mother's beautiful green eyes for the last time.

When sleep finally did come, I saw her. I felt her. By then, the only times I could truly recall my mother's touch was when I was dreaming. I was still a child in my sleep. I could fit on my father's shoulders and wrap my tiny palm around his chin, holding on for dear life. Only when the morning light splashed through my window did I have to let go. The dreams left me with deep sadness and mental exhaustion. Two precious lives eliminated as if they were dust particles on a table, wiped clean away by a hand guided by insolence and swagger.

I had watched the woman become quite successful and well known. I studied her path with a mixture of disgust and admiration. I knew she would be a formidable opponent. I needed to find the one liability that would make her vulnerable. Once I identified her weakness, I would use it to bring her out of hiding.

That was when I would go in for the kill.

Chapter 22: Ella

This feels like a bad case of infatuation. He is so close I can feel his body heat. He smells so good. Like leather and peppermint floating along the breeze that blows in off the ocean. He has me so entranced it actually hurts to take my eyes off him. A little bit like when you are flat on the table having the tension rubbed out of your neck and the masseuse suddenly pulls away. Your achy muscles scream out in protest, come on get back here!

Everything about him is cool. *Of course*, he was a football player, his body is still rock solid. *Of course*, he has a job that takes him all over the country, if not the world. *Of course*, he is close to his family and has an ex-girlfriend who just can't let go. Perhaps best of all, he has even met my BFF! What are the odds you plop down on an airplane during a personal crisis on the way to see said BFF and find yourself next to someone who knows exactly whom you are talking about? Like an old flame that surfaces unexpectedly in the frozen pizza section of the supermarket and tells you he never should have let you go.

Weird, and wonderful and totally not happening to me.

I would say that in itself was the perfect icebreaker, but we're past that. It feels like we've already melted the entire glacier. Wait until Lauren hears about you, Dezi. At least when I tell her about him it might put a shiny coating on my cancer; make it go down a little easier. Like a spoonful of sugar just before you serve up the lumpy medicine that tastes like the fish you accidentally left out on the counter overnight.

I wonder if she would remember him. Granted he did say their photo shoot was a few years ago and half of Los Angeles looks as good as he does. Lauren has well-developed radar for sleazy intentions so she will immediately want to know what I thought his end game was. She'd ask me if he was angling for something. Did he know who I was? Lauren is always defensive when it comes to me, but she also knows I am not some wide-eyed love zealot who thinks every man who buys me a drink is Mr. Right. I am just as guilty as the next girl of trying to use the first couple of dates to gauge just how wonderful the good-looking guy with the smooth lines really is. We go in search of hidden clues that will tell us what is really lurking deep in his subconscious. Through the years, I have developed my own way of reaching in and pulling out a man's true colors. I simply introduce him to Kelby. Poor suckers, I know it's a twisted game but it's always a sure thing. If they start to stutter and sweat, I know they're short-timers who are prone to thinking with what's just below the waistband. If a man can meet my sister and the rest of my family without forgetting my name, I consider myself off to a good start. I get the whole intrigue and allure, but if someone is buzzing around me just for the experience, I wish he would have the guts to be honest about it.

Don't waste my time. Take the White House tour and leave me alone.

Suddenly the flight attendant pokes her lovely face into the area above our heads, asking if we would like a beverage this morning. I figure, hey, its five o'clock somewhere, I have cancer, and a hot guy next to me is acting like he wants in. Might as well throw back something with a little kick to it.

I ask for a glass of champagne with some orange juice on the side. Dezi laughs at that for some reason and asks for the same thing. I notice the flight attendant's eyes lingering on him for a little longer than necessary. I suspect she is quite used to having her pretty little pout get her far in this world, but not today, sweetheart. Dezi politely thanks her then looks back at me. It is juvenile and completely unlike me, but it feels like a small victory, and these days I'll take it because I usually come in dead last.

My hands have moved away from the armrests now. I absently rub them together. They still feel warm from his touch, if not a little softer and perhaps even a touch more feminine. Maybe it's because he is all man, and yet he is so unlike a man. He is not leering at me, or telling me how magnificent and accomplished he is, or even pulling away when I do my usual I'm-not-worthy routine. He doesn't seem to mind that my eyes are red and puffy from stress and lack of sleep. Does he even notice my stained Uggs or torn jeans? Could he possibly be the kind of man who looks at his wife after fifty years of marriage and still sees the girl she used to be the day they said I do? The kind of man who touches her wrinkled face and tells her she is beautiful because he truly believes it?

If he is, then what the hell is he doing sitting here with me?

He smiles when I talk about my family but it's not like he's salivating, waiting for me to drop a morsel of personal information he can talk about at the bar next Saturday night. He does not come off as the name-dropping type. He has more class than that. He has more *everything* than that.

He wants to know all about my work, and the process of getting a book from computer to hardcover. He asks me about my apartment, and my favorite restaurant, and what kind of music I like, and if I ever jog through Central Park. He asks me all of this like I am a normal everyday person with a regular old job and a leaky sink in my co-op.

Ahh, how easy it would be to fall into this perfect pick-up opportunity. Even if it were just for a little while, I would love to be part of his world. I wouldn't even mind if he broke my heart one day because judging by how his hand feels on mine, the good memories would linger longer than the pain.

He is quick to divert me if he thinks I'm not spilling as much as he'd like to hear, but I'm curious here, too. I want to hear about his football days and the injury that ended them. He has been hurt, I think. By an injury that bruised more than just his body. Football did some deep damage here. I try to tell him without being condescending that it impresses me he was able to go on. Not everyone can. When you literally have your hopes and dreams sliced up like prosciutto, it takes an iron will to apply pressure and stop the bleeding. He brushes that aside and tells me it was all for the best. I don't think so. I think his spirit was crushed, and it hasn't been easy to nurse it back to health.

How I would like to have seen him out there, cheering him from the sidelines, listening to his dreams, watching him reach his goals.

Who did that for you, Dezi? Was she special to you? Was she good to you? On the other hand, maybe that's why he's not married. I wonder if he considers himself too damaged to deliver on promises of happily-ever-after. Hey, I can relate. I might not even have an ever after, let alone the happily end of the bargain. How could I allow myself to be so selfish that I would invite a man to hitch his wagon to a carriage with broken wheels? Sure, hop in Dezi, hope the bumps along the way don't make your molars rattle.

I must seem like I'm bipolar, smiling one minute before lapsing back into my introspective coma. I consider another fast retreat when he gets around to prodding me about my dating life, or complete lack of one. How do you tell someone you're one step up from a sad old spinster who sits home every Saturday night knitting afghans? Should I admit that the solitude feels like I am under quarantine? No matter what else I throw into my life, the emptiness is like an annoying co-worker who wears too much perfume. The air is cloying and it's slowly gagging me to death.

I don't know how to evade his line of questioning without being obvious, and there's too much percolating between us. I consider honesty. Do I put it all out there for a man who has just blown in like a category five hurricane? I figure he'll either destroy everything in his wake or shake the cobwebs out of my muddled head. Take your pick Ella, peace and happiness or total annihilation.

Why is everything always so drastic? Why isn't there ever a happy medium when it comes to me? Dezi deserves to know I have my own storm brewing. The placid looking ocean he is dipping his toe into is actually cooking up an underground volcano that is threatening to blow. I wonder why he didn't bolt when he spotted the tears I tried to wipe away, or my capricious and agitated body language, or my attempt at complete anonymity. Those are pretty strong cues most people gladly throw up their hands for. *Okay, you win. You are too much work for me.*

Is it misguided fortitude? Even if you don't believe in the idea of predestination and karma, could he simply be following the blueprint of his life? It is possible, right? How many times have I wondered how two people going about their daily lives cross paths at just the right moment. She drops her keys; he stops and picks them up. They lock eyes and suddenly they both feel as hot as steak sizzling on the grill. How two people both happen to miss the early bus for work one morning and end up stuck on the subway, sitting right next to each other and accidentally bumping elbows?

Bumping his iPod.

Going about our daily lives, crossing paths, catching the other's eye, could that be what we are all sent here to do? Is it what happened when my father needed a lawyer, and out of the trillion available in a two-mile radius, he walked into the exact office where my mother just happened to be on the other side of the front door? Not because I'm convinced of all that, but just in case, I decide that he deserves to know why I'm about to pull out of what could be the best thing that ever happened to me.

To us.

My instincts are telling me he is everything I want, and everything I want to be. Confident and kind, dependable and real, he exudes all of those qualities that don't just come and go in life, and can't be artificially called up at an opportune moment. The qualities no one can teach you how to have, the things you're either born with or spend your life chasing. The only things that have ever appealed to me are the ones I have not yet been able to find. Yet here they are, sitting next to me in row 2B, with tender eyes and a smile that makes me feel like there is melted chocolate running through my veins. In under an hour's time he has made me all soft and gooey, even daring to ask how in the world my cancer cells can survive if there is nothing inside me but saccharine sweet syrup.

Old sayings run through my head. You'll find someone when you're not looking for him. What doesn't kill you makes you stronger. Everything happens for a reason.

I don't want this to be a fantasy, a figment of my overstressed imagination that by now is running on pure adrenaline and anguish. I am vulnerable, and about to square off against something that is so much bigger than I am. Is it fair to try to put a halo over his head if he will only use it to disguise his horns?

Is it fair to deny us our fates?

What if I gave *him* the choice? Stay, or go. No pressure. That way there would be no denial of fortune, yet the ball would land safely in his court. I won't blame him if he freaks out when I tell him my left breast is a goner. Or if he rushes back to the old lady with the tight face in the next row over. I won't follow him if he hustles off this plane and never looks back. But I will let it be his choice. I tell him that before we give in to whatever kismet force is playing with us he needs to know something important.

Am I really going to do this? Am I really going to unload my dump truck on his perfectly manicured front lawn? Whatever happened to slow and steady wins the race? Cancer has a way of forcing you to pick up the pace. Like a swift shove just above your ass. Get a move on already…time's a-wasting. My life is passing me by and I am letting it happen. I hear a voice yelling at me, ordering me to put my goddamned blinker on and get into the fast lane. It's screaming, "Don't let this disease define you, Ella. Don't become a victim. Don't just be someone's daughter, or someone's sister, or someone's work buddy. Be more than that. Be special. Let…someone…in…"

Dear God, have I lost my mind?

Yes, it is long gone, my hand fits so perfectly in his, and I owe him the chance to make this work. Why can't it ever work for me?

"Well," I begin, not a unique start, but a safe word that gives me some time to pause. This is scary, probably not at all wise, and he could blow this up in my face. Spin it right into a death spiral.

"Dezi, there is nothing I would like more than to give in to what I'm feeling here. You are like an unexpected gift to me right now. But I don't think I deserve it."

He looks at me strangely.

"Why would you say that?" he asks. "I'm just asking that you give me a chance. Get to know me, let me get to know you. Obviously, something has you really upset. Maybe I can help. Remember, I have a younger sister. I have seen just about every catastrophe a female can encounter. Maybe if you tell me, we can figure it out together." The grin is so sincere the chocolate already coursing through my body melts even more. Then his irresistible quotient rises, as if it weren't off the charts already.

"Ella, I just want to be around you. If you decide I'm not your cup of tea, then..." he clears his throat as his voice drops, and it is impossibly seductive and divinely sweet at the same time. He finishes his thought, "...just let me be your friend. Either way, I don't want this to be the last time I ever see you. How do I convince you to let me stick around awhile?"

Convince? As in dangle the juiciest carrot I have ever seen directly in front of my face and instead of pulling it away like other assholes do, you let me lap up the entire thing? Wow, what a raw deal. I can't stifle the giggle. Like there is a woman alive who would need a man like him to *convince* her of anything.

"I'm sorry. I'm not laughing at you." Although that was funny, just not in the way he intended. "In fact, that's probably the nicest thing anyone has ever said to me. It's just ironic that you would think *you* need to convince *me*. It's sure to be the other way around, only you don't know it yet. I have a lot going on right now, Dezi. I wish it were as simple as having a bad boyfriend I'm trying to unload, or I just lost my job, or I can't afford my rent, but it's not. It's bigger and badder and more personal than all of that." I pause again, because I feel the tears building back up behind my eyes. I swallow hard to try to push them down but one stray drop makes its way out of the corner of my right eye. I hastily reach up with my sleeve to grab it before he sees it. I am too late. His hand is already there, and his giant thumb feels like a soft tissue as he wipes it away, then trails down so that his fingers wrap around the entire side of my face.

"Ella," he says, making my name sound as peaceful as snow falling at midnight. "It's okay. I would never hurt you. You can trust me. What is going on with you?"

The world is spinning; I can't catch my breath. I try to connect to the ambient noises around me, redirect my brain and get this under control. I listen to the drink cart, to the rustle of newspapers behind me, the slam of the lavatory door.

I slow my breathing, pull in the air, and dial down the hysteria.

"Sorry," I whisper. "I want to tell you, Dezi, but I haven't told anyone yet. That's why I'm going to L.A. To tell Lauren what's happening. She's the only one I've decided to tell. For now."

Dezi asks the obvious because really, who wouldn't?

"Don't you think your family would want to know if it's something big, Ella?"

How do I explain that with them, it's tricky? How this is just the latest imperfection to develop in what has already been a long history of disappointments? Only this one might just close the book for good. How do I explain to him that telling my family I have cancer would be like taking a pocketknife and cutting off my own leg while they tell me I am doing it all wrong?

"A little to the left, Ella, and quit the bleeding for God's sake."

"I know, and I will have to tell them eventually," I say, sufficiently chagrined. "But not right now."

"Okay, I understand. I'm not trying to pressure you, just to get where you're coming from," he says. "What makes you tick?"

Wish I knew. I have been wondering that my whole life.

"What would you say though, if you found out I was sick? Like...really sick. Not like a... take-a-pill-and-call-me-in-the-morning, kind of thing, but a let's-see-if-we-can-get-you-to-your-thirtieth-birthday sick." It is hard to keep my voice from quivering and I feel like slinking away in shame.

He sits on this for a moment, digesting it. *See*, I want to scream. See what happens when you hang around with me too long? It feels like you're being waterboarded. How can you possibly expect to breathe when icy cold water is being force-fed down your throat?

"I would say let's go ahead and book the hall."

Huh? Book the hall? I ask him what he means by that.

"I mean book the hall where I will throw you the biggest thirtieth birthday party you've ever seen." He reaches for my face again, this time to fit a finger under my chin and raise it so I am looking directly into his eyes. "Nothing is ever as big and bad as it seems like it is. Especially when you're trying to be brave and strong and refusing to let someone help you get through it, Ella. Trust me, I've been there. Let me help you."

Okay, Dezi, I hope you're ready. This bite may be way too much to chew.

"I'll just say it, then. But you have my permission to bolt. You're under no obligation whatsoever. Don't worry, I won't hate you. And I won't blame you, either."

He rolls his eyes as if to say, *whatever.* He sits back, folds his hands in his lap as he fits one foot over the other knee. His face is kind, and patient, and deserving of so much more than I am about to deliver.

"About a month or so ago…I wound up at the doctor."

"Figured that much out on my own, Ella. Why did you wind up at the doctor?"

This is awful. I have to force myself to go on.

"Well, because I found something that I knew shouldn't be there. And even though there were no other symptoms and I take really good care of myself …there it was. I knew I needed to have it checked out."

We barely notice the flight attendant return with our glasses. She hands us each a cloth napkin, which is good because it gives me something to wring in my hands. We thank her again, and look back at each other, noting the abrupt break in our heavy conversation. Not exactly the most perfect time to conjure up some sort of toast, but we try. Dezi goes first.

"Here's to chance encounters and good health," he says.

Clink.

"And here's to you. My new…friend."

"At the *very least*, remember?" He withholds his glass until I adjust my toast.

"At the very least..."

Out of nowhere, my arm flies forward. Our glasses come together with such force they shatter, fizzy champagne splashing up and stinging my eyes. Dezi reacts instantaneously. I feel him reaching for me. He brushes the shards of glass away and tucks my head close to his chest as he turns to look behind me.

"What just happened?" I ask, listening now to the other passengers asking the same thing. They must have seen something.

"I don't know," he tells me. His eyes narrow as he cranes his neck to get a better look at the row behind ours. "But I don't think it's good."

Chapter 23: Dezi

Just before things went south, they were going really, really well.

I couldn't help the laugh that slipped out when I heard Ella order a mimosa. How could she possibly know? She cannot of course, which makes this random meeting all the more extraordinary.

Among my best buddies, mimosas are passed around when one of us is tying the knot. We meet up at some bar and start our celebratory night off by knocking back one sweet sparkling glass as fast as possible. The last guy to swallow up all the bubbly is said to be the next in line for the altar. My mimosas always go down like they're supersonic. Today, I thought about sipping it for a while.

Her body isn't quite as stiff as it was when I first sat down, and her hands aren't fluttering in her lap anymore, but I sense a new kind of sadness settle over her. Like a splinter in your finger. You can carry on with your day but you just can't forget there's a piece of wood stuck in your skin. It's unnerving, and it hurts, and you know how much that motherfucker will burn once you pull out the tweezers and go to work.

She's got a great job, and it really matters to her, too. She's not like some of the other spawn of political rock stars who seem to fall ever so perfectly into some man-made position that rakes in huge dough. It sounds like she actually *shows up* for work.

She is introspective, and almost wills herself not to say the wrong thing. Very aware of how she comes off to others, but not in a way that is self-serving. I see her looking at me from under her hat and wish I could slide it right off. Take the stupid thing off and get a good look at her.

You are beautiful, Ella. Hasn't anyone ever told you that?

I prod her when I sense she's faltering, assure her when she wants to turn away, touch her only when I think she can handle it. Her skin is soft, and my hand lingers on the curve of her cheek.

There's touching someone, and then there is *touching someone*. This is somewhere in the middle. It's not just physical, although there's nothing I'd like more than to let my hand travel to places other than her cheek. For some reason I am able to put that aside and focus on what she needs from me first.

Already, she is first.

I think back to the first time. When touching a girl felt like the greatest thing in the world, as if my senses were blowing through the gears faster than I could shift. She was the cheerleader who had caught my eye when I was a lowly freshman trying to hang with the varsity football team. The older guys hated me at first. The quarterback only threw to me when I was as open as a prostitute on a Saturday night.

"Sorry, coach," he'd say. "He can't get open, he's too slow." Bullshit! I was in position before he even took the snap. The coach pulled him out by the chinstrap of his helmet, bellowing at him between the lines of his facemask. He came slinking back into the huddle, snarling at me like a pissed off pit bull. But he called the play that I had been waiting for. The long bomb that made me bolt off the line of scrimmage like my hair was on fire. My legs pumped like pistons, carrying me to an impossible distance so far down the field the ball looked like a pebble. It had floated perfectly, right into my arms. I pulled it to me, and ran it in.

Touchdown.

That quarterback became one of the best friends I've ever had. But he'd made me work for it, made me earn his respect. Like the cheerleader. She was older than I was, and let's face it, in high school older girls were like the Holy Grail. Long flowing hair pulled up into a ponytail, with high kicks that made my stomach hurt. She had ignored me, of course, right up until Thanksgiving of that year. We had played in a freezing rain that turned the field into a mixture of ice and mud. The last game of the season, with a big party planned for that weekend to celebrate our winning record.

After I had washed off the dirt and cleaned myself up that night, she came to me. Her judgment slightly dulled by a few Bud Lights, she was all teeth and perky boobs and long hair that I wanted to wind around my fingers. She told me how she'd been watching me for a while, how cute I looked running around in my tight pants, and would I like to come over and watch a movie sometime.

I did. I came over and over again. She'd made me work for it, too. Like right now. I am working for it here, but that's exactly how it should be. Nothing ventured, nothing gained.

I try to tell her to let go and just give me a chance. Don't rule me out yet.

In her roundabout way, she begins to circle the target. The pain is so obvious she can't help but tear up, so completely tormented she tells me no one even knows yet what's going on. I wonder how that can be. I think of my own circle of people, how I could turn to any number of friends for help with just about anything. But I would always call my parents and my sister if it was as shitty as this seems to be. Why can't she tell them? How in the world do you get to the place in your life when you need your family more than ever, and they are nowhere to be found? Yet, they're right there. Everyone knows exactly where they are. She's running in the opposite direction.

I reach out to grab the tear with my finger. She leans into my hand. The trickle of information continues. I sidestep the grenades she tries to toss back, telling her to stop it already with the friendly fire. I am fully engaged, locked and loaded. Little by little, she shows her hand and the cards are duds. She is flat out petrified and she has every right to be.

She's sick.

For a girl who feels most comfortable in the back row of the family photograph, or under a baseball hat and tucked into a job in the most anonymous city in the world, the attention she's about to get is like rubbing salt in a gaping wound. It's not the sickness as much as what the sickness will bring. Way too much attention.

That must be why she hasn't told them yet. Because once she does, it will start and it won't stop until it has buried her. Like a landslide that washes out a quiet mountain road, she will be lost under the weight of it all. One day, no one will remember the road was even there.

Like hell. I won't let that happen.

With the timing of a sneezing fit during a funeral, here comes the flight attendant with two glasses of champagne and two glasses of orange juice on the side. She hands them off and leaves but Ella has stopped talking, again. I hate the silence. It makes me think she's pulling away.

We toast, hopefully the first of a lifetime full of them. Instead of the gentle kiss of glass I am expecting, there is an explosion of liquid. I react instantly although I have no idea what's happening. My first movement is to cover her, remove her from harm, and protect Ella.

Protect her from what though? What the fuck is going on? I saw her arm jolt forward from the elbow down, so I look up and over the back of the seat to find whatever it was that slammed into her. I pull her into my upper body, but try to fold her head downward so whoever is behind her gets me first.

Go ahead, asshole. Try to get through me.

I see him then, a tall man with a red shirt and dark hair. I lean across Ella to watch him run the short distance up the aisle to the cockpit. I also catch a glint of steel in his left hand as he slams his right shoulder into the door and yells something. Behind me, bodies are starting to stir. People are rising out of their seats to get a better look at the action. Ella mumbles something near my stomach, making me realize I am holding her too tightly. She says she can't breathe.

"Sorry," I whisper, loosening my grip but refusing to let her go completely.

My mind is already weighing options. I can totally take this guy out. He's skinny but he appears to have a knife or a blade of some sort. Maybe he's wearing a bomb on his belt for all I know. Is he alone? I don't know yet. I look back again but all I can see are passengers standing or bending over, probably heaving their breakfasts onto the floor. Some are screaming in panic while others are reaching for the cell phones they shut off when we left.

This is it, they're thinking. We're going down, or we're blowing up. Either way it's happening again. I think of those voice recordings we all heard. The numbers dialed in those final precious moments of life.

"Goodbye, Mom and Dad, I love you both. Thanks for always being there."

"Honey, it's me. Something's happening and I don't think I'll make it out of here. Promise me to take good care of the kids. *Choke.* Tell them their mommy loved them so much."

This cannot be happening right now! How did this shithead get on a fucking plane in the first place? The man yells again, and the thick door bursts open. The co-pilot comes out first, his eyes downcast and registering shock. Instead of terror, however, I think I see…disappointment? The man with the red shirt grabs him roughly by one arm and pushes him toward an empty seat in the first row directly across from Ella and me. He barks at him to sit down, then he waves what I first thought was a knife in our general direction, warning us all to sit down. It's actually just a small silver cell phone.

You little bastard!

He tells the flight attendants to strap themselves into their seats. They stand their ground, ignoring him until the pilot emerges from the cockpit. He whispers something to them I can't quite hear. They both stare at him for a couple of seconds then return to their seats snapping their belts back together in a stupor. One of them lowers her head and starts to cry. The other places a hand on her back and tells her everything will be fine. Then she starts to cry herself.

The pilot looks away from them, unfazed. He then looks over at the co-pilot sitting in the first row. The co-pilot shakes his head, as if in disbelief. He refuses to hold the pilot's level gaze, and looks down at his hands.

Wait a minute, I think. Back up the fucking bus here. Aren't you all on the same team? What's the plan? Tell me we are *not* going to let this scrawny fucker take us out! And, if you're all out here, then who's flying the goddamned plane?

I realize I am still standing when the dark haired man rushes by me and reaches for Ella. He gets a hand on her and slams her straight into the floor, her head connecting with the armrest before she goes down. I lunge at him with the full weight of my body. I land on top of him, but beneath us both is Ella. We are a tangle of arms and legs as I wrench his hand back until I hear the pop of bone.

Motherfucker, you will not hurt her!

"Enough."

A voice is above me now, and there is cold metal pressed to my forehead. I refuse to let go of the guy beneath me until he is completely off Ella. But the metal is digging into the space between my eyes, and the pilot speaks to me again.

"Get up," he says. "All of you. Get up."

Slowly, we rise. I still have the man by the back of his shirt, making sure as he gets off Ella he can't get to her again. The pilot doesn't try to pull me off him, but he does keep the gun firmly on my head. I get a sinking feeling he is not one of the good guys. He pushes me aside telling me to sit back down. In some other language, he speaks to the man, who is whimpering and holding out his damaged arm. *Good, hope that fucking hurts!* He moves back down the aisle as the pilot extends a hand down to Ella. I want to rip it off, but I figure he would shoot me. Then what good would I be?

Ella is bleeding badly near her temple, and she is shaky, but instead of taking his outstretched hand, she swipes it away. All on her own, she gets first to her knees, then rises to her full height. Even though she is a tall woman, he dwarfs her. She stands mere inches away, lifting her chin up so her head tilts back and she can make full eye contact with him.

"Give me your phones, Ella. I won't ask nicely again."

Jennifer Vaughn

"How do you know my name?" She refuses to cower away.

"In good time I will explain all of that to you, but for now I need your phones. *Both of them.* Don't play games with me. It will not end well if you do."

Her hand twitches a little then, but she holds her ground. Heart of a lion in this girl.

"I will give you my phones only if you promise not to hurt anyone else," she declares. Her eyes remain locked on his, a counter-offer even though she has no real estate left.

"You have my word. I do not intend to harm anyone on board this plane, including you. But I am prepared to, if I have to." With that, he turns to the man still cradling his injured hand. He mutters something I can't understand then raises his hand and fires off a single shot at point blank range. The man's eyes go wide, just before he takes the bullet in the head. He goes down without a word, but not before landing squarely on Ella again, showering her with brain matter and bloody chunks of what used to be the back of his skull. She turns her body toward mine, but does not make a sound.

I feel like I'm on a movie set, watching a stunt double take the hit that no actor worth his twenty-million dollar paycheck would stand for. This can't be real! Who the fuck fires a gun on a plane? The bullet does not stray from its intended target. The dude is done for. And it is very real. Too real.

"Trust me," he says, as calmly as if he had just peeled back a banana. "He would have killed all of you."

He puts out his left hand palm up, impatiently waiting for Ella to deliver to him what he wants. She wipes the man's blood from her face with the back of her sleeve. She has a look of pure fury mixed with horror that she directs at the pilot. Slowly she bends down to find her bag. I can't help but think it's the same bag that first brought her into my life as it followed its wayward trajectory straight into my iPod. She unzips it, fumbles around inside and produces two cell phones. One is a standard issue flip type, the other a small black and silver Blackberry. The man takes the first one, opens it up, and tosses it aside.

It lands directly in front of the dead man. The other cell phone is the one he is really after. He takes it, slides it into his pocket, and steps back to address the passengers. Raising his voice slightly he tells everyone to sit down, totally unperturbed that no one past first class can actually hear him. I suppose he figures we'll spread the word. He tells us not to bother attempting to call out because our phones won't work right now. He also advises us not to storm the cockpit or try to take the plane back.

"This has nothing to do with any of you," he states. "Once we get where we need to go, I will allow everyone off." He looks back at Ella. "Except you."

The pilot takes several steps backward. He reaches the cockpit door, reinforced to keep the thugs out, now working against us to keep him in. Irony strikes gold yet again. No good deed goes unpunished. Give you the good cockpit door, but you get the psychopathic pilot to go with it. I can just hear the buzz at the next aeronautical engineer convention. *Hey guys, maybe we need to rethink those reinforced cockpit doors. Or rethink who the fuck we issue pilots licenses to.*

He closes the heavy door with a thud. I can hear the metal lock glide safely into place on the other side. We won't be getting in there anytime soon. We're on our own.

There is a sudden rush of movement all around. Passengers who had been holding their breath trying to listen to what the pilot was saying are now regurgitating a blend of shrieks, moans and sobs. I don't blame them, but this is no replay of history. This guy is an American for Christ's sake, a fucking American pilot.

Is nothing sacred anymore?

I turn back to Ella. She is covered in blood, some of it her own, but most is from the man who is lying dead in the aisle. Thankfully, the co-pilot has just jumped out of his seat and is asking me to help him drag the body away before passengers in the back see it and really freak out. We hustle over, picking him up by his shoulders and his knees and sliding him into the space directly next to the cockpit door. He reaches up into an overhead bin and drags down several blankets, handing one to me and motioning with his head back to Ella.

"Here, use this. Clean her up a little," he suggests. He lays another blanket over the length of the crumpled goon and then turns to the two nearby flight attendants as they unbuckle their straps again and stand up for a group hug. The tears flow again.

Wow, I think. Talk about being betrayed by someone you trust. It's like the moment you walk in to find your wife in bed with your best friend, the same friend who told you that you deserved better than her. How many hours had they spent in flight together, sharing pictures and stories of their families? This must feel like a knife in the back.

I quickly make my way back to Ella. She has moved back a row to escape the gore that has seeped into the cushions we had been sitting on. Her face is as white as a sheet, making the red streaks of blood stand out like a bad case of the measles. She is as still as stone, staring straight ahead. She doesn't even look at me as I approach.

"Ella, let's get you cleaned up." I move toward her face, thinking how absolutely disgusting it must be to taste the blood of another human being on your tongue. She is literally covered in him. She doesn't even flinch as I begin to wipe away the carnage.

"This is my fault," she begins, her voice low with remorse.

"No. No, Ella. Don't say that, this is not your fault..."

She jumps back in, her voice rising, her eyes getting a little wild.

"Dezi, you don't understand. It *is* my fault." Her hands brush through her hair, and I notice that her hat has been knocked off her head. Who knows where it is now. Her hair is half attached to a ponytail, half hanging free and tangled in red. She doesn't notice. She is barreling toward DEFCON 1, point-of-no-return, in the red-zone.

Pull up Ella, pull up before you slam into the mountain. I yank her chin toward me, trying to force her eyes to lock onto something solid again. She continues explaining this theory of hers that places our predicament squarely on her thin, already tapped-out, weary shoulders.

"This is *exactly* what my mother has been warning me about for years. That some sick asshole out there will think he can use one of us to destroy the world. Or at least try to. Didn't you hear him? He knows who I am, Dezi. He knows about my phone. No one knows about that phone. And now he's got it. He is here for me."

Got to admit here, I'm a little stumped about the frigging phone. "Okay, Ella. Okay, calm down. So you've got two phones. Lots of people carry two phones. I get it. He's probably got your mother's office number or your brother's private line, and that sucks. I totally get that. But what's the big deal, your mother's office number is probably available on Google, or in the phone book, or whatever. So there is no way this is your fault."

"Dezi, no, you don't get it. It's much more than that. And he knows it. That's why this *is* all my fault." She covers her face with her hands, then breathes in and tries to calm herself, make things as coherent as possible given the gravity of what's churning around in her head.

"That phone is special. And it does a whole lot more than just connect me to my mother's office, or my brother's private line. But Dezi, he already knows that." Her left hand juts out to point a finger at the cockpit door.

"For some reason that pilot wants a direct line to the White House," she says, soundly defeated, her eyes steeped in sadness.

"And I just handed it to him."

Chapter 24: Ahmed

I despise the notion of chance. When at all possible I leave nothing to chance, preferring to design my own fate. There have been moments when I have had to let go and hope things fall into place. This was one of those moments. In the death of his son, I aimed to give the man back his honor. The honor with which he had lived his entire life had been wasted by his own offspring. For all these years, I have saved the small pistol he placed in my hand the day I left his village. The same gun I just used to put a bullet in his son's head.

He was not completely without purpose. If not for Malik I could not have made it this far and for that I am grateful. I said as much before I pulled the trigger, passing along my proper gratitude for his intellect and his tutelage. His hatred had become uninspiring to me, ruthless, and far too broad. He believed I was of the same mind. I was not. I never have been, but I have been good at pretending.

It is what my entire life has been up until this point. An optical illusion. I am not what I appear to be. My colleagues will wonder how they missed the signs. They didn't. This is not their fault. I have been very convincing and they could never have interpreted my true intentions. They had praised me as an immaculate pilot, a perfectionist with a flawless record. It needed to be that way, so that I could ensure I was onboard this plane, at the exact moment she was.

I have been following her life without her knowledge for quite some time.

Several years back I arrived on the East Coast of the United States ready to further my education and find Malik. By that time, opportunities were abundant for such effulgent minds as ours. I had shared with Malik the details of the work I had been doing in Kuwait. He used it to develop the next generation in virtual security, becoming a pivotal innovator of a worldwide network that sent him abroad for complicated jobs. He was the best at what he did, and he taught me everything I had not already known. This was very different from the smaller operation I had been a part of. The clients were wealthy and powerful, willing to pay exorbitant amounts of money to ensure their computer exchanges were kept confidential. We cooked up ways to guarantee a client his information was not only tamper-proof, but also unable to be copied for publication, or to collapse. We provided the client with immediate notification of any unauthorized activities within the entire network. That way they were always one step ahead of anyone who would try to do them harm. In knowing how to eliminate just about every firewall known to man to let us in, we could then design them in such a way that we could keep everyone else out. No one ever had any idea that both Malik and I were living double lives.

He was earning a great deal of money for his work, and funneling most of it back to the unsavory assembly of criminals in Iraq. He had become almost maniacal in this pursuit. The men who had appealed to him when he was a teenager had become supreme leaders in this underground organization. I learned his group was responsible for many heinous acts inside the country, but was searching for a way to launch its own devastation abroad.

I grew weary of his propensity for bedlam, the bloodthirsty way in which he would watch via his computer the images of someone's beheading. The group videotaped each event in an effort to persuade foreign nationals to withdraw from the country.

I no longer accompanied Malik on his trips back to Iraq. I knew he was recruiting young boys and girls barely old enough to leave their parents' homes. The children were promised a stake in the future of their homeland if they helped fight for its survival. Malik plied them with lies, telling them his organization was a legitimate political group and once duly elected its leaders would place great value in their early sacrifice. Innocent young beings promised a better life, were then killed for believing in it.

I did not ask him any longer if he still saw his family. I hoped he didn't. How ashamed the good man would be if he could see what his son had grown into.

A savage.

After inflicting chaos in Iraq for many years, Malik and his organization began to discuss the best way to spread their perceived influence to the rest of the world. Malik began to delve into the world of satellite tracking, global positioning, and radar interference. He wanted to do it bigger, better, and more thoroughly than ever before, as did his associates. He came to me one night with a plan. Wild-eyed and animated, he was as excited as I had ever seen him. I had developed a palpable disgust for him that was growing more difficult to hide. Malik had become a menace that would carry out unspeakable acts if he were not stopped. That could wait. His plan was tempting.

I had become a technician on his security team, having graduated hastily from the university. Everyone I met believed I was much older than I actually was, and that was exactly as I had hoped it would be. Malik never broke my confidence by revealing the truth about my past. He did this not to protect me as much as to safeguard his own future. I knew too much, and he could not risk my wrath. With a simple phone call, I could disrupt his entire pipeline, and he respected that.

While he chose to send money to the terrorists, I invested in the technology I would need to complete my mission. I designed a computer for my home that was far more advanced than even what was available at the university. I had learned how to remove the central processing unit long ago, when mainframes were basic and simple. By using innovative derivatives that were not yet commercially available, I could command it to function as several different computers capable of thousands of applications and tasks at the same time. I learned how to make my computer anonymous, an enormous development that had exponential potential.

Malik was working on his own tangle of sophisticated theories that confounded even me at times. The sheer power of his brain was astounding. There was no hubris in his intellect, nor any pomposity or contemptuousness. If I asked for an explanation, he would give it thoroughly, until I was able to contribute again. Malik was without a doubt the finest instructor I ever had. Unfortunately, his talent was wasted long before I shot him dead.

His design was simple yet extraordinarily obtuse. It took years to master, which was good because I needed this time to develop my own course of action. Malik knew nothing of what I was working on, even though eventually our plans would bring us to the edge of the cliff together.

I was extremely careful not to arouse the suspicion of those who would be watching. As I developed my skills and learned how to circumvent the layers of protection around this famous woman, I began to tease the system. How close would it let me get? How quickly would it sound the alarm? How much time would I have before the walls began to close in?

Eventually, Malik and I assumed control of the global security team, entrusted to dispatch it to specific regions of the world. The travel demands led me perfectly to the next hurdle in my long-range strategy. I could inconspicuously attain my pilot's license. It also coincided with what Malik and his cohorts were developing, but I insisted I be the one to learn how to fly. I looked up my former colleague in Kuwait, inquiring whether the flight school his father ran in the south was still operational. He told me it was, and gave me his father's contact information and his best wishes for my new career. He was now a multi-millionaire, using some of the same security techniques in Dubai that we were using in other parts of the world. I bid him farewell, thanking him for his time. I was glad to hear that he had a family now, two young girls and a wife. He deserved his success; he was a good man.

His father was a seasoned old pilot who was quick to welcome me as a pupil. Soon after I arrived, he took me aside for private lessons. He told me he saw great promise in me. I worked hard, but flying an airplane was inordinately easy for me. I studied the instrument panel in my head at night, visualizing the perfect takeoff, the impeccable landing. It did not take me long to become certified. The old pilot insisted on accompanying me on many multi-hour flights and applying that time toward the hours I needed in the air. As I was completing the flight time mandates, he would put the plane in various stages of distress and teach me how to recover from them. This was challenging, and quite physical. I had not yet engaged in this type of work before, and it exhilarated me. Better yet, it exhausted me. During my flight training, I slept more peacefully than I had in my entire life. My mind was so weary it filtered the dreams out.

Time had made them almost unbearable. The colors I saw in my sleep became vulgar and raffish, blown far out of real life proportion. I was always an arm's length away from my parents, held back by an invisible, malevolent force. Crying out in anguish and despair, I was unable to reach them in time. I watched them die night after night, awakening in a cold sweat, my breath labored, my heart sick.

It was good this was approaching a conclusion, because I did not think my mind could withstand it for much longer.

One day, the old pilot asked would I mind if he brought someone along on our next training flight. This would be a longer journey because I was approaching the end of my lessons. I agreed, of course, it did not affect my concentration to have another person present. On this day, somehow it did.

She was lovely, that I noticed immediately. Small frame, with long dark hair, she and I were complete physical opposites. I greeted her politely, shook her hand, and helped her into the back seat of the plane. She explained that she was just beginning her lessons, and thanked me for allowing her the chance to watch. The hours in the air went by quickly that day and before I could stop myself, I asked her if she would like to see me again.

I had been renting an apartment near the airstrip. She knocked on my door exactly when she had said she would, her arms full of homemade food she had prepared for our dinner. We talked late into the night, mostly about her. Abandoned as a child, her dark hair had come from her father, who had died many years before. Her mother's new husband had not liked the idea of raising some other man's children. Another family adopted her and her brother, but her brother was later killed in an accident. Aside from occasional calls home, she was entirely on her own.

Our relationship fell into a comfortable pattern. We flew together from time to time, and I taught her what I had learned up to that point. Occasionally, the old pilot allowed us to train alone together in the simulator. It was during these hours when she would try to press me for details about my life. I kept them simple. I explained my job and spoke briefly of Malik, though I described him as a work colleague. Everything else remained a secret. She was a perceptive woman and I do believe that right up until the day I kissed her on the forehead for the final time, she knew I lived in a state of unrest.

After our boy came, she would find me in his nursery very late at night. It was there, rocking my son gently back and forth in my arms, that I would find a sense of calm. She would smile at me, leaning against the doorway of his room. A lack of sleep would reduce her voice to barely a whisper, and she would tell me how lucky he was to have me as his father.

I knew better, and soon so would she. It was the closest thing to regret I have ever felt.

Just before I became a father, it was time for me to leave the security firm and acquire a commercial airline pilot position. I had been flying privately by then for some time and had more than enough experience to become a desirable hire for any airline. This was where I had to be selective. I was inching closer to the woman I had been seeking out my entire life. I had identified a pattern in one of her children, a possible fissure in her wall that would lead me straight to her. It had come to me so easily it felt almost like it was fated to be this way.

Malik stayed with the firm, but only to assist in funding the massacre he was planning. I, of course, knew there would be no massacre in the sky, but I needed him to believe we were on course. For many years, he worked to perfect the technology that would allow us to gain control of the plane. Even after I eliminated him, I would need his tools to help me arrive at my final destination, under the cover of darkness, in the most literal of ways.

I knew them as if they were a part of me. I studied them voraciously for many years, this unique, indomitable family. At first, I had followed a flash of possibility that the son could be my opening, and I pursued that lead for some time. Then, unexpectedly a new target emerged. My specially designed software began to notice a method of travel with her that could give me some level of predictability to work with. Once, twice, even three times she broke the rules, which meant she was off the grid for several hours. The next time, I would be waiting. I had to be prepared to move at a moment's notice, as did Malik who was far more difficult than I to get into position.

Recently, I had noticed aberrant queries in her internet activity. My computer followed every move her mouse made, giving me a daily report of her activities. Usually, they were predictable. Lately, they were anything but. I started watching closely, preparing myself for the possibility that the time had come. Although I am quite certain she considered herself fully protected, she was wide open. They all were. How comical that they thought they were truly safe.

She was the least despicable of all of them. In spite of myself, I felt empathy toward her, especially as I learned the nature of her online searches. She did not seem as though she fit comfortably into their world, she was not nearly as vapid as her farcical sister was, and she did not seek out unnecessary attention.

Nonetheless, she was the perfect conduit. By the time her personal credit card numbers pinged my computer again, I was ready.

Ella Sheridan would lead me straight to her mother.

Chapter 25: Mel

The alarm sounded like a nuclear warhead had exploded directly above my head this morning. It has been like this too much lately, fighting blinding exhaustion isn't quite as easy as it used to be. Brett would tell me that I am only as old as I feel. This morning, I put that at downright ancient.

Today my plate is full, as it always is. I will have approximately forty-two minutes before the car will pull up to whisk me off to the West Wing for the first meeting of the day. All present will appear fresh and alert even though the sun will barely be visible over the Mall. Just my luck to serve under a president who does his best work before breakfast.

The education secretary will be leading a summit today at which I will be presenting the results of a new study aimed at lowering the nation's dropout rates. It is a relatively light agenda, but heavy on numbers and most of them were just delivered to me late last night. I'll need to be sharp and focused, so before I step into the shower I reach for my first cup of coffee. The staff here is wonderful, completely attentive and dedicated to our needs. I try to keep it simple: coffee by five, breakfast by six, car warmed up by 6:30.

I reach for the cache of cell phones sitting on the ornate end table next to the bed. I remind myself each day to take a moment and appreciate my surroundings. Each family to have had the honor of making this place its temporary home has added its own personal touches. Colors have come and gone, wallpaper put up then taken down again, carpets changed, artwork updated. Timeless, though, is the old millwork. I often run my finger along the great arching doorways, or along the soaring molding surrounding the brick fireplaces. The original artisans, who used rudimentary equipment and raw talent to create all of this, awe me. Human capability is fascinating. What hands can do when they are guided by a vision.

I stifle a yawn as I click through the dozens of messages on one cell phone, noting the "urgent" nature of more than half of them. *Everything* here is always urgent. Marjorie can address most of them once I arrive at the office. I pull on my robe and detour from the bathroom to make my way over to the six-foot windows that face the east. The scene is breathtaking. From the quiet of my private quarters, with my husband still snoring behind me, I often find myself most at peace with the events of my life. Before the sun rises each day, I stand in the glow of daybreak and take stock of it all. For a fleeting moment, my shortcomings do not haunt me. My transgressions seem temporarily suppressed by my successes.

On a good day, the people I have hurt only *slightly* outnumber the ones I have helped.

On a bad day, they line up like a firing squad.

I grab my other cell, and like usual feel a small sense of gratitude that at least as far as I can tell from the empty message folder, my children are safe. Inevitably, I will hear from at least one of them during the course of the day, but they will not use this line unless there is something momentous unfolding. Thankfully, the phone is silent.

I finish off the day's first cup of coffee, brewed nice and dark just as I like it. The house crew has become indispensable to me, for the job is all-encompassing. Not that I expected any different, I had been fully indoctrinated in the pace of this town for many years. Although I usually do not allow myself too much time for personal introspection, over the past few months I have begun to rethink the way in which I got here. I must repeatedly remind myself that my private regrets must wait, because right now I owe my country more than I owe myself.

I put each phone down on the end of the bed and walk into the bathroom. I refuse to open my laptop. That can of worms can wait.

I make a mental note to talk to Brett again about Ella. She has been disturbingly distant as of late, not completely uncharacteristic of her, but enough so that I have begun to worry. Unbeknownst to her, I have a special place in my heart for Ella, my often sullen yet sweet girl. Of the three, she is the most unlike me in every way possible. Completely unselfish, Ella has asked for absolutely nothing from us, a simplistic quality that is as refreshing as it is rare. Concerning, however, because Ella shrivels under the spotlight like a raisin in the sun.

I worry that will be my legacy, the damage I have inflicted upon the well-being of my own daughter.

I shake the contrition away and hurry through a shower. My wardrobe assistant has laid out today's suit, perfectly pressed and ready for me to step into. The only accessory I choose on my own each day is my simple wedding band that I have not taken off for decades. Brett insisted on buying me an enormous diamond when he first proposed, but I am happiest when only the thin band is present. The diamond tucked away in our personal safe will await the finger of one of my daughters should the day ever come. Of course, Kelby would think it was much too small, and Ella would consider it flamboyant and embarrassing. Perhaps Kass will pass it along one day, as long as it is not intended to be the lipstick applied to one of his pigs. Forgive me my vulgarity, but my son has been sowing his oats in some rather distasteful fields. To think he believes I am completely ignorant of his behavior! Brett assures me it is a passing phase, but I have my doubts. I stand by my rule that no woman accompany him to official White House events if she has so much as a late library book. My good-natured son abides by it all, but in private, I know what he is doing in all those hotel rooms.

I get dressed and hurry down the stairs, greeting the staff I see along the way. Finally, I hear the car pull up, grab my overstuffed briefcase and a light jacket, and pull the heavy wooden door shut behind me. I say hello to my driver, and settle into the plush leather seats. Marjorie is already here, sitting directly across from me, ready to brief me on overnight developments across the globe. There has been a small earthquake along the Pacific Rim, but no significant damage. Investors are anticipating the monthly jobless report, so the White House will be watching the opening bell closely for reaction, and the president is expecting a call from the Joint Chiefs of Staff for an update on tensions along the Arabian Peninsula.

I look up as Marjorie stops speaking. "Is that all?" I ask.

"And, so far this morning the tabloids are clear," she adds. A good measure of where my children were last night. She reaches over and hands me a full page of notes she has prepared for my meeting today. I scan the line-by-line break down of all the talking points on the dangers of high school dropout rates. I make special note of the phrases "economically unsustainable," and "a threat to national security." There are asterisks next to each term, and several more lines beneath them detailing the report's perceived significance of each. I thank her, fully aware that given the late release of this information last night, and the quality of the notes she just handed me, Marjorie likely has not slept a wink. Yet she is as bright-eyed as a teenage girl on the eve of her first prom.

I ask her how her daughter is feeling. Marjorie and her husband have a six-month-old baby who has been battling a double ear infection.

"Why, thank you for your concern, Madam Vice President. She is feeling better this morning. At least I think she is. She was still asleep when I left."

Of course, I think. Of course, your sick little girl was sleeping. You keep the hours of a vampire. *Everyone* is sleeping when we are not. I know from experience, she will call home as often as she can, but Marjorie will not see her child again until she has already been tucked into bed for the night. She will worry about her fever, and whether her husband gave her Tylenol at the right time, and if she drank her entire bottle. Otherwise, she will be entirely focused on my needs.

There is a great deal wrong with this picture. Welcome to D.C. Land of the perpetually sleep deprived. Not to mention leading candidates for parent of the year.

"The education secretary is waiting for you with the agenda for the meeting today, and I expect the president will drop in for part of it."

"Thank you, Marjorie. I think once the meeting breaks for lunch you should sneak home and check on her. Seeing her mommy might make her feel a whole lot better." I wait for her to tell me that's unnecessary. She attempts to, but I stop her.

"I insist." End of story. Marjorie quietly thanks me. We both glance out the window as we approach the drop-off area near the back rotunda of the West Wing. The guards quickly hop into their formal salute as the car sweeps around the corner and pulls to a stop. They swing the door wide, stepping back to give us room to disembark.

"Good Morning, Madame Vice President," they say in quick formal tones. I know each of them by name, where they live and the ages of their children. I ask them how they are all doing, but I always get the same answer. They tell me they are just fine, and thank me for inquiring. They would never burden me with the truth. That their teenager is driving them crazy, their wife is engaging in an online affair with her high school boyfriend, and their property taxes just went up. I always get the standard old line.

"Fine, we're fine. Thank you for asking."

Just once, I would like a pinch of honesty. They make me think of Ella again, my daughter who is also always "just fine." Have I become so untouchable that she doesn't feel as though she can tell me the truth? Surely, Kelby does not have that problem, I hear about *everything* that is bothering her. Kass genuinely doesn't have any problems, but I think if he did he would at least tell his father.

But Ella won't. Or can't.

I think back to my own sleepless nights when Ella was first born. Her tiny head was as shiny and bald as a bowling ball, which made her eyes seem enormous. They were beguiling, even back then. Somehow, genetics had taken my blue eyes and Brett's hazel ones and spun the color wheel to come up with something smack dab in the middle. I would lose myself in the green of them. Her eyes literally took my breath away.

The child never cried. *Never.* If she was in pain or was upset, she just grew quiet. There were never any tears, tantrums, or even shrieks of displeasure. Only when Ella was unusually quiet did that serve as my cue that something was wrong. Sure enough, at the delicate age of four months she wound up at the doctor's office after two days of sheer silence. Laying on the white paper covering the examination table she looked up at our pediatrician with a wobbly little grin, grabbing at the stethoscope that swung from his neck, just out of her reach.

"Jesus, Mel," he said after shining his light inside her ears. "She's bright red in there, totally infected on both sides." I was shocked, and mortified. I explained to him that Ella had not cried once, not in days. He wrote out a prescription for antibiotics and sent me home with a warning.

"Watch her," he said. "Kids like her have very high pain thresholds, and they won't give you the obvious signs when they're sick or injured."

Which is why right now I feel like something with her is not right. She has grown very quiet again, the biggest warning sign I know to watch out for.

Call her, I tell myself. *When Marjorie goes home for lunch with her baby, call yours.*

The hallway leading to the president's private residence is bustling. Bodies in motion everywhere you turn. I greet them all, passing papers along the way, accepting new files while dropping off others. My phone is buzzing on my hip, so I detach it from its case and hand it over to Marjorie. I tell her there are several emails that need her attention as I turn the corner into the Oval Office. When the president is stateside, he insists we begin each day with a formal Pledge of Allegiance. The Stars and Stripes hangs between the three large south facing windows that run the length of the wall directly behind the president's desk. It has actually become one of my favorite traditions here.

From there we move as a group through the east doors, walking past the famed Rose Garden, which has become slightly ropey by the approach of fall. We head toward the northwest door that will take us along the main corridor of the West Wing. We move past the president's secretary who stands primly by the door of her office, greeting each of us as we walk by. The click-clack of our heels along the marble floor shakes the last bit of fog from my head this morning, helping me at least temporarily push my concern for Ella from the forefront of my brain.

Finally, we reach the windowless Roosevelt Room. No framed glass panels to distract us, we often meet here when we need all minds focused and present. I notice all other parties have arrived and they stand almost simultaneously to greet us as we enter. I shake hands with the ones closest to me and nod slightly at the others flanking the ends of the long table. It comfortably seats sixteen, but additional staff members line the space along the walls. They are the aides, pages, and assistants who have done all the work on this presentation, but will get none of the credit.

The president has not accompanied us here. He stayed behind in the Oval Office, telling me he will stop in just after the lunch break. I told him I would be prepared for his arrival.

Marjorie rejoins us then, sitting in the chair directly behind me as I call the meeting to order, acknowledging the presence of the officials gathered before I ask the secretary to begin his presentation of the findings. I turn slightly back to Marjorie, asking her quietly to bring me a cup of coffee from my office. She will know to put a single drop of skim milk, along with just a sprinkle of sugar in the cup before passing it off to me. Is this my fourth cup today? Fifth? I have lost count, but I figure I had better eat something soon or my stomach will begin to growl like a wild animal.

The meeting drones on. Thanks to Marjorie's notes, I am fully prepared for my part. We discuss strategies for inner city schools, urban schools, every school in between. Grandiose ideas that will inevitably be scaled back by the financial realities of the president's budget. We will then agree to take our proposals back to the various committees for study. Half of what I do is sent back to some committee. No wonder voters think Washington moves like it is firmly planted in cement. Most of the time, it is. And I'm partially to blame.

I think I had better grab a bagel or fruit then before the excess caffeine completely burns through the lining of my stomach. I make a move to stand up and walk over to the refreshment table when I hear a buzz begin to spread. One by one, I notice everyone reaching for his or her Blackberry, even though that is a major faux pas in the presence of the vice president during a meeting. But here they are, scrolling down, then staring back up at each other with gaping mouths. Marjorie immediately takes my arm, which is highly unusual for her, too. She *never* touches me. With surprising force, she whisks me out into the hallway.

"Madam Vice President, there has been an incident," she begins, but I notice the direction in which we are moving. I follow pace, and we travel together down the hallway and through the door that will lead us straight to the Situation Room.

Oh shit, this is serious.

"What do we know?" I ask.

"The FAA has reported a plane that took off from JFK a short time ago has disappeared from radar," she says, her voice slightly higher than usual but completely in control.

"Is the president safe?" I ask, thinking that one of us will be required to stay in the bunker until the threat has passed.

"Yes, he is in the Situation Room already. He will expect you to move to the safe location." I already know that, but first things first. I intend to find out what the hell is going on.

"Yes, of course, in a moment." I take the lead as we turn down the final hall leading to a pair of oversized doors. I swing them open and ask for an update before anyone can tell me to leave.

"It's untraceable, Madam Vice President." What?

"What do you mean, *untraceable*?" I demand. No modern plane in a post-9/11 world is *untraceable*.

He says it again, with more authority this time, and a hint of dread.

"So in other words, you're telling me a plane has taken off from JFK this morning, with hundreds of souls onboard, and the government has virtually no way of knowing where it's headed?" I speak calmly but I am fuming inside. How can this be happening, again? Shame on us.

"Yes, Madam Vice President. That is exactly what I'm telling you. But we are doing everything possible to make contact."

I look over at the president who is standing across the table from me. His face has gone devoid of color. He turns to speak to me just as Marjorie groans audibly behind me. It is such a shocking sound at this dire moment that I turn to face her.

"What is wrong with you?" I say sharply.

Just then, I notice the wall of televisions has come to life with word of the missing airliner. Breaking news crawls are snaking across the bottom of the screens, and anchors are reading copy of Associated Press bulletins that are apparently crossing the wires.

"How long have they known about this?" I demand, dreading the thought that the news organizations are pressing the panic button already. We are entering a national emergency, folks. Buckle up, it's about to get bumpy.

"For several minutes, actually," Marjorie says, but her eyes are cast downward, she is staring at the phone in her hands. My phone, *my emergency family phone.*

"Madam Vice President, Kelby has called several times. She says it's an emergency."

"Well you'll have to tell her I've got my hands full right now...and to..."

She flat out interrupts me then. "No, you don't understand, Madam Vice President." Her voice begins to shake, and I can tell she is near tears. For God's sake Marjorie, pull it together here.

"What exactly are you trying to tell me?" I ask while walking the few steps it takes me to stand directly in front of her. I am woefully unprepared to take the hit that comes next.

"Madam Vice President. It's Ella. Kelby says she was flying out to Los Angeles today. She thinks Ella is on that plane."

In front of the leader of the free world, my mind fades to black and shuts down. My knees buckle and I sink to the floor of the Situation Room.

The sum of all my fears has just been realized.

My entire world is imploding.

Chapter 26: Ella

I taste metal, and bile, and wonder if I've thrown up on myself. I look down but all I can see is red. I feel the stubbly wool of a blanket on my face. Dezi is trying to clean off the pieces of flesh, bone, and hair that have begun to coagulate on me. Long stringy strands of blood that now stink to high heaven. I heave again, trying to swallow down whatever is left in my stomach.

He is reaching for my face, trying to get me to look at him. It's okay, Dezi, I'm still here. I haven't retreated to my safe place yet, but I am close. I try to explain to him again why we are in deep shit, deeper than the regular old run of the mill shit. The pilot is on a mission, and I'm thinking he's looking down the barrel of a direct strike on the White House.

"No, I don't think so, Ella," he says, and I can see the wheels turning. He mutters something about us being way past Washington D.C. by now. "It's only a short hop from New York, and our altitude is too high." By now, we have settled into the row of seats behind the ones we were in. First class passengers have been moving freely toward the back of the plane, spreading the pilot's message. Just as he expected, I suppose. He is playing us like puppets.

Somehow, not a single cell phone onboard can get a signal. I think back to Computer 101 class and realize how pathetically inept I am when it comes to technology. I certainly won't save the day by outsmarting him. None of us will. I shudder at what is likely happening on the ground. My mother knows by now, for sure. The FAA and NORAD will have immediately notified the White House that a plane is off course.

Or are we off course? He is the pilot after all. Maybe the rest of the world has no clue what's happening up here? My mind scrambles through what I know about airline security. I try to remember each step in the process of alert when you're a couple miles up and everything goes haywire. But...wouldn't *he* be the one to press some red button or something to tell the guys watching the radar screens that we're

Jennifer Vaughn

screwed? Clearly, the co-pilot is out, because he's sitting across from me right now with his face in his lap.

Thanks for the help, buddy.

I chime in on Dezi's ongoing stream of thought. I tell him there's a chance no one knows yet that we've been hijacked, especially since we can't call out and he's running the ship. But he's got *my phone* so what is he waiting for? Alert the masses already, let's get the show on the road.

Oh, Mom. I am so, so sorry. All those long-winded explanations of how we are vulnerable. She was so right. She knew it all along. How stupid I was to think I could float through this life undetected by the loonies who are hell bent on bringing us down any which way they can. I have been so naïve. I have put these people at risk. Behind me, I hear a baby wailing and that makes it even worse. I shake my head in utter disgust. Ella Sheridan, baby killer.

How could I not have known that all it would take was a smart person with bad intentions and a powerful computer to find me, flagrantly booking clandestine trips with a stupid fake name? I kept doing it, over and over again, handing him my personal information with a big fat red bow on top. Here you go, you crazy fuck, come and get me.

And so it seems he has. He has come for me. But I will not go down without a fight. I will be damned if I can't wield just the slightest bit of power in this situation. He has told me he will allow the passengers off the plane when we land wherever it is that he is taking us. Good. I will refuse to speak to him until I can personally check each goddamn row for human life.

"Don't even go there, Ella," Dezi says, as if he's been listening in on the conversation I've been having with myself. "He just *shot him!*" He motions to the front of the plane. So that's where the guy went, apparently. Too bad he left half of himself back here with me. "Don't think he won't shoot you, too. Maybe the phone is the only thing he wants from you. Look at me, Ella, you have no bargaining power here. Don't be a hero."

Billy don't be a hero, don't be a fool with your life. The lyrics of that old sad song jump in my head. Bizarre how the brain behaves in moments of extreme stress. I think of Kelby years ago, bouncing around with a hairbrush in her hand pretending it's a microphone as she belted out that song on top of our parents' bed. She was crushed when she found out at the end that Billy had died. Crushed not so much for poor Billy, but for the girlfriend he left behind.

"How unfair," she had said. "Didn't he know he could die? That's really selfish. To go and die on her. Billy sucks."

"Ella!" Dezi is in my face now. "Stay with me here. You will not attempt to hijack the hijacker, understand?"

I have to do something. *Think, Ella, think.* How did he do it? How did he blow right by the most sophisticated, hack-proof technology available courtesy of the United States government, and sit right down at the controls of this airplane?

Houston, we have a problem.

He has bypassed the entire system. How? Why did he shoot that guy, weren't they working together? I feel blindfolded, trying to feel my way out of a burning house. All this heavy thinking makes me realize suddenly how badly my head hurts. A steady trickle of blood is seeping out as I put my finger gently on top of an elevated lump of skin.

"Ouch," I say softly, but loud enough for Dezi to pounce.

"Oh my God," he begins, "you're bleeding again."

He jumps from his seat with such force heads turn to see what the hell else could be happening now. He finds the co-pilot and the flight attendants in the row across from ours, who look to me like they are still very much in shock, asking them to help him locate the first aid kit. He also tells them it would be a good idea for them to walk through the cabin and check on the passengers in the back of the plane. He rummages through the tiny kitchen at the front of first class, clanking through soda cans, juice bottles, filling his arms with as much as he can and walking it back to us. He does this repeatedly until finally

I see other men jump up to help. They ask each other for information, asking who saw what. At this point, it's just a matter of time until they all realize who I am, and that I have single-handedly put their heads on the chopping block.

I hit replay on my brief encounter with the pilot. I go over his words. He told me he won't hurt anyone else. It's me he wants, *and my phone.* I'm puzzled that we are now well into our unchartered course and yet there are no F-15 fighter jets roaring alongside. That is the new normal these days. If an airliner drops off radar for even a moment, the FAA alerts the White House. If after a designated amount of time passes and there is still no contact with the cockpit, jets are dispatched from the closest base on the ground with instructions to locate the plane, and flank it until further notice.

Until they get the order to shoot it down. Oh God, could this get any worse?

I start to feel a little woozy, like I'm underwater and everything is floating by me. My blood is dropping in little splats onto the armrest of my seat. How much blood have I lost? I know that head wounds bleed a lot, but how much is too much? Before I can contemplate that any further Dezi is back, kneeling in front of me and whispering my name.

"Ella, Ella, can you hear me?"

"Of course I can hear you. Tell them I'm so sorry."

"Who, Ella? Tell who?"

"All of them, here and back there." I motion with my hand to indicate the back of the plane. "Please tell them I never meant for this to happen and I will do everything I can to get them off this goddamn plane." Now it feels like wind is whipping in my ears, my eyes are heavy, and my head is pounding as if the monkey with the cymbals is sitting on my shoulders.

"Okay, Ella, I'll tell them, but you rest now. You close your eyes and rest now. I'll be right here." He is wiping my head again and it hurts but I can't raise my arm to push him away. I can't do anything but give in to what's pulling me down.

I think I pass out, because when I wake up there is a thick bandage on my head and I hear voices around me.

"Where are we?" they are saying. "Look at that water, it's so blue. We're in the Caribbean, right?"

Dezi is next to me, one arm wrapped around my knee. He has laid me down on the row of seats and has squeezed himself into the one closest to the aisle. He notices me shifting, trying to push myself up.

"No, Ella. Don't move. Your head will start bleeding again. Just lay back down. Nothing's changed, he hasn't told us yet where we're going."

"What are they talking about, blue water? Dezi, tell me what you see?" I ask.

He looks over me, craning his neck to stretch his gaze out over the bottom of the window. "They're right," he says. "It does look like turquoise water, but no land yet. We've only been airborne a few hours so I don't think we'd be too far down past the Keys by now. Who knows for sure? Lay back Ella, that cut on your head looks nasty. I think you passed out because you've lost too much blood."

"Do they know?" I demand.

"No, they don't. The crew saw what happened, but they didn't hear him speak to you. They haven't recognized you yet. Maybe it's all that blood, keeps them from staring at you for too long. You'll make 'em all throw up." He smiles at me, but it hurts to smile back.

"You didn't tell them?" I ask. "Why didn't you tell them?"

I was fully prepared to wear my scarlet letter. Let the shame game begin. Dezi knows exactly what the pilot said to me, and he knows this is happening to him and everybody else here because they had the misfortune of booking themselves onto the same flight that I hopped on today.

Hey, welcome to my world, I feel like shouting. Because the truth is, if I don't crash and burn right here right now, the cancer coursing through my body will probably take me out soon enough anyway. Either way I promise I will suffer for my sins. Is that consolation enough? I think not.

"So why haven't you told them Dezi? They deserve to know the truth. Otherwise, they probably think we're heading for some tall building somewhere. Maybe he really will let them go. They deserve to have hope right now."

"Ella, right now *you* are my biggest concern. I don't know what he's planning, or where we're going, but you are in a bad way, kiddo." He gently touches my head again, so I figure the cut really is bad. He shakes his head. "Can you believe there's no frigging doctor on board? When is there *not* a doctor onboard a plane?" He's right. There is always a doctor, or at least a vet somewhere on every plane. Or does that only happen in the movies? He leans back over me, moving his hand from my head to my hand. He squeezes my fingers, and tries to make me smile. *Me,* like I deserve to smile at a time like this. Or ever again for that matter. "But," he continues. "I've looked around at the passengers and there is a priest, and a baby. I feel pretty good hedging my bets that God wouldn't take out a priest and a baby at the same time, right?"

I push up on my left elbow, bringing it slowly upward until I am sitting with my back straight against the seat. Dezi tries to keep me prone but I am not having it. I need to see what's going on. I need to look at the faces around me, burn them into my memory so I can properly mourn their losses if I make it to the other side. I think that maybe I will be stuck in purgatory. *Here Ella, sit and stew in this for a while.* I picture myself in a giant bubbling pot of humanity, having to hear the dreams and wishes of every person onboard this plane retold to me for a million years.

This is what my carelessness brought to bear. They are the true victims here. I am just a victim of my own stupidity.

Why, Dezi? Why don't you just blurt it out to them all? Tell them that Ella Sheridan is sitting right here next to you. The vice president's daughter lied. She wanted you to believe she was just like you, but she's not. She's every fruitcake's wet dream. She brought one straight to us like Hansel and Gretel's breadcrumbs. She is the reason you may never again kiss your spouse good night, pack your son's lunch for school, or taste the salt of the ocean.

Ever again.

Maybe I'm mumbling all this, maybe I'm not even coherent anymore because Dezi looks at me strangely and gently uses his thumb to push my mouth closed so I can't speak.

"Shhhh, Ella," he says. "Your secret is safe, you have my word. I will tell you for the last time that this is not your fault. There is no way you could have expected someone to trail you for however long he's been trailing you. Yes, your mother will be really mad at you and you've got some explaining to do once we get out of this, but you are not to blame. Got it?"

I nod dumbly at him. I will accept this for now because my head hurts too much not to.

He gets this mischievous look in his eye as he comes in closer.

"So, let me get this straight. You obviously bought yourself a ticket, so you had to pay for it somehow. You don't want your mother to know about it, at least not right away. You figure that eventually she'll find out because the phone is *government issued* and all." He uses air quotes and a mocking tone, making me grin in spite of the pain that rips through my head.

"So she can, like, track you down?" I nod, but he's not done yet. "So she can track you down, but you were hoping that she wouldn't until after we landed?" I nod again.

"Okay, but why wouldn't your name just pop up on the manifest? She'd know before you even arrived at the airport, right?"

I realize I am about to incriminate myself further but I do it anyway.

"Well, yes, technically you're right. She would be notified if I appeared on an airline manifest because we are forbidden from traveling commercially unless it is cleared first by her office. So, I just give myself a head start." I am sheepish, but he doesn't seem to notice that. He's smirking at me again. Go on, he tells me.

"So I use *my* credit card to book the ticket but I use a fake name. The numbers won't jibe with her security people for at least twenty-four hours, and by then I'm airborne. It has always worked. Till now." I trail off at this last part, because I really should have learned my lesson. If I had, none of this would be happening. Dezi is on it like he's reading the first page of a mystery novel. He's working the problem.

"Okay, so by now if history repeats itself your mother's people may have noticed a transaction. But if they're calling your phone, *he's* the one who's picking it up." He motions toward the cockpit.

"Yes, or...*he's* been calling *them*." I flip-flop the scenario because that's how I think it's unfolding in there. "I think he knows exactly who will pick up that phone."

"He looks young, almost like he's around my age." Dezi is talking aloud but mostly to himself. "He's tall, I think I could hit him at the waist, but he's got a gun. That fucking door is like Fort Knox, we can't get to him until he comes out. Obviously, if he wanted to bring us down, he would have already, so he is taking us somewhere. And, he thinks he's keeping you with him once we get there."

"I will let him if that means keeping all of you safe, Dezi. It has to be that way." I will not let him play the martyr, although he probably thinks I am trying to do it myself.

"No way, Ella. That's the first rule, never go with your abductor. You're as good as dead if you do. Besides, I won't let you. Don't get all I-am-woman-hear-me-roar on me right now, we're in this together. You and me, long after this asshole is out of our way. I will not let you walk out of my life, especially on the arm of a lunatic. It is *not* going to happen. Period, end of story. Got me?"

I don't have the energy to argue anymore. He reaches for a bottle of water and tells me to take another sip. He rips the side of a tiny package of aspirin, pops the capsules out and hands them to me.

"These may help take the edge off," he says, "but once we land you're going straight to the hospital. I think you need some stitches up here." His hand goes softly again to my head. He brushes back a strand of red gnarly hair, and tells me how nice I look without my baseball hat on. His voice drops, sexy and low.

"You are so beautiful, Ella. Where have you been all my life? I feel like I've been waiting for you forever."

The water rushes out then. I think of what he just said and I start to cry.

When we land, go to the hospital. They are words that we say when life is carrying on like it should, when there's a bump in the road but otherwise logic is still intact. The tears flow out of me, brought on by trauma, and tenderness. They are so fierce I can't contain them. They sting my cheeks on the way down, but I don't feel anything but deep, wracking sobs of guilt and sadness.

I don't deserve him. I reach for him then because I have to feel him. I wrap my arms around his strong neck and cry into his shoulder. I cry because I am so scared, because I have cancer, and because I have summoned forth a mad man who may soon cut my head off with a butter knife. I cry for what seems like a long time. Dezi never lets go. Not once. He holds me until I start to pull back. He lets me, but immediately dips his hand under my chin, already anticipating that I will lower my head and refuse to meet his eyes. How does he know me so well?

"So tell me something," he says, once he seems satisfied that I can breathe again and the torrential downpour has stopped.

"What?" I reply weakly.

"What's the name you used to book your ticket?" How does he do this? Make me cry one minute and laugh the next.

"Julie. Julie Roberts." He closes his eyes as a broad smile breaks out across his face.

"Really?" he asks me. "Why?"

"Because the TV was on in my kitchen at the time, and she was snapping the snail out of the shell, and Pretty Woman always makes me feel good." And *nothing* makes me feel good anymore, until you came along.

"Well, *Julie*," he rolls the name off his tongue, "I may not be nearly as cool as Richard Gere and I don't know a thing about polo, and…" he slows, stroking the side of my face, not even noticing the dried blood caked there.

"And…*what?*" I ask.

"And, you really don't strike me as the hooker type."

We laugh together, we laugh until we stop almost at the exact same moment. He becomes serious. I feel like he's making me the most solemn promise of his entire life.

"I won't let anything happen to you, Ella. We are going to make it, and then we're going to learn everything there is to know about each other. No objections here, let's quit the bullshit and get down to business." He folds my hands into his, binding our fingers together until they are meshed entirely. "As incredibly absurd as this sounds, given the, uh, circumstances we find ourselves in right this moment, I will dare say, Ella Sheridan…that I like you. I really, really like you." A gentle grin warms the corners of his eyes. I feel hot liquid rush through my internal organs, spiking my temperature from the inside out. "Right here, right now," he continues, his face so close to mine it blurs around the edges, "with you all glammed up in the latest designer threads from the murder scene runway collection…I think that…I…love…you." It is not that he hesitates on this declaration; he is just slow and careful. Almost like his heart is doing the driving and his head is content to simply follow along for the ride.

There is movement just beyond Dezi, and it catches my eye. The older woman, rich bitch incarnate, is speaking to another woman on her right. They are two people with nothing in common suddenly thrown together in crisis. They hold each other's hands and I lean forward to catch part of their conversation.

"…and I've taken everything from him for all these years and he's been so kind and patient." She looks at the other woman, giving in to a basic human need to connect to another person as she confesses her bad deeds. Does she imagine she is speaking to him?

"And I've never even told him that I love him. That I *truly love him*, and I'm sorry I've never made him feel like I do."

Why does it have to work like this? Only when we are faced with our own mortality do we achieve our highest level of personal clarity. What a waste.

Let him in, Ella, something inside is screaming at me. *Let him in!* Let him make this less terrifying. For the first time ever, before I can stop myself, I let go. I reach for him with the kind of passion and longing I have never felt before. His may be the last face I see before I die. Even if I don't have much longer on this earth I am grateful. I have just felt the purest kind of love there is. Even if it is happening while we're sitting on a bridge to nowhere, about to be thrown off the edge without a parachute to break our fall. At least it is finally happening. To me!

I try to forget that even if we do make it out of this alive, and I am spared the dead-woman-walking kind of punishment my mother will be prepared to dole out, there is still a wolf roaming around my backyard waiting for me to step out so it can pounce. On my left breast.

I make a snap decision that none of that will matter right now. I will be honest with myself and with him. The words rise on my next breath.

"I think I'm falling in love with you, too." There is no hesitation as we both lean forward. Our lips meet halfway, a gentle first kiss that solidifies everything.

"We will live," he says.

I pray then. I pray first for the people on this plane who are completely innocent. They are the people who don't know me, who deserve to sleep in their own beds tonight. They deserve to smoke a cigarette if they wish, or eat too much at dinner, or even drive their cars too fast along a country road. They don't deserve to die right now, and neither do I. Like the phoenix rising up from the ashes, I am suddenly renewed. I zero in on the face of the man behind the bolted cockpit door, telling him in my head that I will not let him take this all away. You want a piece of me? Well bring it on.

Almost as if he hears me taunting him, the click of the in-flight intercom system interrupts the plans I am making in my head. His voice is entirely calm. "Please fasten your seatbelts. We are about to land. I will remind you again that I do not intend to harm you, and I will allow you to leave the plane once we are on the ground. But until then, don't try to get up or move around."

I look over at Dezi again. He is staring at the back of the cockpit door, his hands on mine. He turns toward me, smiles, but all I see is boiling fury just below the surface. The cabin breaks out in low mumbles again, everyone staring out the windows trying to figure out where in the world we are, and how the pilot will put the plane down because all we can see is ocean.

Dezi's fingers twitch when the pilot issues his final reminder.

"And if anyone tries to storm the cockpit…

"I will kill you."

Chapter 27: Mel

I do not entirely hit the floor, thank God. I am able to catch myself just before I go down, and by grabbing the corner of the table in time, I ease myself into a leather chair. I try to switch gears to survival mode, shut down all unnecessary systems to preserve the core. I will not feel this just yet. I will not think of her.

Of my child.

I will think as the vice president, now called upon to help lead us out of this crisis.

"I'm fine, everyone. I am fine. Tell me what we know."

They have surged toward me, I feel arms reaching for me then pulling back when I defensively throw my elbows out to signal that I am all right. Someone puts a glass of water in front of me but I hesitate to take it because my hands aren't steady enough yet. I focus on the top ice cube, how it moves against the glass. I keep my eyes locked on the ice. I watch it melting. I feel like I'm melting right along with it.

"We know it's still airborne. Communication with the tower was interrupted shortly after takeoff. The pilot confirmed altitude and course then went silent. Last they saw him he was making a left hand turn out over Long Island. Unfortunately, most aircraft do if they are on a southerly or westerly route, it would be very difficult to tell if he completed the turn only to double back to the east. Therefore, we are working with the assumption that he is likely moving to the south. Or perhaps the west."

"So in other words, you're clueless." It is not a question, but more of a statement full of repulsion. The president's voice rips through the room like a crack of lightening.

"How in God's name can a plane just disappear?" Arms outstretched, his eyes blazing.

"This is *unacceptable!*" The table convulses as he slams his fist down. "I want the goddamned owner of the airline, the tower, every air traffic controller who spotted the dot on the screen. Get me the FAA and NORAD. I want to know *everything* about every single person onboard that plane." He moves toward me. "Melanie," his voice is only slightly less cutting. "Who would have known Ella would be on this plane?" He sidesteps the admonishment, for now. I thank him with my eyes for sparing me the public lambasting. There will be plenty of time for that later.

"I'm not sure, Mr. President," I begin. "Apparently, Kelby was aware of this, but as far as I know that's all. I certainly wasn't." Those last three words shame me for so many reasons. First and foremost because my daughter is living a life that I know nothing about. Where were you going, Ella? And why in the world is *Kelby* the only person who seems to know about it? If this was supposed to be a secret, what were you thinking telling *her* of all people? Kelby keeps a secret like most husbands hide their porn. Not well. Secondly, I am personally horrified that somehow my daughter has stumbled into a quagmire of monumental proportions. She has unwittingly put an entire planeload of people at risk, *exactly* what I have warned my children about for all this time.

This is no coincidence; someone wants her. Or wants *us*, and is using her. Did I really expect it would ever happen? Was I truly anticipating this? What else could I have done to ensure their safety? What have I missed?

By now, every network and cable operation is in wall-to-wall breaking news coverage. There has been no mention yet of Ella, which is promising. She must have used some silly name again when she bought her ticket; otherwise, security would have tagged her immediately. Just like all the other occasions, she scoots off before we know she is gone. Only this time, she may never come back.

Congress has been evacuated. Members of the House and Senate are shown from some helicopter shot scurrying down the steps, skirts snaking up chunky middle-aged legs, ties flapping loose from beneath blazers that no one had time to button back up. The president flies into a rage at this.

"Shut down the goddamn air space, for Christ's sake," he bellows. "Get those choppers out of there." Movement on the phones, someone is putting forth the president's orders. There is near panic outside, but this is protocol. Local police will know to close the Mall, remove tourists from monuments and museums, and shut down access to all roads leading to the White House.

It won't be pretty. Getting thousands of people to leave at a moment's notice is like lifting the picnic blanket and shaking off all the ants. They fly in every direction, some more graceful than others. Even though the mass exodus may look like a stampeding herd of buffalo, there will be less collateral damage if this thing comes at us at five hundred miles per hour.

With my daughter strapped inside.

Oh God, how do I tell Brett? Has Kelby called him yet? Does Kass know? Is he safe? Endless questions run through my head.

"Are all other aircraft accounted for?" the president demands. "Figure out if this is an isolated plane, or if we've got more to worry about."

The president is pacing the sides of the long table, his shirt sleeves rolled to his elbows, tie loosened so his top button can open. There are a dozen or so laptops open and crunching, phones are buzzing, and short bursts of information are whizzing by like machine gun fire.

"No other aircraft as of this minute," we are told. "Radar is up and running at JFK, except on this plane," they declare. We look frantically at one another, stumped by how that could be. Finally, we determine someone must have figured out a way to disrupt the signal from the aircraft, because the tower is functional. That must be the only way this is happening. How have we missed it? I look around the room, packed now with our country's finest minds. We have been entrusted with the preservation of our great nation, and today we have failed you, our fellow Americans. It is an astounding realization that ultimately we are still as vulnerable as a puppy let loose on a highway during rush hour.

Two tiers of computer terminals turn into each other. Along the top members of the twenty-four hour watch team are trying to figure out how they missed this, while along the bottom row the duty officers are consulting with the intelligence analysts and the communications assistants to find *something* to contribute here. I'm sure many of them are thinking that after today they could be slinging burgers at the greasy spoon down the street.

I see on your resume you once worked for the government, why were you let go again?

Well, sir. That would be because I let a psychotic genius slip through my highly trained and security cleared fingers.

The president puts the country on alert, which really means the military will be ready to launch a preemptive or defensive strike. I am aware that as soon as we are able to discern the location of this plane, fighter jets will launch to assume positions on either side of it, and behind it. I also know that they will be prepared to fire on the president's orders, which tells me because of the executive privileges I hold during this event, I will hear the exact moment that my child dies. Whether it's a missile launched into its fuselage, or a deranged crackpot at the controls, I will *watch* the destruction of this plane.

Perhaps it is fitting. I was there to witness my precious girl enter this world. And now, there is a high probability that I will witness her leave it. I am glad I haven't had time to eat yet today because I don't believe it would have stayed down very long. Marjorie appears behind me, ready to escort me to the bunker.

"Madam Vice President, it is time to go," she says close to my ear, firm but respectful.

"No," I tell her. Although I am breaching my contract in every way imaginable, I cannot allow myself to be removed from this room. I have to know what is happening to her. Just in case she reaches out to me.

Call me, Ella. Use that phone I moved heaven and earth to give to you. It was unprecedented and expensive to equip my family with these specially designed gadgets. I had insisted. I thought they would keep them safe. Now, of course, I realize the phone may have made my family tantalizing targets to sick yet ingenious individuals. How arrogant to think no one could crack our codes. In reality, it seems they are as soft as boiled eggs. That reminds me to speak up then.

"What about cell phone transmissions from the aircraft?" I ask. They are all aware of Ella's phone. Did she take it with her? Is the damn phone tucked into her hole-in-the-wall apartment, not even charged, completely useless right now?

"Madam Vice President, there have been no traceable calls from that plane. No contact in or out. It's almost like it's disappeared off the face of the earth. We have no idea where it is and no idea where it's going."

How can this be? I yank my elbow back from Marjorie, raising my voice now to a level that I would consider utterly caustic in any other situation.

"Stop it, Marjorie! I am not going anywhere." I don't intend it to but my declaration echoes through this insular chamber. Glances pass around me, but no one will dare to tell me otherwise. Finally, the president reaches over and taps Marjorie, pulling her close enough to hear him without the information passing beyond the two of them. I see her nod and resume her position near the wall. She will not move again unless told to. The president walks behind me and squeezes my shoulder.

"It's all right, Melanie," he says. "Stay here, for now. But if I tell you to go, you go. Understand?"

"Yes, sir. Thank you, Mr. President."

Radio transmissions hiccup over one another, we patch in to the JFK tower again as it repeatedly checks in with every craft in its airspace. All air traffic has been advised to divert to the nearest available airport, and remain grounded until further notice. Satellite space is dangerously full as cell phone use quadruples before our eyes. The White House clears out enough space to guarantee uninterrupted contact for all lines assigned to official staff and world leaders. We are aware that at any moment, this could turn into a global event and the president instructs his chief of staff to begin reaching out to allied nations.

I wonder if he will tell them my daughter is right in the thick of it. I envision several world leaders shaking their heads and muttering about the ineptitude of women. If they had just stayed home in the first place we wouldn't be in this fix.

I shudder involuntarily as the image of Ella's face fills my head. When was the last time I told her I loved her? Did I hug her or did I tell her she had worn the wrong shoes, again?

Damn it, what have I done to you, Ella?

"Mr. President, there's a development." One of the communication analysts has his ear bent into his neck as he struggles to balance one phone on each side. "We're getting info on the flight crew," he says, putting one of the phones back into its holder on speaker.

"Go ahead, Mr. Malone. You have the president, and the vice president. Tell them what you know."

The owner of the airline is clearly shaken. He begins by telling us his crew has a safety record second to none, and we can be assured they are doing everything they can to protect the passengers and the country. The president interrupts him sharply to forego the commendations and stay on track.

"Yes sir, my apologies. Uhh, we just had a very strange phone call come in to our headquarters. I thought the authorities…or uh…you guys…uh…would want to know about it," he stammers.

"Mr. Malone. This is the president. I will remind you time is of the essence here, please get to the point." I can see his patience evaporating like the sand through an hourglass.

"Okay, sir. Sorry. Anyway, uh…the pilot is a young man, who is married and has a son. He is actually a very skilled pilot who is always the first one to volunteer to cover a shift if need be. Uhh, this is the part you need to know."

The president rips his hand through his hair violently. "Go on," he says sharply.

"Yes, Mr. President. Well, uh, he doesn't typically fly the JFK-to-LAX route. He volunteered to take today's shift. We have learned that he called the pilot slated to run the route and offered him a day off. Out of the blue, for no apparent reason at all, he asked to take today's flight. Told the pilot to take a day off and spend it with his family."

Revelation sinks in like a rock. The president looks up from the desk where he had been scrawling out notes as the owner spoke.

"Please, go on," he urges. Because there has to be more. There is. The owner continues.

"Well, Mr. President. Normally, we wouldn't think anything of it because pilots cover each other all the time. But then we got a very unusual call from his wife."

The president's fingers stop moving. He puts his pen down, and bridges his hands under his nose. His voice is dangerously low as he prompts the man to continue.

"Sir, he had some sort of elaborate computer system set up in his house. His wife said the door to the room is always locked, and he was pretty private about it, telling her it was just a project he was working on but that she should stay out. Anyway, they've got a baby, and the wife says she was walking to the kitchen to get the kid another bottle…"

"Jesus Christ! Just tell us what the hell she said."

The air was electric as the president's voice cut through the small space. Then a silence fell over the entire room. Someone temporarily turned down the volume on all the gear around us. You could hear a pin drop, or my heart shatter into a million pieces.

"I'm sorry, sir…I'm sorry. So the wife has to walk by the door of this computer room to get to the kitchen. It's always locked shut, but today she says it was *wide open*. The computers weren't on. She told us they were all black except for one image that was on every single one of them." He pauses, and takes an audible breath. I can hear his voice quake. He really doesn't want to have to tell us this, because it's bad, it's really bad. I prepare for impact, but none of us could be prepared for this. It feels like the oxygen has been sucked out of the room. I can't breathe.

"Mr. President. She said every computer screen had a picture on it. A picture…sir…of Vice President Sheridan. Her picture was on every single computer in that room."

Every eyeball in the room finds me. I'm on fire, the heat is unbearable.

"Is there anything else, Mr. Malone?" the president asks, although I don't know how I heard him. It sounds like a freight train is following a course in my head from one ear over to the next.

"No sir, that's it. That's all I know." Mr. Malone is dismissed as an analyst transfers him to a separate line to continue his interrogation.

To imagine I had the audacity to think that hearing my daughter was onboard an airliner that had just been hijacked would be the *worst* thing to happen to me today. Before I can even form a response to this windfall of enlightenment, a sudden movement diverts me to the table just to my right.

My cell phone. My family emergency cell phone.

It's buzzing again.

Chapter 28: Ahmed

The sky is azure. The ocean is a deep teal. From this far up it appears almost as if there is no interruption between heaven and earth. One simply slides smoothly into the other. I am perfectly on track. Just as we had anticipated, the Trojan program Malik implanted shortly after takeoff worked exactly as it was designed to, flooding the tower with a blast of manufactured traffic. As it temporarily crashed the system, Malik implanted a denial of service program into our aircraft so the network in the onboard computer system went into default. The ground and the airplane became so out of sync they would be unable to locate each other again until the program was reinstalled. Even though the tower's sophisticated servers immediately recognized the attack, it took awhile to shift to auxiliary power. By the time they were back online, we had become invisible.

Malik's magnum opus was faultless when it needed to be. In fact, this has been a flawless operation so far. The solace of the empty cockpit has given me time for reflection. I had to move quickly over the past couple of days. Once Ella's credit card numbers pinged my computer, I put the final pieces into motion. Malik was put on alert, though he thought it was for an entirely different event. Sorry to disappoint you, my friend.

Malik was prepared to die. He just thought I would be going with him at the time. Perhaps I still will. I am also prepared to die. I prefer it to be by my own hands, at my own time, but I will accept it either way.

I pull out a single photo I have tucked inside my jacket. I am one of the few pilots who prefer not to be distracted by photographs taped to the long visors just above the control panels. They use the pictures of their families to stay focused and alert up here. I purposefully keep them away for the same reason. The faces of my people make me feel impuissant.

Today, I gaze down at him. I gently stroke the paper, as if by doing so he will know I am thinking of him. He has given me so many gifts, this tiny boy. Lately, I have received his final one. As I grew to adore him more each day I felt closer to my parents than I ever have. He has brought me mutuality with them that I did not have before, or at least not on this par. I have only known love as a child. My son has allowed me to feel it again as an adult. Now I know exactly how my parents felt on that last day. I *know* what my father thought when he spoke to me in his operating room, as the lights were flickering and he was torn by his duty to save the sputtering life before him, and his desire to tuck me safely into his body and remove me from the danger. I feel it now when I touch my own boy. I understand why my mother told me to run. Even as she gasped her final breath, her thoughts were not of herself. She thought only of my safety, as she let go and drifted away.

My boy has given me a surprising burst of strength to see this through. I should expect no different fate than my own parents suffered, and I have begun to accept this as my preordained expiration. I will never see him grow up, just as they never saw me grow up. I am about to round the final arc to complete this unfortunate full circle.

I put his picture back inside my jacket, and reach for Ella Sheridan's cell phone. I run my finger over its buttons. I know every function it has by now. I have been decoding it for as long as I have known it existed. They used a relatively innocuous firewall given its capabilities. It took me no time at all to disengage the GPS program and throw off the trackers. It was not difficult to attain, yet it was imperative that I do.

Ella is most definitely single, yet the man seated next to her came at me as if he was prepared to defend her to the death. I will have to watch him, because he seems somehow invested in her. Why? Do they know each other, or is this just a relationship of convenience? Is he a warm body to comfort her as she loses control of her future?

People are interesting creatures. I know there is a level of terror among the passengers that is incomparable to anything they have ever experienced before, and yet some of them, *that man next to Ella*, are quick to display a certain prowess. He did not cower, even when I pressed the gun to his head, ready to fire if need be. I had trained with the tiny pistol to ensure I would hit only my target when I pulled the trigger. A misfire could bring the plane down. He knew he was outmatched, and was wise enough to step out to save his own life.

Would he do that again? I know there will be a moment of vulnerability when I dislodge the cockpit door and expose myself again in the main cabin. That cannot be helped.

I do not wish to hurt her daughter; I never have, especially as she now appears to me in person. Photographs do not do her justice. She is by far the most alluring of the Sheridan children. I found myself staring into her eyes, a bright mix of greenish gold. They are not the same shade as my mother's, but unique nonetheless. They could distract me if I am not careful. Ella is a sympathetic figure who obviously is already engaged in a fight for her life, but I need her. She is not a coward. She is quite admirable actually, and I will allow her a certain measure of legitimacy with me. Perhaps that will provide her the fortitude she will need to watch the death of her mother.

Just as I had to all those years ago.

I know there will be much dissection done on the maladies of my mind. They will label me a sociopath, or a schizophrenic, or simply a murderer. All of which, I suppose, have a level of merit to them. I am none of those things and yet I am likely all of them. I fully expect Madam Vice President will defend her actions, and there is measurable truth in the fact that she is hardly singular in the events of my life. But to the extent that she should be held responsible for her actions and her words, she will be. By the law of the land and of most Gods, I do not have the authority to dispense punishment to others. I accept that I am going beyond the boundaries within which humankind is expected to exist, but I am at peace with that. If there is a place beyond this one, I will accept whatever consequence awaits me. Just as she needs to accept hers. She needs to understand the consequences that come from looking into the glass of a camera lens and telling a little boy on the desert sand of Iraq that she considers the death of his parents a justifiable loss, a small sacrifice in the larger pursuit of her nation's call for freedom. Maturity has taught me she was merely one of many proprietors of the country's rhetoric at the time. Though she may believe what she speaks, she is not solely in ownership of it.

Although logic has dictated much of my life and professional achievements, I have never been able to apply it to the death of my family. This woman has singularly changed the course of my existence, and I very much look forward to our first and only encounter. I have prepared to meet her as an equal, and I certainly hope she will give me some of the respect that I deserve back. The respect she never showed to my parents.

I will not disclose to her that her daughter is ill. I will also give her peace of mind by telling her that I will release Ella unharmed once she has been eliminated. That will be my final offering of good will, and it will come only after she hears all that I intend to tell her.

Chapter 29: Mel

Immediately, someone grabs my phone and slams what looks like a tiny black sticker on it. I assume it is some kind of tracking device, though the phone should already have one. Perhaps it's been disabled already.

"Is the call from Ella's phone, Mel?" the president asks me.

"Yes sir, it is. Should I answer it?"

"Yes," he says, "we're ready." He gently places his hand on the space between my two shoulders. Support, I realize, in case someone is about to tell me my daughter is dead. My hand reaches for the cell. I wish Brett were here with me--no parent should have to face this unspeakable dread alone. However, here I go.

"This is the Vice President of the United States, to whom am I speaking?"

"Hello, Melanie." A male voice comes over the phone's speaker. The pilot. The man who has my picture plastered all over his computers.

"Identify yourself, please." We already have his name, address, and social security number as it appears on his pilot's license, though by now we are certain it is an alias. I remain on task, but part of me wants to give in and beg. Get down on my knees and beg him to let my daughter go. Let them all go.

"I will do that a bit later, but first things first. I can assure you the passengers are alive and well and I am quite certain you have all been wondering where I have taken them. For your purposes, Madam Vice President, where I've taken Ella."

I struggle against blind fury. *How dare he even speak her name?* I press on with the pre-approved dialogue.

"The well-being of each soul onboard that plane is the concern of this nation, sir. We are prepared to discuss the scenario under which you will release them. *All* of them." I say it without having to really say it. My final offer before I do everything in my power to bring him down. *Release my daughter, you bastard.*

"Well, there's really only one scenario that's acceptable on my end, so let's not waste each other's time. Are you ready, Melanie? Because if you do not follow my exact instructions, I will kill her. The rest of them perhaps, but Ella for sure," he pauses, as if to milk his big moment for all it's worth. "So really now, it's entirely up to you whether your daughter will live or die. Your call, Madam Vice President."

Someone I don't recognize is rolling his finger forward in small circles, a signal to me to keep the pilot talking because they haven't traced the signal yet. Not that I think they ever will. If he was able to take this plane and make it virtually invisible to our technology, then find some obscure satellite space that the United Stated government hasn't yet locked down to make this call, he could be hovering in the skies directly above us and we wouldn't know it until he landed on our roof.

Knock, knock. Anyone home?

There is a script I should be following right now. I should be doing anything I can to keep him talking, give our team some more time to try to figure out where he is. I can't do it. Even though the president is counting on me to fulfill the duties of my office, I veer sharply off course. Because all of the sudden *I see her.* She is everywhere. Her toothless second grade grin beaming up at me from the picture I refuse to leave home without. Her long blond hair flowing behind her as she dances with the waves along the beach. Her hand in mine as she meets her little brother for the first time, dipping her tiny face down ever so carefully to place a sweet kiss on his forehead.

"Hello, bay-bee." I hear her little voice like she's right here next to me. Barely four years old at the time and her touch was as gentle as a flower petal. Now she is in the presence of evil. I realize I have to get to her before it is too late. This has nothing to do with the men and women in this room right now, or even the passengers he's scaring the daylights out of. This is about me, and him.

"I'm listening," I say, though my voice sounds dead.

There is a rustle of fabric behind me as the president releases his hand from my back and pulls himself around to catch my eye without speaking aloud. He mouths... "What the hell are you doing?" I wave him off and wait for the pilot to continue.

"Good choice, Melanie. I have to admit I wasn't sure which way you would go. Ella is but one citizen of an entire nation you have sworn to protect. It is almost as if she could have been considered a justifiable loss, yes? One or two discarded in order to save the entire lot. Sound familiar, Madam Vice President?" He is playing with me now, dropping clues. *Justifiable loss.* What is he trying to tell me? What does he want me to know? He doesn't give me time to respond. He throws out a list of coordinates then clicks off. I think he's telling us how to find him. To find her.

The information is scrawled on pads of paper and entered into keypads on laptops. I hear from someone toward the back that the coordinates are off, or they're encrypted, so they get to work on dissecting his little riddle. Surprise, surprise, he's fooled us again. He has the country's most skilled technicians spinning in circles. I hear frantic discussions break out.

"He's on VOR," they say, which I know is some sort of radio navigation system for aircraft. They scramble some more to figure out how he's using it if there's no landline station giving off a signal.

Or is there?

Someone gets the bright idea to plug his coordinates into something that would parlay them into VOR navigation language. *Oh, you think you are so clever, you crazy fuck.* He must still be airborne. By the time we figure out where he meant to send us, he'll be there already. Within twenty minutes, they have it.

"Mr. President, we got a hit on his coordinates. He's heading to Florida." All heads turn toward the data analyst who just cracked the code.

Sudden movement breaks out. The president points toward his national security advisor, bellowing out bullet point instructions.

"Assemble tactical teams, sniper units on alert. Go, go, go!" he screams. They scurry like deer that have just heard a hunter's rifle explode. I remain in my seat, eyes locked on my cell phone sitting on the table. I can't move. Not yet. Not until I know how I will get my daughter off that plane, because I do not believe it will be a well-practiced hostage release plan that puts an end to this. He's too smart for that.

Almost as if he is piped into the room, the cell phone buzzes again. He is back on the line and saying something that slams the brakes on everything.

"Melanie? Are you still there, Melanie?" There is a slight lilt to his voice now. He's enjoying this, I think.

"Yes, I'm here."

"Good. Tell me now. Have they gotten a location out of those coordinates I gave you yet?"

"Yes, you're going to Florida. We see that. "

"Perfect. Good work. Now here's the thing, Melanie."

The president has moved back toward the table, so close now I can hear him breathing just behind my ear. I know that if he could reach through the phone he would throttle this belligerent asshole. He holds the cards at the moment, and seems to be quite comfortable calling the shots. He sends me his final message over my daughter's cell phone.

"I want you to come alone."

Chapter 30: Dezi

Goddamn it, there is still so much blood. Every time she moves her head, it splits open again. We have run out of clean gauze so now I'm ripping up those fuzzy blankets and wrapping the shreds around her head. Not that she's letting me. She very quickly unravels the fabric and tells me she would prefer not to look like Rambo.

I have stuffed airline-issued ibuprofen down her throat but the pain must be awful. Not to mention the mental anguish she is in. She has convinced herself this is happening because she tried to literally fly under the radar and get herself out to Los Angeles without her mother's permission, which does not sound all that easy to attain, by the way.

The asshole has spoken again, telling us to buckle up and get ready to land. I wonder why, if he's going to kill us anyway, he'd give a shit if we get bumped around back here. Why in the world tell us to fasten our seatbelts if you're only going to squash us like beetles? I try to formulate some sort of strategy when and if the time comes when we are let off this plane. I figure by now he isn't the blow-you-up-with-the-bomb-I-made-in-my-cave kind of terrorist. And he looks like someone you'd see modeling bathing suits for JC Penney. All-American dude who just happens to be one demented fuck.

He wants Ella, or he wants her mother, or maybe he wants the goddamn President of the United States. But why? He could have flown us right into the Capitol by now, but he didn't. So if he doesn't want to take us out in a blaze of glory, what the hell does he want?

I wonder what the rest of the world knows by now, if there's some live stream of the plane beaming across the airwaves. These days, TV stations go live if someone on Capitol Hill so much as farts. I can only imagine the hysteria being whipped up once they get word that an airliner has been hijacked. The absurdity of it almost cracks me up if it weren't so deadly serious.

Jesus Christ, I think. I am onboard a fucking hijacked plane, sitting next to the vice president's daughter. And here's where it really gets weird. I'm falling more in love with her as each moment passes.

It is a helpless feeling. I think back to when my sister's baby was born prematurely. She fell down the stairs of the back deck chasing after her two-year-old, landing smack down on her seven-month pregnant stomach. She was rushed to the hospital where the baby was delivered via emergency c-section. Weighing in at barely three pounds, poor kid didn't stand much of a chance. She was hooked up to a bunch of plastic tubes with her eyes taped shut and a machine doing the breathing for her. One by one, at some point we all had to leave. Her husband had the other kid at home, my parents were too old to curl up on the worn leather chairs in the waiting room, and I was working. But my sister never left her daughter's side. Not once. The NICU nurses would stop by and tell her to go get some coffee or a sandwich, but she refused to budge. Just when I thought she'd collapse with the stress and heartache of it all I made a final attempt to drag her away, just for a good meal or a quick nap at home. She pulled her hand from inside the incubator and reached for mine.

"Dezi," she said, a single tear sliding down her cheek. She looked like a different person to me, hardly the carefree, pain-in-the-ass little sister I had known my entire life. She was so tired, her eyes ringed by black circles. I stared at her, thinking that if a person could be rocked to her very core by grief and despair, this is what it would look like.

"How can I make you understand? I can't leave her. I just *can't.*" She motioned back to the tiny being, encased in plastic. "The doctors tell me she may die, but they don't know when. So what happens if I step out because I'm hungry or tired, and my daughter dies?" Her chin quivered as she took my other hand briefly. She looked down at my knuckles, trying to make me see her reasons.

"It's the only thing I *can* control right now. I can control who is here with her in this scary new world, even if she only stays for a few days. She will know that I was here. She will know her mommy never left her alone. Not even once." With that, she let go of me and turned back to the infant who was struggling to survive. You should see that girl kick a soccer ball now. She's an animal. The thought of not seeing her again, or my nephew, or my parents, is sickening. The thought of leaving Ella behind with this lunatic is even worse.

Her mouth was sweet like a summer strawberry. I look back over at her, suffering in her own personal concoction of regret and penitence. Obviously, her phone is a big deal, he needs it to pull off whatever it is he is trying to do. He has also figured out how to make sure no other cell phone can call out. How do you even do that? Somehow, he has managed to fool a lot of people because there are so many variables at play here.

I think of all the serial killers we have known through the years. How so many of them were attached to families, and jobs, and never so much as hit the dog before they slaughtered their victims. Has this guy been hiding in plain sight waiting for just the right moment to strike?

She's watching me run through the possibilities and grabs my arm to steer my attention back to her.

"Dezi, I'm begging you not to jump him, or pull a Chuck Norris when he comes out. Honestly, let me handle it." She is trying to sound both earnest and strong in spite of the trickle of blood running down the side of her face. It takes the punch out of her bravado, and she knows it.

I ask her then where her green eyes came from. Her mother flashes in my head and I can't recall that she has green eyes at all. I'm thinking blue, maybe. As for her father, I guess I never looked at him that closely. They are both good-looking people, but Ella is stunning, unique, with her very own look. She looks at me strangely, as if to say, "Seriously, we could be up at bat in the ninth inning with two outs, two strikes, the ace on the mound, and you want to talk about my *eyes?*" She plays along, telling me she has no idea, neither of her parents has green eyes and both Kelby and Kass have blue eyes. I tell her again that she is beautiful. Maybe I am trying to fill a lifetime of compliments into whatever time we have left.

She looks so pale. I think she is approaching some danger zone because she is breathing faster and her hands have gone cold. She tries to ask me again about the L.A. job, which by now feels like it was happening to another person. How simple my life was just a few hours ago, when all I could think about was striking gold with a good photograph. I wonder if someone has alerted the senator. Did his

Blackberry buzz just before his spray tan appointment? Has some aide called to tell him to back off on the summer glow because the shoot is in jeopardy? He is probably pissed, or he's thanking God for small favors. Nothing better than a national emergency to shift the attention off the dirty tramp he messed around with.

You're welcome, asshole. Glad I could help.

I have no reason to believe I will live beyond today, and I guess in some ways it is nice to get a warning that the end is near. It gives you pause, makes you dig up thoughts and feelings you tend to blow off when every day is a mad dash from start to finish. I think briefly of Bridget, who will probably milk my demise like the fourth wife of a ninety-year-old billionaire on life support. I can hear her now, sitting on some talk show couch, dabbing her lovely eyes gently so her lash-lengthening mascara doesn't smudge. *"But I loved him, and we were going to be sooo happy together. I can't believe he's gone."* Then she'd eagerly accept a check for her appearance fee and move on to the next "exclusive" interview.

How different Ella is, not just worlds apart from Bridget, but from the vast majority of all the women I have ever met. If anyone ever had a reason to feel a sense of entitlement it would be her, but she is about as real as a newborn. I study her profile. She is gazing out the window, watching the ocean below. We have no idea where we are or what is about to happen, but I have to find a way to keep her safe.

You could pluck a hundred people off the street and fifty percent of them would have some beef with the government, but who hijacks a fucking plane to make a statement? If he has Ella's phone and he is patched in to the people he is so pissed off at, what does he still want with her?

Or is she bait? Is he using Ella to draw someone out?

Of course, I suddenly think. Of course, he is. He is going after the big fish in the pond, and he's using her little minnow to lure her to the surface.

Chapter 31: Mel

"Melanie, don't even think about it. We do not negotiate with terrorists. I will not allow you to go anywhere. By yourself, no less." Every cell in his Type A body is fuming. To think someone would dare order a sitting vice president to appear anywhere is infuriating to him. It should be to me, too. But it's not. It's the only chance I may have to get to Ella.

The coordinates put him at the southern tip of Florida, but there is no identifiable airstrip in the area. Although he has offered us no proof the passengers, and Ella, are alive I believe him. I don't think he wants to harm anyone.

Except me.

Maybe he's a tax cheat, and considers me the personification of big government. Perhaps he's a chauvinistic hanger-on from the dark ages when women belonged barefoot and chained to the dishwasher. I look at one of the many TV screens perched along each wall of the room. His image has been frozen on one of the plasmas ever since we got notice of whom we were dealing with. My eyes narrow as I find myself staring at his face again. Blue eyes sit beneath heavy blonde eyebrows, a slight dimple in his chin, perfect line of white teeth. His pilot's hat sits straight on his head, and there is not a single wrinkle in his suit jacket. I despise him. Someone is trying to get in touch with his wife. I think that is a waste of time, she's already given over all the information she has. This man was living a double life. She is a victim as much as every person onboard that plane is.

Who are you? More importantly, what will it take to convince you to let my daughter go? I think back to some old movie with Demi Moore in it. She is pregnant, and has some weird guy living over her garage while the world seems to be falling into a cycle of biblical Armageddon. Just as good is about to make way for evil to reign, she goes into labor. Someone is shouting at her, asking a single question.

"Will you die for him? Will you die for him?" Life's biggest question asked in cinematic glory.

Will a mother die for her child? She says yes, and mankind is saved.

Why should I expect it to be that easy for me?

If this is how it ends for me, then so be it, but I will not sit idly by while someone else decides the fate of my daughter. She has suffered enough. Ella never wanted any of this. She didn't want the fame, or the glory, or the place in history. All Ella ever really wanted was a mother, and for one reason or another, I left her. I let her think she came second. I let her think she was strong enough to go through her life all alone. I am a failure at the most important job I will ever have.

I rise so quickly the chair almost topples over behind me.

"Mr. President," I say. "I will go to him. It may be Ella's only hope." He is shaking his head before I even finish my sentence.

"Not an option Melanie, we're prepared to intercept him with-"

No, no, no! Stop and *listen to me.* "Forgive me Mr. President, but I insist." I hold my ground, even though he is going toe-to-toe with me now, glowering down at me a mere inch or two from my face. David and Goliath squaring off in the Situation Room of the White House.

"Melanie, what are you thinking? That won't end well. For you or for Ella, you know that."

"I understand your concern, Mr. President," I say, because I do understand, and logically speaking, he is probably right. I refuse however, to leave her again, at a time when my showing up could actually save her life. My daughter needs me and for once, I will not let her down.

"Sir, I have no choice. It's my *daughter.*" I clear my throat because my voice feels too thick. I prepare to deliver the words that will reverberate across the nation. The words that will allow me to become what I should have been all along. A mother first. "So with all due respect Mr. President, please accept my resignation. Effective immediately."

His face registers shock and awe. I see him asking himself, did she just say what I think she just said? He closes his mouth sharply and looks down. He nods without looking at me.

"Mr. President, may I make one final request?" Time is of the essence here, I have to get to her now.

"Yes, of course, Melanie."

"May I borrow a plane?"

A second goes by, and another one. Then he's back, and he's fiery, and he's on my side.

"I want my plane ready to go... *Now!*"

Chapter 32: Ahmed

She could have refused. She could have followed protocol and denied me our meeting. I realize that once she arrives she will not be alone for long. I remind myself to have the passengers pull the shades down on their windows before they disembark. That way the snipers I am certain will assemble along the perimeter of the airstrip won't know for sure where to aim.

Opportunity allowed me to choose this location for our meeting. The old pilot had died last year, and because his son was still working abroad, there was no one to maintain the flight school. After a few months, it shut down. They had notified us of his passing, his two favorite students who had found love in the cockpit of one of his planes. We attended his funeral. I properly mourned his loss and privately asked his forgiveness for the day when I would use his property for my own purposes.

I knew it would be a perfect place to meet my mortal enemy face to face. Although it would take a bit of effort to land this airliner on a strip not built for something of its size, I knew a skilled pilot could pull it off. The landing strip sits directly next to the ocean, in a beautiful southern Florida town. It is innocuous and unknown, and not easy to access. All of that works in my favor, at least temporarily.

Once the plane is safely down, I will instruct the flight crew to open the doors, engage the emergency chutes, and help the passengers off. They are fearful, so I am certain once they are on the ground they will scatter like dry leaves in the wind. That is how it should be. I would prefer none of them see what will unfold here. It does not involve them. Once they are off the plane, their cell phones will be of use to them again so they will likely flood family, friends, and authorities with overdue calls. It will take awhile for even the local police to dispatch to this location so Madam Vice President should have plenty of time to land and board my plane unobstructed.

In these final hours, I pray for strength. By now, my wife has found the only clue I have left behind. I have destroyed everything on my computers, knowing that even though they will pull apart the guts of my system they will find nothing. I meant to take it all with me. They were not intelligent enough to block me, and therefore not worthy to learn from me. They should not rest easy. For even after I am gone, there will be others and most of them will have far more evil intentions.

I take back control of the plane, switching off autopilot and pulling back engine power to prepare for landing. Just a hint of land below, I purposely flew in from the east to keep the plane over water for as long as possible. Malik's denial of service attack on the tower at JFK, triggered as inconspicuously as possible from his seat in first class, allowed me enough time out of radar to reach an altitude where I could safely bank right and cruise out over the ocean. Once we were imperceptible to sonar, he downloaded a GPS blocking program directly into the plane's onboard computer. Because GPS signals cannot permeate stone or water, Malik fooled the program into thinking it was experiencing something akin to a very heavy snowfall. With the receiver essentially shut down the plane has been under an artificial cloud cover for several hours. Risky, I will admit, but otherwise the perfect way to become untraceable.

Then there was the issue of passengers' cell phones. I had to find a way to make them unusable during flight, while maintaining the satellite signal I would need to make the call from Ella's phone. It is relatively simple to jam a cell phone, but I needed something commonly used by law enforcement to shut down service up to one mile. That would cover the entire length of the plane, and provide me safe distance from above and below. Of course as a civilian, I would not have access to such a jammer, so I designed my own. It worked exactly as I planned it to, but I did hold my breath for a moment as I was dialing out on Ella's cell. Ideally, satellite signals bounce from a ground station to their final destinations. I was concerned that as I blocked access with my jammer, I would interrupt the route the call would take. Another moment of chance that had unnerved me, but the call went through just as it was supposed to.

Her voice sounded reposeful. I wonder if she had considered sending a tactical team first. Eliminate me because I was a security threat, but allow the demise of her daughter in the process. How deeply did she struggle with her dueling identities? The vice president would do what was best for the greater good, but a mother would kill with her own hands to save her child.

I asked her to come alone, although I am not so naïve as to think they will not be far behind. On board her plane will be my executioners who will be waiting for the opportunity to take their shot. I will make them wait as long as it takes, but I will not deny them their moment of triumph. However, it will only come after I achieve mine.

Once we land I will instruct the flight crew to exit after the passengers, but I expect Ella's man could make a final effort to reach me. If I had my choice, I would opt not to kill him. I know he is being noble and brave for her, and frankly, she deserves that.

Just not today.

I drop the landing gear, slow my speed, and lock in on the short runway. I will have to reverse the engines almost immediately to guarantee I don't overrun it. It will be a jarring landing, but that cannot be helped. The airstrip is deserted, as I expected it to be. Not a single car in the parking lot, not a single employee left to operate the tower. I know the coordinates like the back of my hand, having perfected my abilities at this very airport. I alter direction to approach from the southwest, angling the huge plane carefully because I know the width of the strip is narrow. As gently as possible, I set it down. The engines roar as they work now to slow us down, and with little space to spare, we come to a stop.

I speak into the intercom again, issuing my final instructions.

"You will be allowed off momentarily. I will ask each of you sitting next to a window to reach up and pull down the shade entirely. Flight crew, activate the emergency exit chutes and help the passengers off. Then exit yourselves. I will be opening the cockpit door, but I will remind you that I have a gun and I will not hesitate to use it. Please use common sense and get off the plane, otherwise I will be forced to kill you."

I click off the intercom, and shut the power down on the plane. I reload the pistol to its full bullet capacity and prepare to unlock the door and check on the exit of the passengers. And, of course, to make sure one of them stays behind. Alone.

I am facing another moment of chance. I hope the passengers are bright enough to follow my instructions, and simply get off the plane. Of course, I need to be prepared for the possibility they will attempt to take me down first. Basic survival instincts will have most of them running as far from me as possible, but as in any conflict, heroes will emerge. I admire their spirit, and it will pain me to shoot them down. It is my fervent hope that does not happen, or if it does, I am able to limit the casualties to one or two. Malik notwithstanding, there is only one person who deserves to die today. Two, if you count me.

She heard me tell her she will not exit the plane with the rest of them. She knows I have likely made contact with the White House, and her mother is aware of her situation. I have known Ella Sheridan only through her computer activity, but I believe she is of strong character. She will not try to rush out; she cannot bear the thought of bringing harm to any of the passengers. Because of that, I will spare her the knowledge that by booking herself repeatedly on the same airline, on the same route, with the same credit card, she was as easy for me to find as a black crow on a white fence. She is the reason I took the job with this specific airline. By then, she had taken the JFK-to-LAX route multiple times. I knew her habits; I knew her preferences. All I had to do was prepare myself for the next time.

My colleague appreciated the day off. He had been meaning to take his wife out to celebrate their anniversary but work had been too busy lately. He told me he would return the favor someday soon, so I could take my own wife out for a nice quiet dinner. I told him that would not be necessary, though the extent to which this was true was lost on him. Lost on all of them, really.

I prepare to enter the plane's main cabin. There is a series of numbers only crewmembers are aware of that unlocks the cockpit from the inside. I punch them in, and I hear a metal click. The door is unlocked.

I step outside, leading with the pistol. I scan both left and right. The crew has done as I asked. They are walking the rows, telling passengers to move orderly toward the emergency chutes on either side of the plane. Just inside the galley lies the body of Malik. I feel no remorse for his death, only a sense of loss because he was one of the greatest minds I have ever known. Now, he is nothing more than a bloody heap crumpled into the corner, a waste of monumental proportions.

No one sees me yet. Perhaps the din in the cabin was too loud for them to hear the heavy door unlock and swing open. This works in my favor. I spot her still sitting, a row behind a now red and matted section of seats that must be where Malik bled out before they moved him away. Covered in blood herself, she has a vicious head wound that has left her looking like she went through the windshield of a car. Malik's doing, I recall. He had reached for her just before I shot him. He did not know of my intentions with Ella, and probably did not even recognize her. I had not anticipated he would become violent with any of the passengers. It is unfortunate that Ella, of all people, was harmed. A strange irony.

I look for the tall man who rushed to Ella's aid. I need to mitigate the threat of his attacking me as quickly as possible. With that in mind, I edge closer to the area at the front of first class. The crew is at the middle of the plane, assisting the passengers in the emergency rows with the bulky hatch doors. Every eye is turned to the back as they await the rush of outside air that will signal the chutes are down and they can exit the plane.

Except her eyes. She notices me then, her green eyes looking slightly dazed. I walk forward keeping my pistol visible to anyone who sees I am out of the cockpit. I speak softly enough to avoid panic as I tell her to get up and come with me. I wait for the man to notice me, prepared to fire if I must. He feels her subtle movement, senses her getting up before she even does.

"Ella, no. Sit down." He does not see me yet; he is just trying to keep her still. She does not respond. I see him bend his head closer to hers as he says something softly in her ear. Ella's head twitches forward only slightly, yet it is enough to move his gaze toward me. He sees me, and tenses like a panther getting ready to pounce.

"Please don't," I say. "She needs to stay. Get off this plane, or I will kill you. I would hope you would prefer to spare her that."

He glares at me with raw hatred. I respect the man somewhat, for I realize that he would fight me to the death to protect this woman. *His woman?* How odd they would fuse like this in just a matter of hours. In any case, I need to remove him quickly. He reaches for her then, brushes her hair back and kisses her temple. I hear her begging him to go, and him telling her he will not.

"Move it along please, I want you off this plane now." I step in closer with the gun aimed directly at his head. I raise my voice, fed up with his stubborn refusal to follow my instructions.

"Get off." I relay my final warning.

He hugs her tightly, whispers something else in her ear that I cannot quite hear. She nods back at him and squeezes his hand before she lets go and motions with her head for him to move by.

"One more thing," I say, as I notice the window shade behind him is still wide open. "Reach over and pull the shade down."

He looks at the window, shrugs back at me and says, "Do it yourself, asshole." I sigh loudly because I have no tolerance for his arrogance.

"You are getting on my nerves. Either pull the shade, and get off this plane, or end up dead. Your choice, I could go either way." I watch him move from hatred to something even more sinister as he slowly turns toward the window, lowers the shade, and turns back to Ella. He stares down at her, then back up at me. He needs to have the final word.

"Motherfucker, let me tell you this. If you so much as put a finger on this woman, I will find you. I have no idea what you want with her, but whatever it is you think the world owes you, I do not care. It doesn't matter. All that matters is that I see her again, and if you deny me that I will *rip your fucking head off.*" His lips have pulled back in a severe snarl and tiny beads of sweat are falling off his forehead.

I level my gaze at him. "Fair enough," I say. "Now get off."

He touches her face one last time, moves gently by her and fixes one last look on me.

"Bastard," he says.

"Indeed," I tell him, and motion with the end of my gun the direction in which I want him to move. Reluctantly, he goes. He is among the last passengers to get off the plane. I watch him slide down the chute and then turn back to help the woman behind him. She is quick to run off, but he stays beside the chute until the very last person slides down.

The plane is quiet. I ask Ella to get up so I can walk through the aisles. I don't think she would run off now, but I can't risk her trying to escape. With my free hand, I loosen my tie. The cabin air is getting warm.

"Are they all gone?" she asks me. "Because I won't speak to you unless they are all safe and off this plane."

Although I appreciate her gallantry, there is little time for it now.

"Get up, Ella," I say again. She rises slowly, gripping the headrest of the chair in front of her. She is badly hurt, I think. The blood begins to trickle down her face again. She looks almost grotesque, covered entirely in red. Not exactly how a mother would want to see her child, but that can't be helped now. I move behind her, putting the gun near her back although I do not intend to use it. She is as weak as a kitten, and much smaller than I am. It would take no effort to overpower her, and I believe she realizes that as she moves forward. I scan the rows of seats, check the window shades, and open each lavatory door. The plane is empty.

I turn Ella around and instruct her to move back toward the first class section at the front of the plane. I deflate the emergency chutes, disconnect them from the doorways and close each door. I trained specifically in how to do this because typically this is something the crew would do in case of emergency. I lock the doors again from the inside. An emergency ladder can be deployed from just outside the cockpit. This would ensure the safe exit of the pilot and copilot if for some reason the cockpit door were jammed shut. This will be how Ella's mother will enter the plane. Once she is onboard, I can retract the ladder. No one else will be able to get in. At least not until I want them to.

"What do you want with me?" she is asking, though her voice is low and she sounds very fragile. I have sat her down in the middle row of first class, far enough away from the growing smell of death and carnage. She grimaces a bit as she speaks; her head must be pounding.

"This is not about you, Ella. You were a means to an end, nothing more. If I could have done this without you, I would have. I don't enjoy watching you suffer." It is true, although I do not believe it serves as any comfort to her now. For all she knows, I could be lying. I look around for something to stem the flow of blood. I reach up into an overhead bin for a pillow. I pull it apart, giving her clean pieces to apply to her head. She stares at me. I can almost hear the questions churning about in her mind.

"How did you know about my phone? It's not public information. How do you even pull off something like this?" She has taken a sliver of pillow from my outstretched hand and is holding it against her head, but her face is streaked with fresh blood.

"Well, the phone is hardly private to someone who knows how to look for it. This is not your fault, Ella. I would have found some way to get to her eventually. As for pulling it off, it's not over yet."

"You want my mother, I get that. Why though? I figured that if you wanted my phone, you wanted the whole kit and caboodle. The big guy. The president. Why stop with just her?"

"That's a long story. One I do not wish to repeat. We will wait for her to arrive."

"My mother's coming...*here?*" She lifts her voice on the question.

"Yes, she is," I tell her. "In fact, I expect her any minute now."

Chapter 33: *Mel*

Marjorie has appeared behind me, handing me a neatly folded pile of soft clothing.

"Here," she says, "change into these." She also hands me flats. Good, I think, no need to head into battle with four-inch heels slowing me down.

"Thank you. I will need you to find my husband." She tells me she already has, and that he will be meeting me at the plane.

"He has been told he will not be allowed to accompany you, Madam Vice President." I notice the title she still uses to address me. Technically, it is no longer necessary or appropriate. Marjorie stays with me only until I reach the door I will exit to take the brief walk to the awaiting chopper. The White House bars media from the grounds during times of national crisis so there is no risk of photographers waiting to pounce. I board the chopper that will take me to the airport where the president's plane is waiting.

We lift off.

Soon enough, the president will have to address the nation and acknowledge the situation unfolding. He has promised me he will wait. The command center is already up and running inside the jumbo jet, though it will be manned only by one person on this short flight to Florida. I have insisted the crew stay grounded, refusing to put any more lives in danger. Reluctantly, the president agreed. The specialist I am traveling with is fully capable of monitoring the onboard electronics that will protect us from an electromagnetic pulse. In other words, nothing short of a direct hit by a nuclear bomb will bring this plane down, so even if this loon is planning a runway ambush, we're safe.

I disembark the chopper and climb the stairs of the jet leading to the hatch. I immediately head to the president's private suite to change clothes. I instruct the pilot to alert me when my husband arrives. Once I say goodbye to Brett, we will leave.

Just as I am stepping into my loafers, the pilot tells me he is here. I zip up the velour sweatshirt and pull my hair back into a low ponytail. I may look ridiculous, but for once, I couldn't care less. The only thing that matters anymore is Ella.

I open the door and turn back up the long aisle. It is eerie how quiet this plane is, it is usually buzzing like a hive. I see him entering from the stairs and I almost lose control. My husband, my best friend, my closest adviser, he is all of those things and yet right now he can be nothing more than a worried father. His eyes are watery and his face looks drawn. For the first time in all the years I have known Brett, I don't recognize him.

I go to him, as an equally worried mother but also as a wife who may be touching the face of her beloved husband for the last time. We reach for each other, hoping to find strength in the familiar feel of our embrace, but on this day, fear controls us both. The kind of unbridled terror a parent knows when her child is in danger.

I remember a day when Ella was about five. She had learned to ride a bike without her training wheels but she was still wobbly. She worked up some confidence and begged me to let her ride ahead of her sister, brother and me trailing behind her on the sidewalk. I was pulling the younger two kids in a red wagon, so I told her she could go ahead just not too far. Of course, she couldn't tell how quickly the distance between us had spread until she swiveled her head back to check where I was. The movement threw her off balance and she tumbled off her bike, off the sidewalk, and smack into the middle of the road. I could see the car approaching before she could. I took off in a dead sprint, guided by panic and a desperate need to get to her in time. Just as the car was closing in, with an apparently dense driver behind the wheel who couldn't see the slumped child directly in his path, I caught the edge of her pink sweatshirt, pulling her off the street and into my body at the exact moment the car cruised on by. Her little face looked up at mine, filled with guilt as she said the three words that would become her mantra in life.

"I'm sorry, Mommy."

She has been apologizing to me her whole life, and yet she has never done anything wrong.

I'm sorry, Ella. Forgive me.

Brett starts to pull away first. I have never seen this man cry before and yet his cheeks are streaked with tears. They flow freely, as he reaches out for my face and runs his hand down the length of it. He closes his eyes and whispers something only I can hear.

"Go get her, Mel. Bring our girl home."

"I will. I promise you, I will get Ella out of there."

He steps back, takes his forearm and wipes it across his eyes. He opens them back up and finds me. It's just Brett and me now, just as it was in the beginning.

"And Mel?"

"Yes, Brett."

"It would be really good if you could bring yourself home while you're at it."

"I'll try."

He turns and leaves me. Exiting the plane without looking back, he returns to the open door of the awaiting limo on the tarmac. His driver closes the door and returns to the front of the vehicle. It quickly pulls away.

The pilot closes the hatch. He tells me to find a seat, buckle up. He returns to the cockpit, fires up the engines, and we turn out onto the runway. I look out the windows and imagine the flood of press inquiries that will come after the plane lifts off. I hope that by the time the president makes his initial appearance today on national television there will be good news to report.

"Ladies and gentlemen, I am happy to report a peaceful end to what has been a dramatic day for the family of the former vice president."

Of course, it could easily go the other way.

I think of my other two children, so different from Ella. If they have to lose one of us today, I hope it is not the sister who has been more like a mother to them both. How lucky they have been to have Ella in their lives. Through her, they have known true goodness. I fold my hands tightly as I call up each of their faces behind my closed eyes. I search my memory for the last time we were all together, as a family. Not for some state dinner or White House sanctioned event, but just to be together. What did I say to them? Did I tell them how proud I am? Did I hug them close and whisper in their ears that I loved them? Or did I criticize Ella's dress, and wipe the excess lipstick from Kelby's mouth? Did I tell my son that I think he's great, or did I remind him of his obligations not to impregnate some slutty cocktail waitress from the bar at his team's hotel?

Oh God, what have I become?

I guess I have been soul searching for longer than I thought. Although it feels like we just left D.C., the pilot's voice is clear as he tells me we are approaching our destination. He asks me to buckle up, even though as I look down it appears I never unbuckled.

I look out the window. There is nothing but ocean on all sides. Where are we?

The pilot is coming dangerously close to skimming the surface of the water, but suddenly the wheels catch earth. He throws the brakes almost as soon as the landing gear connects with the runway. The engines roar and we quickly slow to a crawl. He is back on the intercom, alerting me that he will be opening the doors, setting down the ladder, and then he will pull away again. Just as I have instructed him to do.

I have told them to leave me here alone, but I know there is a plane following closely behind us that will be setting down soon. I promised the man holding my daughter I would come to him alone. I intend to keep my promise, but the cavalry is not far behind. I suspect he knows we won't be alone for long.

Only in the quiet of night do I ever speak to God. I ask him for strength and for clarity, and to lay a gentle hand on the shoulders of each of my children. Although the brilliant sunshine of a Florida day is surrounding me, I find darkness behind my closed eyes and pray one final time.

"Please, God. Please walk beside me today. Take me if you must but protect my daughter. There is far too much she still needs to do here. She deserves to know happiness, Lord. Please, let Ella live. Amen."

The specialist at master control stands as I exit. He salutes me a final time.

"Good luck, Madam Vice President. I will see you and your daughter soon."

"Thank you, Steven. Get out of here. As soon as I leave I want you airborne."

"Yes, ma'am."

The pilot is standing next to the cockpit door, his hand next to the brim of his hat.

"See you soon, Madam Vice President," he says, offering me the hint of a wink.

I look out onto the smallest airstrip I have ever seen and the passenger jet sitting idle on the other end of it. I walk down the ladder, feeling a blast of humid air on my face. I breathe deeply, filling my lungs and pushing myself forward. I walk toward the plane.

Toward my daughter.

I see her pink sweatshirt again, how it felt to reach the soft sleeve in time to whisk her out of the car's speeding path. To hold her shaking body in my arms, stroke her soft cheek and tell her everything is okay now.

Hold on, Ella. I'm coming.

Chapter 34: Ella

We are alone now. He has taken off his hat and undone the first button of his shirt. He is extraordinary looking and yet I can't stand the sight of him. My head aches and my throat feels like there's dirt lining the route to my stomach. Swallowing is painful.

He has tried to help me stop the bleeding, handing me ripped up pieces of pillow. He has gotten me a bottle of water, though I refused to accept it. He told me it would be wise for me to stay hydrated.

It would be wise for you to fuck off, buddy.

Dezi barely got off this plane alive. I made him promise he wouldn't jump the pilot, or risk a hail of bullets let loose in our direction. He left only because I begged him to. Otherwise, I have no doubt Dezi would have died for me today, laid down his life for someone who is almost a complete unknown to him.

To think I don't even know his last name, yet I can close my eyes and feel him.

At least in these last moments I have felt something I doubted even existed. If I never see the light of another day, that will be all right. I must be hovering somewhere between present and passed out because his voice sounds muffled, even though as I look up he's just a couple feet away.

"What?" I say.

"I asked you if you were thinking of that man." He cocks his head at me, and again I am amazed at how lovely this man is. Physically, at least, because on the inside I'm certain he is loaded with night crawlers and maggots. He is staring at me now. His eyes so intently focused on mine I feel nauseated. I inadvertently shrug backwards. He notices.

"Am I making you uncomfortable, Ella? I apologize. It's just that your eyes remind me of someone I used to know. Someone who was quite incredible, actually. She had the greenest eyes I had ever seen. Until I saw yours."

Ewwww.

Although he is ultra-attractive, he reminds me of the creepy uncle who should be kissing you on the cheek, but he always tries to get too close to your mouth.

"Tell me, Ella. Tell me what it was like for you growing up. Was she a good mother to you?"

"Why do you want to know that?" I ask. Where is he going with this? What does he want with my mother?

"Because I am curious. I myself had a wonderful mother. She was killed a long time ago. I watched her die, in fact. Right there in front of my own eyes. I was only a child."

I make a mental note to focus on what he is telling me. If by some act of God I get out of here alive, there will be many people who will need to know as much about this man as I can tell them. If he's going to open up to me, then I'm going to be ready.

"I'm sorry to hear that. Tell me about her."

"Oh, I will, but later."

"What does my mother have to do with this?" I ask, because he still hasn't explained the connection to me. What did my mother ever do to him? More likely, what does he think my mother did to him?

"Not that I doubt your clout or anything, but my mother's not the easiest person to order around. How did you manage to get to her?"

"Actually, she surprised me. All I had to do was tell her I had you, and she agreed almost immediately."

"Agreed to what?"

"Agreed to come here, Ella. You seem to have trouble following me. Are you sure your head is all right?"

Please, I want to tell him. As if my mother would hop on a plane and hustle right down here just because you asked. I couldn't care less if you were holding the Dalai Lama on this plane. Protocol is protocol. The vice president does not jump when someone tells her to.

"No, no trouble, it's just that even though I hate to be all Debbie Downer on you right now, I hope you realize you won't actually get my mother. You'll get the marines, and you'll get special ops, a few SWAT teams and perhaps even some army specialists, too, but the president will never allow her to come here. Sorry, pal, what's your Plan B?" He smiles with what I perceive is amusement.

"Ella, you have no faith. I can assure you, she is coming here. Better yet, she promises to come alone.

"Alone?"

He nods. I force another bit of saliva down the sandpaper of my throat. He notices me swallowing hard, and goes on. He tells me he is sorry to have done this, but he threatened my life if she didn't agree to arrive by herself. He also tells me he knows the rest of them won't be far behind, and that's all right. He doesn't expect the meeting to take long.

"I've been waiting my whole life for this moment, Ella. See, it is because of *your* mother that I lost *mine*. Did I mention I had a father, too? He was a successful, kind man who loved me with his entire being. He died the same day she did, in the same place. Can you imagine what that feels like, when you are just a small boy? Can you imagine, Ella?"

I'm too hot now. My jeans are sticking to me and my feet feel like they're simmering in my boots. I open my mouth, but I can't speak. He is truly crazy, delusional, living in his own tortured past. He wants to kill her. *He wants my mother dead.* Somehow, he blames her for the death of his parents. Driven by some warped need for revenge, he has hijacked a plane, stolen my phone, and ordered the vice president of the United States to answer to him.

Then he plans to put a bullet in her head.

229

I cannot let this happen. I cannot let him murder my mother, while I am sitting right here.

How do I stop him?

Suddenly, I remember what Dezi whispered to me right before he got off the plane.

The window. He told me if I had the chance, to reach over and open the shade of the window. Just a crack, just enough for someone to get off a shot without him knowing it was coming.

For now, I have to keep him talking.

"No. No, I can't imagine how that feels, especially for a child. I'm sorry you had to go through that. But how did my mother cause the death of your parents?"

He wasn't ready to tell me yet, or he lost his train of thought because he stops talking and does his weird staring thing at my eyes again. Freak, I think. How in the world is the system so broken this maniac slipped right through it?

I switch gears. I look away; try to break the spell.

"Tell me more about your mother." It's a new approach. At least try to get him to stop staring at me like I'm some mouth-smacking appetizer.

"No. Not yet," he looks down at the floor. He sits quietly for a couple of minutes, and then comes at me again. "How are you feeling, Ella?" he asks. A totally bizarre question given the circumstances under which we are having this conversation.

"At the moment, not so hot. I'm sure you can understand why."

"No, not at this moment. In general. How are you *feeling?*" He annunciates the last word crisply, though I still don't catch his drift. "Ella, I know. I know that you are sick. I am asking how you feel. Do you feel sick yet?"

Son of a bitch! Of course, he knows. I figure to know what he knows he must have been trailing me, probably on my computer, for God knows how long. The emails from Dr. Sturgis's office, the Google searches I've been doing, all of it going straight to him.

Asshole.

I won't let this go any further. I can at least control what I give him from here on out. He may be able to infiltrate my online activity, but he can't read my mind. He will never know how I feel. I won't let him.

"I have no intention of discussing that with you. Ever." My head pulses with pain as I feel the anger well up.

"I understand. But for what it's worth, I'm sorry about your cancer. Perhaps you will beat it."

"Or it will kill me, if you don't get the job done first." He looks insulted.

"No, Ella. No. I have no intention of killing you. I promise that if you die today, it will not be my doing."

"I'll be sure to hold you to that." I am swallowing tacks now, and trying to breathe through my nose because my mouth sounds like it's forming mumbles instead of words.

"Will you tell me how you did all this? I mean, I thought it was impossible to hijack a plane these days. And why couldn't the passengers use their cell phones? And why did you kill your friend, even though I agree he was a jerk."

My hand goes to my head again, remembering how he took me down. I come away with a fistful of blood. Damn cut just will not close.

"I don't mean to insult you, Ella, but I doubt you'd understand how all this came together. Suffice it to say it was a lot of work, and you can feel some comfort in knowing that most of the people in the world would not have the knowledge or capabilities to do something like this. I imagine the nation will use this as a learning experience, as it should. It would be horrible if someone like him got through again." He motions to his dead friend who is really throwing up a stink now that the heat is blasting in here. "He was brilliant. He did most of the work, but he would have taken all of you down today. He was pure evil."

I want to tell him that he's pulling off the role of the antichrist quite nicely himself, but I don't. He goes silent again, for what feels like another couple of minutes. He sits on the armrest of the seat facing me. He reaches over to the window, raises the shade slightly and looks behind the plane. A slow smile begins to spread. He sees someone approaching, slams the shade down with force.

"Ah, she's right on time. I need to help your mother aboard, Ella. Stay here, don't do anything stupid. I'll be right back."

He leaves me. Heads into the cockpit and I hear metal clanking.

I am alone. He's not watching me.

This is it.

This may be my one moment to save my own life, and possibly that of my mother. I think of Dezi, already hatching his own plan to get me off this plane alive.

Do it, Ella. Do it if you can, give us a chance to help you.

He won't let me down. Dezi will find someone who has eyes like an eagle, who can squeeze off a bullet at a thousand paces, have it tunnel through the thick glass, and take this psycho out.

Okay, Dezi. I'll do it.

I lean over the aisle. His back is to me as he fumbles with some rope cord that I assume is a ladder. Good Lord, my mother is supposed to climb up that thing? At any other moment, I would laugh, but I can barely even breathe. Sweat is pouring down my face, mixing with my blood, and making me gag as the stream flows into my open mouth. I silence a cough, preferring not to grab his attention and make him look back here. I reach the other way, toward the shade he just slammed down.

Please, please, please. Let me do something right for once in my stinking life.

I grab the plastic handle, it squeaks like a mother, and feels like it is stuck in place.

Oh, shit!

I yank with more force. It moves up. I pull harder, just one…more…inch…

Voices. Two voices now. He's talking to her. She is onboard this plane. My mother has arrived. Crap, my mother has arrived! Part of me wants to collapse in her arms, a bigger part of me wants to turn her around and get her the hell out of here.

Seconds go by. Then she appears in the aisle, finds me with her eyes, and rushes over in flat heels and what looks like one of those track suits old people wear to the mall. Jeesh, I think. My mother is wearing velour? But then, it doesn't matter, because I am folded up into her, my head under her chin. I still fit perfectly there. She is whispering to me that I need to be strong. I know, Mom. I'll try.

I tell her the words I always have to tell her. Because I can never live up to her expectations and this is by far my best fuck-up to date. She shushes me like only a mother can, tells me she loves me. *She loves me?*

I wait for fire and brimstone. They never come. A moment of stillness between mother and daughter because neither of us know if this is all we'll get.

"I'm going to get you out of here. I promise."

She touches my head, pushes my shoulders back into the seat and turns her body so she is entirely in front of me as she faces him.

The Florida sunlight shines across my leg. A sliver of hope through a partially open window shade that makes me believe we just might survive.

Chapter 35: Dezi

I watch the last passenger scurry off the plane, one shoe falling off as she runs as far away as possible, grabbing at the cell phone in her purse mid-stride. By the time I turn back toward the plane, the emergency chutes are being detached and the hatch is closing. There's no one left here. They have all run away, although none of us knows where we are.

There could be a 7-11 around the corner, or more likely a jungle because this feels like the middle of nowhere. I hesitate to reach for my own cell now because something is telling me not to. The voice that has guided me through peril before, is speaking again. Logic leads me to believe I should let someone know that a psycho pilot is holding Ella prisoner. Instinct tells me that if he has her phone than the people who might actually be able to help her should know that by now. I don't think anyone else on board the plane knew who she was; even when her hat was knocked off her head she was covered in so much blood she was pretty much unrecognizable.

Besides, they were all too worried about saving their own asses to worry about hers.

I hold off on the call. I worry again about her head. Blood has been pumping out at an alarming rate, and by now, it must feel like a sauna inside that plane. I jog off the side of the runway and take cover just inside the line of nearby trees. My knee is pulsing with pain, but my nerves are so jacked up on adrenaline I can mostly ignore it, for now. By tonight, it will swell up like a balloon. I try accessing the internet from my phone, shocked that in this seemingly desolate place I can get online. I search around for news on the missing plane. *What the hell?* They have the headline, but they're missing everything else. All they know is that a plane took off from JFK earlier in the day, and promptly disappeared from radar.

My God. No one knows we've landed. No one knows where we are.

More importantly, no one knows Ella was onboard.

This leads me to believe there is some high level operation underway, and I don't have the security clearance to be in on it. *Bullshit!* Try keeping me out. Whatever they *think* they know, I know more. I was there for Christ's sake.

Just as I am trying to figure out how the federal government is keeping this under wraps, I hear the echo of jet engines in the distance. I whip my head up as the sound gets louder. I see it coming in, getting close enough for me to make out that distinctive blue stripe. As it lowers even more to prepare for landing, I can see small black letters along the side.

United States of America.

The famous plane roars just above the short strip of concrete, kicking up a blinding swirl of dust as it touches down. Almost immediately, it grinds to a halt. I keep my eyes fixed on it, pretty sure by now who will step out. The pilot opens the door nearest the cockpit and lets down a set of stairs. From my vantage point, I can see two legs start walking down. Only when she turns the corner at the front of the plane and begins to walk toward the other one can I tell for sure it's the vice president, and she's all alone.

Almost as soon as she steps off that last stair, someone hoists them back up again, revs the engines, and starts to taxi back for takeoff.

Why are they leaving? Don't they know he'll kill them both? Goddamn it, who the hell is in charge here? *Jessica Simpson?*

She walks without hesitation straight to him. Straight to her daughter.

Just as I thought, she has come for Ella. He used her phone, called the White House, and demanded the vice president come alone. I imagine the anguish she must be in, what he said to her, what he told her he would do to Ella. It makes my own body twitch, and I'm just the guy who's known her all of half a day. Her mother must be in agony.

I watch her make her way to the front of the plane, and begin to climb the set of stairs he just threw out for her. She walks up, disappearing from my view. I swallow hard, hit by the gravity of what I am watching like an open palmed smack in the face.

Holy shit!

I feel useless out here, what am I doing? *Do something, Dezi. Do something to help them.*

It's now or never. I pull out my phone again, disconnecting the internet to dial up 911. I stop, because there is more noise coming from the air. Another plane is heading in, though this one is compact and entirely white. It lands abruptly and pulls in close to the back of the 747. Immediately, its doors burst open and guys in black race out in all directions. They take up positions just outside the plane, while another crew borders the outskirts of the airstrip. I see the gray steel of their automatic weapons cocked and loaded.

Finally, I think. The good guys have arrived. I just pray they're in time.

The scary part in all of this is that by now he's gotten everything he wants. I think back to what I said to Ella as the asshole had his gun on me telling me to get off. I was working off the assumption that eventually, other guys with bigger guns would arrive.

I had an idea.

"Crack the window, Ella," I'd told her. "Just open the shade a crack so they can see in. Do it only when he isn't watching you."

Did she hear me? Can she get to a window without him seeing her?

Be careful, Ella.

I exit the woods slowly. I am careful to hold my arms in the air so they don't shoot me. I holler to one man with his back to me, telling him I'm here. He swivels around, aims directly at my chest. I scream back, telling him I was on the plane and I might be able to help. Still leveling his rifle at me, I scream at him again, telling him I was onboard, I was sitting next to Ella, and there may be a way in. He rushes over to me, pats me down roughly then grabs my arm and pulls me toward the smaller plane. Head down, he says. Move it. I *move it*, because we have to. He could have killed them by now. He knocks on the door loudly and it swings open, giving me a glimpse of the technological playground set up inside.

"Who are you?" someone else is shouting at me over the buzz of the electronics.

"I was on board that plane, in the seat next to Ella." He registers surprise that I refer to her as intimately as I do, and motions with his head for me to continue. I do so, fully aware the guy with the AK-47 is still behind me.

"She's hurt. She was whacked on the head and is bleeding pretty bad, but she may be able to give you an opening."

"An opening?" he asks, not willing to trust me yet. For all he knows, I could be working for the other side.

"Please, just listen," I beg him. "I was next to Ella Sheridan." He weighs this for half a second, figures it just might be wise to listen to me.

"Go on," he says.

"Okay, listen. If one of your guys is steady and he can get off a shot he might be able to get the pilot. Ella is near the front of the plane, just outside the cockpit in first class. If he doesn't move them back, and if she can do it without him noticing, I told her to lift the shade on one window. It's a big if, everything has to line up just right but at least it's something."

He nods his head, and talks into the walkie-talkie type thing attached to a loop on his shoulder.

"Give me the approximate size of the pilot. How tall is he?"

I tell him he's a tall dude, maybe six-three, six-four. Good build, not scrawny. He relays everything I tell him to his shoulder, converting it into lingo I don't completely follow. He asks me for my name, tells me he's John. I tell him my name and then ask if there is anything else

I can do to help. He asks me where the rest of the passengers were, if there were any left onboard the plane.

I tell them they have all gone. I also tell him the pilot only wanted Ella, but I think he wanted her mother more.

He tells me he is aware of that, wants to know why I stayed.

I'm not sure how to answer that. He might take me into custody if I tell him the truth. Consider me just another fruit loop with a twisted interest in the Sheridan clan.

So I keep it simple, and more *on* the side of honest than *off* it.

"Because I sat next to Ella, sir. I sat next to Ella and I care about what happens to her."

He looks at me for a long moment, then nods once and tells me to climb onboard.

"Find a seat, Dezi. I don't want you running around out there now. You might get shot. Just don't touch anything." I hurry up the steps and slide past the heavy equipment to the opposite end of the plane where there are seats. I settle into one that gives me a long view of the plane, from the back. I can't see the area where I think they are. I can't see if Ella managed to inch the window shade up.

Doubt rushes in. Maybe none of what I told her even registered. Ella may be halfway to la-la land by now, bleeding uncontrollably, wracked by guilt, sick with worry.

I will her to fight. *Come on, Ella. Fight for you, fight for us.*

It will take an act of God for this to end well.

I think of all the times fate has fucked me. Turned me upside down and wrestled me to the ground. Please, not this time. Please, let something work out. Please, don't take her. Not yet, not until she has changed my life like I know she is meant to. Until I have changed hers. Let us have our time.

What am I thinking? She's already gone. I have lost the only woman I have ever loved. The only one I have ever wanted to love. I feel like I'm about to throw up. I start to rise out of the small seat, figuring I had better get the hell away from this place before someone tells me she really is gone.

All at once, the metallic clicks of noise coming over the speakers sound like explosions. Quick fire verbal volleys ricochet across the small space inside the plane. It's getting smaller in here, *impossibly small.*

I start moving toward the door. John lifts his chin a couple inches back from his shoulder mic, straight-arms me, and stops me in my tracks.

"Hold up, Dezi," he starts, his flat palm landing on my chest. "Sit down. I think she just gave us our opportunity. My guy says there's one shade that just cracked open. We may have a shot after all."

I sit down again. Not because he told me to, but because my legs don't work anymore.

Chapter 36: Mel

I want to rush to her, hold her, and feel her chest rise and fall in confirmation that she is alive. I know I could be walking straight into a trap. I know Ella could be dead by now, and I could get a bullet in the face or something even worse the moment I step foot on this plane. The only peace I feel is knowing that his demise won't be far behind mine, given the level of fire power arriving on the next flight in.

They have told me I will have ten minutes before they storm the plane. Ten minutes to convince him to let my daughter go.

Ten minutes to soak up every little detail of her face.

Ten minutes to tell her how much I love her, how much I have always loved her.

He has thrown out a rope ladder from the cockpit window. Christ, a rope ladder. Really?

I am certainly not as agile as I used to be, so this will take some doing. One by one, I step up the rickety rungs, hanging on tightly with both hands even as sweat loosens my grip and I struggle to quicken my pace. Finally, I reach the open window and haul myself into the cockpit.

He is waiting for me, watching me huff and puff with exertion. Taller than I imagined, with a thick chest, and broad shoulders, he is remarkably handsome.

"Well, hello there, Melanie. Glad to see you could make it. Come on in."

I try to steady my breathing. I want to meet him as his equal, not some winded old lady. I make sure my voice is strong as I tell him I want to see Ella.

"Sure thing. But before you do, prepare yourself. Ella's got a bump on the head, but not all that blood is from her."

All that blood! Dear God, what has happened to her?

He steps back, and I notice his small pistol for the first time. As he steps into the cabin of first class, he moves left, giving me access to the right side of the plane where she is sitting in the aisle seat of the third row. My heart skips a beat, and then starts to pound with relief as I see her smile at me and mouth the words, "Mom, I'm so sorry."

Oh, Ella. He stands away from us, but close enough to remind me he is there, with his gun.

"Go ahead," he tells me. "Go to her."

I'm not sure if he'll fire a bullet into my back, but I risk it for the chance to hold my daughter for what could be the last time. I take her gently by the shoulders, pulling her into me and running my hand down her back. I whisper into her ear, "Be strong, Ella. No matter what happens here, be strong. I love you more than you could ever know. And *I'm* sorry."

I pull her back to get a look at her face, her glorious green eyes, *her bleeding head.* I run my finger softly over the gash.

"This is bad, you need stitches, soon." The sudden movement opens the wound and the slow trickle turns into a swift red current.

"Sit down, Ella. Let me see what I can do here." I help her sit back down, before I turn to face him again. I rise to my full height, straighten my back, and prepare for war.

"I want her off this plane right now. She needs a doctor. I am prepared to give you what you ask for, but you must give us something in return. Give me my daughter."

I plant myself squarely in front of Ella now, blocking her from him. If he fires, I will take it first.

"In a moment. First, I think there are some things Ella should hear. The kind of person her mother really is. The kind of person who praises the murder of innocent people in the name of justice."

Here he goes again with this whole murder for justice thing. What is he talking about?

"Then get on with it. I'm listening."

He doesn't like my tone because his face darkens and I can see the hatred churning just below the surface.

"My name is not Seth Baxter," he begins. "I was born Ahmed Thomas. My mother was Iraqi, my father a Brit. They were both brilliant doctors."

How proud they'd be of you right now, I would like to say, but I keep my mouth shut, not wishing to antagonize him further. I think we're around eight minutes and counting until the saints coming marching in.

"They studied in England but returned to Iraq because there was a need for their skills and their compassion," he looks beyond us, into thin air. I wonder whom he sees there. "They saved many lives, you know. *Saved lives*. Is that a foreign concept to you, Melanie? The idea of protecting another human being by any means you know how to use?"

He's taunting me again, hostile, insulting. Clock is ticking; get to it.

"I was a boy when they were killed. A boy who was quite good at school, loved by his family, with potential to do good things in this world," he looks down briefly, examining the small gun, leveling it on his leg before he looks back up at me. "I wasn't always this way, Melanie. I wasn't always guided by my hatred for you." I try to keep him talking, six minutes until they take over.

"You are a young man, Ahmed. There is still hope for you. Just let Ella go." He either ignores me, or can't hear me anymore.

"It has taken me years to get to you. I have sacrificed everything for this moment." His voice is low, and I'm not sure if he's congratulating or disparaging himself. He is the picture of madness as he looks back up to find me. His hand steadies on his small gun, and although it is broiling in here now, his grip is tight. He won't miss. "Before I put a bullet in your brain I want you to speak their names. I want you to acknowledge they were human beings, and they were precious to me, and they didn't deserve to die in the rubble of a hospital, knowing they were leaving their little boy alone in this world."

What hospital, I think. What part of his life is he reliving? I will give him anything he wants if it means getting Ella the hell out of here.

"I will do as you wish, but only after Ella is gone." I remind him again that there has to be an exchange here. He can't control everything. He has become vacant. His face is getting red, sweat falling in lines down each cheek. His eyes are like the deep blue of an arctic ocean, simmering beneath a cold glacier. He is growing more and more agitated. He raises his gun at me now, teeth bared, his voice barely there.

"Say their names, Melanie. *Say them,*" he is growling at me, and I believe whatever strands of sanity he had left are gone. Four minutes to go, how can I stay upright for *four...more...minutes?*

"I don't know their names...Ahmed...I don't know...tell me, just tell me..."

"*Shut up! Shut up, Melanie!* Don't you understand?" He is wild-eyed, his pupils look huge, transforming the blue into something almost as dark as night. "You denied me a life. *A life!* You took it away. And now, I'm going to take yours. While your daughter watches you take your final breath."

He exhales on a huge sigh, dropping his voice into a near whisper. He is begging me now, pleading with me to give him what he thinks he needs.

"Say their names. Say their names, Melanie. I want their names to be the last words you ever say."

I reach behind my back to grab Ella's hands. We wrap our fingers around each other's and I squeeze her. I may die right in front of her. How does anyone ever recover from that? This man has suffered. He deserves retribution. I will give him that.

"Tell me their names, Ahmed. I will speak their names, and I will honor their memories. But only after Ella is off this plane. Otherwise, you won't get a thing from me."

He can't hear me anymore, he's somewhere else now. A wry smile twists his lips up.

"She was so beautiful, Melanie. Her eyes were green. Like Ella's, but even greener somehow. She was so good, and so brave. She deserved to watch me grow up. They both did. My father used to take me fishing." He takes the hand that isn't wrapped around the gun and raises it at me. He looks at it, as if he is seeing it for the first time. "I remember his hands, Melanie. He had the biggest hands I'd ever seen."

I stay quiet as he revisits the memories of his life.

"They did not die peacefully. They died worried about me. Like you will die now. Worried about Ella. It is only fair, Melanie. Don't you see?"

"Yes, Ahmed. I understand. It is a terrible thing, but the past is the past. You still have a chance to do one good thing before this is all over. Your parents would want you to let my daughter go."

He explodes with anger. I have somehow infuriated him. He jumps closer to us, leaning in with his chest, face beet red, eyes blazing with fury.

"Don't you dare tell me what my parents would *want!* They would *want* to be here today! They would *want* to know their grandson. They would *want* to have survived your country's brutal attack. They would *want* justice, Melanie."

He cocks his gun, aims it straight between my eyes.

"Time's up, Madam Vice President. Judgment day has arrived."

His eyes are watering, his tears flowing in a steady rhythm. His chin quivers as his emotions begin to stumble over each other. Insanity ruling completely now, his words are reduced to a tortured moan.

"Say their names."

I prefer to close my eyes as I meet death. I think of my children, my precious Ella sitting just behind me. She will have no choice but to carry on with life after this horrendous event. I think of my husband, who is so strong and so kind. I am ready. I am ready to die.

"Say...their...na-"

Gunfire explodes in my ears, as I feel a body cover my own. I immediately fall to the floor, but I feel no pain. I swing my arms blindly, feeling for my daughter who is spread-eagle out in front of me. She is heavy, dead weight.

"Goddamn it! Ella, what did you do?"

Only silence. She is silent. Unconscious? God forbid, *dead?*

Where is he? I struggle to move Ella off so I can find him.

He is down. His eyes are open and his breath labored. I scan his body, looking for wounds. I see it then, a circle of red growing wider just above his waist.

Chapter 37: Ahmed

Light comes at me first from behind. I can see it along my periphery. My knees buckle but I never feel myself hit the ground. There is no pain, just quiet.

Through the brightness, I see fog, a haze of cloudy air that reminds me of how dawn used to break in the misty English village. Gray sheets dance just above the ground.

I see them then.

Two shadowy forms that are so close together they appear almost as if they are one, but as they separate, I can begin to tell them apart. One is much larger than the other, approaching me with outstretched arms. The other is more delicate, more feminine.

She is standing before me now, reaching for me. I have to look up at her, for she is much taller than I am. Her face is above mine, her green eyes sanguine and peaceful.

As I reach my own hand up to find its place in hers, I notice it is small.

The hand of a child.

She takes it gently as I am scooped up from behind, hoisted carefully to the place I had known so long ago. I feel safe, and deeply content as I wrap my hands around my father's chin. Familiar stubble roughs my skin.

"Hey, Yellow. We've missed you. Welcome home."

From my perch atop his strong shoulders, I kiss the top of my father's blonde head.

I reach for my mother's hand again.

Holding them both, I find the place inside myself that is finally still.

I am so high now I can almost reach the heavens.

Or perhaps I am already there.

48 Hours Later: Ella

I hear them before I see them. Voices as soft as a butterfly's wings flutter next to my ear. I struggle to reach up to them but it's like climbing out of icy water. Every muscle in my body fights me, tries to hold me down. I work against myself, pushing up, up, up.

"Brett, she's trying to open her eyes." My mother's voice. *My mother's alive, she's talking.* Or maybe she's dead, and I'm just getting there.

"Sweetheart, we're all here. Open your eyes, Ella. Open your eyes."

One blink, darkness. Two blinks, three…fuzzy light, lots of faces.

I try to reach beneath my rear end, propel myself upwards. I am tangled up in plastic tubes.

"No, honey, don't. Just lie still. It's okay. You're in the hospital. We're all right here."

Now I can see. I do a slow scan around the edges of my bed. My parents are on either side of me, reaching over to take one of my hands in their own. Kelby is next to my mother. Kass is peering anxiously over my father's shoulder. He speaks to me next.

"Girlfriend, you are a heeee-ro!" Kass's pimped out compliment makes me laugh. *Ouch,* note to self, laughing equals instant headache. They are fussing over my head, stroking my hand, worried I am slipping back into the deep end of the pool again.

My eyes find Kelby's. She looks lovely as usual, but tired. Worried, perhaps? Nah, just tired.

"For sure, Ella," she nods at me. "You saved Mom's life. After you almost got her killed, of course."

Of course. Thanks for reminding me, soul sister.

Just beyond Kelby, more toward the foot of the bed, hanging back a bit, is another person. My distance eyesight isn't the best anyway, but throw in a major head injury and he's really just an orb. But it is a *he*. That much I can tell. He's tall, and thick, and I squint at him, trying to pick up more detail. He moves closer to me, comes up on my side just above my mother's shoulders.

"Hey, you," he says softly. "Remember me?"

I try to blink him away, because surely he is just something my injured brain cooked up. He doesn't go anywhere. He stays right here, next to my hospital bed with that impossibly cool yet sexy smile of his that made me love him almost instantaneously.

I start to cry. He stayed with me. He didn't run away.

"Dezi. How could I forget you? You saved my life."

"No way, Ella. You did that all on your own." He's next to me now. Somehow, my mother made room for Dezi, just stepped right out of the way. This is new. My mother does not step out of the way for anyone. Dezi reaches over and trails a finger down my arm lightly. He stops at my fingers, closes his hand around mine.

"How's the head?"

"Hurts. Someone is going to have to fill me in here. I think I fell asleep before the movie ended."

They all look at each other then, but no one speaks just yet.

"What *do* you remember, Ella?" my mother asks. I tell her that I remember her getting on the plane and something about the pilot wanting her to speak someone's name. Then, it all goes blank.

She tells me the pilot is dead. She also tells me that somehow, someone with nerves of steel managed to fire off a bullet that must have been on a course guided by the hand of an angel. It penetrated the thick glass at just the right angle, at just the right moment, to find him and no one else.

"You did this, Ella. You opened the shade for them. Otherwise, they would have had to storm in and fire blindly."

I look over at Dezi. "No, Mom, *he* did it. It was all his idea. Right before he got off the plane, he told me to do that. I'm not smart enough to come up with that on my own."

"But you saved *me*, Ella. He was ready to fire. He had his gun pointed at my head, ready to kill me. You threw yourself on top of me, giving the sniper a clear shot at him. Otherwise, you were blocking the window. If you hadn't moved, he would have killed me first."

Wow. My one shining moment and I don't even remember it.

Typical.

A nurse knocks on the door now, responding to the button my father just pushed on my bed.

"She's awake?" she asks.

"Awake and talking," my father reports.

"Good, the doctor will be right in. We'll take a look at her."

Where are we?

They tell me we're in Florida. I was rushed to the hospital after losing consciousness on the plane. I have been out for almost two full days.

Jeesh, the whole world must know by now. It feels like a lifetime ago that I boarded the plane at JFK. This brings me back to the purpose of the trip in the first place.

They are all here. I should just blurt it out. They say the best time to drop bad news on someone is after they have just survived a major trauma. Like, "Good news, Mrs. Smith, you survived the crash but we had to cut your legs off."

They are happy I'm alive. No better time than the present to tell them it might not be for much longer.

I look at them again. One by one, I spend several seconds looking into the faces of my family. Then I stop on him. The most amazing man I have ever met. Honest and real, brave and strong. He is the stuff little girls dream of. The kind of man who has a starring role in fairy tales, the one parents hope to see when they open the door for their daughter's first date. Yet for some reason, he is standing on my front porch. He has found *me*.

Only to lose me. To cancer this time.

"There's something you all need to know. I wasn't just going to see Lauren for a vacation. I had something to tell her that is really hard to say..." I gulp, as I feel my face getting hotter. "...it's scary and it totally sucks and..."

It's Dezi who speaks first. Out of all of them, Dezi goes first.

"Ella, we know. Everyone knows. And we're going to be right here for you every step of the way."

We. As in you...and them?

"But...how...can you...possibly know?"

He looks at my mother now, a subtle signal for her to pick up the story.

"Honey, we couldn't keep things quiet for very long. The president had to address the nation once Ahmed was killed and you were taken to the hospital. Dr. Sturgis called my office when he heard you were hurt. He told me about the cancer. Don't you get mad at him now, he was very concerned and offered to fly down here to help the trauma team treat you."

I feel ashamed. As I look around at them, I feel ashamed that I felt like I was alone. I am hardly alone.

I look at her with a new question. Who the hell is Ahmed?

I must have mumbled that aloud, because my mother turns to the others and explains that there are likely parts of the ordeal that my brain is blocking out. She turns back to me, tells me he was the pilot.

"Remember now, honey?"

"Huh," I say quietly, as I begin to recall how tall and fair he was. "He sure didn't look like an Ahmed, and why was he after you, Mom? And what were those names he wanted you to say? That was totally weird."

She nods at me, tells me Intelligence has been piecing his life together.

"His mother was Iraqi, his father born in England. From pictures we have been able to find, he resembles his father almost identically. It seems he was around ten years old during the first Iraq war. His parents were doctors in Baghdad, killed when a missile hit their hospital. There is no record of Ahmed after that, so we figure he was raised in some desert village. At that time, I had just been appointed to the Senate Armed Services Committee. I was doing many interviews, daily briefings on TV. We think he somehow associated me with the deaths of his parents. He had a couple of aliases but no record whatsoever. His friend, however, the one who hurt you and was later shot, he was real trouble. He was the front man for a terrorist group inside Iraq. We are still looking into what his role was." She takes a breath, and sighs softly. "As for Ahmed, it seems he spent his entire life plotting his revenge. It is a shame, really. He was a technical genius; he completely bypassed our security. On every level."

She looks down, her face soft, thoughtful. She is sad, I think. My mother, *is sad?*

"He had a wife. And a son," she says softly as we all feel the tragedy in history repeating itself. Another boy who will grow up without his father.

A technical genius. It comes back to me then. How he hacked into my life. How I lead him right to her. *Whoops, my bad.* She must recognize the look of utter mortification, because she cuts it off at the pass.

"There will be plenty of time to…*uh-ummmm*…discuss that, Ella. Our security team will want to talk to you."

Of course, they will.

"First things first," she says, leaning in to brush a stray strand of hair from my forehead.

"Let's get you well."

Oh yeah, about that.

Epilogue: Dezi and Ella

"Hey, Q," he throws himself down next to me. Everything Dezi does is big. His whole being is big. And it's wonderful, and it is entirely mine.

He has taken to calling me "Q," a reference to my now entirely bald head, something he tells me looks just like a cue ball from the back. I guess I have to laugh, because when you're with Dezi, there is just no reason to cry.

"She'll be here any minute, time to get up," he tells me, helping me shift into a sitting position on the couch. We are squeezed into my apartment, although recently we have been looking at bigger apartments. To share. It is a monumental step forward for both of us, but something we feel like we have been waiting for forever.

He has never left my side. In the nine months since we first met, I haven't had to look far to find him. He has sat through countless doctors' appointments, pulling out his little notebook to write down things he thinks I'll need to remember. He has knelt beside me as I hurled into the toilet after my very first round of chemo. He wiped away the single tear I allowed myself to shed as I took his old pair of clippers and shaved off my own hair before the drugs did it for me.

He even shaved his own head as a sign of solidarity.

As did Kass.

Kelby? Don't even think about it. Although she did offer to wear a ponytail for a week if I thought that might make me feel better.

Try as I might, there is nothing I can do to make him leave. I have told him to, too many times to count. He just shakes his head and smiles.

"As if I ever could, Ella. You're stuck with me now."

My left breast has survived the journey. Doctors say once they opened me up they found the cancer was contained. They removed the lump, shot me up with some radiation, and only put me through chemo because of my age. They tell me even though it might make me feel like crap for a little while, it will just about guarantee the cancer is fully zapped.

At this point, I am approaching the finish line, and even though I might be a little bruised and battered, I am still standing.

Dezi is the best cheerleader in the world, though my mother is pulling a close second.

He clicks on the TV. "Is today the day? I forget if it's today, or tomorrow."

"*Duh*, tomorrow. She'd be really pissed if she knew you forgot."

"I didn't forget. And she wouldn't be pissed. Not at me. She loves me. She'd probably blame you anyway."

He's right. My mother loves Dezi. Why not? *Everyone* loves Dezi. As far as they're concerned, if we ever have a fight, *I* should be the one sleeping on the couch.

"Turn it off. I don't want to be distracted when she gets here."

Tomorrow, my mother grants her first and only exclusive interview as the former vice president of the United States. She has promised to reveal details of the incident, as well as how she made the difficult decision to resign in order to try to save the life of her daughter. The president practically begged her to reconsider. She declined. She said her family needed her more. She has been front and center in my life ever since.

She also plans to update the nation on my health. The network is teasing the interview in a way that just might make you believe I am already dead. Sorry to disappoint you folks, rumors of my demise are greatly exaggerated. I am like the proverbial cockroach. Sole survivor of what has felt like a nuclear winter.

He clicks the TV off just as the doorbell rings. He jumps up. I move in behind him as we both walk to the door. It swings open to reveal a petite, dark-haired woman holding a baby in her arms. I welcome her in, feeling her discomfort and guilt as she faces the two of us here.

Ahmed's wife reached out to me several weeks ago. By now, she knows the truth about who her husband really was. There is something she has asked me to have, though I have no idea what that could be. Despite my family warning me against it, I insisted on meeting her. I think there's a part of me that needs to see her. Maybe in some way, she needs to see me, too.

"Hello," we both say at the same time.

She has traveled all the way from Florida, where they had been living. Ahmed, who she knew as Seth, had been flying for the airline for two years, taking the Atlanta to Chicago route mostly, but filling in when someone needed time off. She told me she didn't think twice when he left her very early that morning, telling her he was covering a New York to L.A. route for a friend.

"He loved our boy very much," she says once we've exchanged niceties, getting to the real reason why she's come. "A part of him was always missing. There were secrets he would never share. Obviously..." she trails off. "I have researched his life as best I can. I have found relatives in England. They are good people. I plan to bring my son to them, soon. I think I may stay there for a while. I have no family of my own."

I nod mostly, letting her do all the talking.

"Ella, although he was consumed by a need for revenge, there were parts of Seth...I mean Ahmed, that were good. He was a good husband, and he was a loving father. I don't think he ever would have become this madman if he hadn't lost them when he was just a little boy. He started his life with so much love. His parents were both such wonderful people. I have learned just how much they loved him."

"Yes, I know. Sometimes our lives change without us knowing how to stop it. He was a sick man, but I'm sure he loved you. And your son."

"He did, Ella. So much." She fumbles around in a bag hoisted sideways across her chest, looking for something inside.

"Here," I offer, holding out my arms. "Let me take him."

She looks at me, holds my eyes for a couple of seconds before she slides him forward to me.

"Okay." His child fills my arms, the offspring of a man who could have killed me. I look into his tiny face. He is beautiful, actually. He looks just like his mother.

The light coming in from the window behind us shifts, and the baby's eyelids inadvertently close to keep it out. Then he blinks them open again, giggling at what he must think is a game designed just for his amusement.

"My gosh," I say. "His eyes are gorgeous." They are the deepest shade of green I have ever seen.

"Yes," she says without looking up, as she continues to sift through the contents of her bag. "He got my brown eyes."

"Brown?" I say back, surprise registering in my voice. "Not *brown*. You mean green. They're a beautiful deep, dark green."

She stops moving her hand, and looks at me strangely, as she shakes her head and leans in toward her son. "No, his eyes are not green...they're..." She can't deny it as she looks at him then.

Sure enough, in the light of day, her child's eyes are *green*. She is stunned into a moment of silence. She stumbles to explain. "I uh, I...must appear clueless to you right now. A mother who doesn't even recognize the eyes of her own child. But I swear to you, he has brown eyes. They must be...changing."

I can see her trying to figure out how in the world this is happening. Green? But how?

"Hey," I say, trying to lighten the moment. "I have weird green eyes myself. Even though my mother's are blue and my father has some variation of hazel, I got green. It happens." I shrug, still holding the now squirming boy in my arms.

"Yes, maybe someone in Seth's...uh Ahmed's family..." she trails off again, trying to stay focused on the reason she is standing in my foyer. "Anyway, I brought you something. I don't know why, Ella, but I think you should have it."

She pulls a tiny blue case from her bag, hands it over to me.

"Oh no, I don't think I could..." I hesitate to reach for it.

She interrupts me. "Please, take it. I think it came from his mother. From what I know about her, she was fearless, and strong. A survivor. Just like you."

I feel my chin pull up. Her kindness takes me aback. I gently open the box. Sitting inside is a slight golden bird, its wings outstretched, sparkles of diamonds on the tips. It is simple, lovely, and very personal.

"I don't know what to say." Because I don't. I have no words for this woman.

"Just go live a long, happy life, Ella. You deserve it."

I reach for her then, hold her gently next to me. Somewhere in the middle, I hand her back her son.

"Thank you," I whisper. "This means more to me than I can ever explain."

"As it should be." She pulls back, prepares to leave.

"No, don't go yet. Come in, sit down."

"No, Ella. We're on the last flight out. It's been a busy time for us. I'm looking forward to going home."

"I understand. Take good care of yourself, and your boy."

It dawns on me that I don't even know his name. I ask her.

"Easton," she says, running a hand softly over his dark hair. "His father named him."

With that, she turns away and walks to the elevator. She never looks back.

"Wow, that was intense." Dezi had been standing just far back enough not to interrupt us. He comes up behind me, wraps one arm around my shoulder, looking down at the bird sitting in the palm of my hand.

"She's right," he says softly.

"About what?" I ask, still slightly dazed by this unexpected bequest.

"You are fearless. And if anyone deserves a long, happy life, it's you."

I start to turn into him then, to squeeze myself around him because I need to feel his strong arms. I have just been touched to my very core. I feel this strange connection to a set of parents I will never know. Ahmed's parents. I tear up again with the sadness of it all.

But Dezi is not there. He is looking up at me. What are you doing down there?

I start to ask him, but he speaks before me.

"And I would like nothing more than to share every moment of it with you."

He is on bended knee, and there is another box, an even smaller one that he pulls open.

"Ella Sheridan, you are more than I deserve. I have loved you from the moment you fell into my iPod, and I will love you until I take my last breath."

Tears stream down my face. It is not as I imagined it would be, and yet it is perfect.

"Will you marry me?"

I surprise myself with how strong I am as I reach down pulling him up to me. The bandana I had wrapped around my bald head flies off, but neither of us cares. He swings me around and around, until I laugh more than I cry. As he steadies me, I look beyond him to the wall where I have hung his now famous shot of the senator on the cover of *Time* magazine. I am so proud of him. He is so much more than I ever could have hoped for.

For the first time in my life, I am at complete and total peace with who I am, and who I'm about to be.

Dezi's wife.

I have survived a plane trip from hell. I am on the road to surviving cancer. I have held up under scrutiny and criticism from every direction, and I am still here. *Right here!* I haven't gone anywhere.

Oh my God! I have to call Lauren! I have to tell my family! Of course, Kelby will tell me to wait, that there is no way I can get married with no hair. I'll have to tell Kass he can't bring the porn star we all know he's secretly been dating to the wedding.

I have to...

"Ella!" he says sharply, snapping me back into the moment.

"What...?"

"I asked you a question. You haven't answered me yet. Will you marry me?"

I feel a grin spread across my entire face. I want to shout it from the rooftop.

"Hey, world. This is Ella. I'm back, and I'm getting...*married!*"

"Yes," I say. One little word that fills every part of me with joy. I slip the ring on my finger. It is glorious.

And I deserve it.

A light flashes. Dezi is behind his camera, snapping the moment our lives fused together forever.

He pulls me over to look into the viewfinder. There I am. My grin almost as bright as my bald head. I see myself then, perhaps for the first time ever. I look objectively at the shot.

And I smile.

Because finally, I see my worth, I see my beauty. I see what Dezi sees.

I see me.

THE END